THE DARK RISES

THE KILLIAN BLADE SERIES

STELLA BRIE

Cover Design: Covers by Jules

Editing: Kaye Kemp Book Polishing

❀ Created with Vellum

Playlist

"UNDONE (FEAT. FLEURIE)" - TOMMEE PROFITT

"COMING BACK STRONGER (FEAT. SARAH REEVES)" – SILVERBERG (NIGHTCORE)

"IGNITE" – UNSECRET X NEONI

"BRAVE" – NEFFEX

"WHAT WE CAME TO DO" – OUTSKRTS

"WELCOME TO THE FIRE" – WILLYECHO

"FIGHTER" – THE SCORE

"BACK IN THE FIGHT" - ZAYDE WOLF X EDVN

"RETURN OF THE GREATEST" - MANAFEST

"BLACK SKY" – WAR*HALL

"WATCH THEM FALL (FEAT. TEDASHI & SAM TINNESZ)" – UNSECRET

"REVOLUTION (FEAT. RUELLE)" – UNSECRET

"WILD ONES" - SAM TINNESZ X OTTO BLUE

"SOUND OF WAR (FEAT. FLEURIE)" – TOMMEE PROFITT

"BATTLEFIELD" – SVRCINA

"ETERNAL ECLIPSE" – COSMIC ENTROPY

"KING OF THE WORLD" - WAR*HALL

"RISE UP" - CLEAR BLUE FIRE

AUTHOR'S NOTE

This is a Why Choose romance, which means the heroine does not have to choose between male interests. The book is a spin-off from The Killian Blade Series and includes fictional characters and places introduced in that world with little additional explanation or backstory.

The story contains violence, death, battles, cussing, and other mature content. Please take care of yourself and read at your own discretion. Recommended for 18+ years.

Killian Blade Series fans – this is it. The last book in this world.
Enjoy!

CHAPTER ONE

<u>MERI</u>

Betrayal doesn't hide in the dark like a thief in the night. It hides in plain sight, waiting for the right moment to strike. This time it struck at dawn in the light Fae court. Solandis saved, crown gone, traitors vanquished; I step from the portal into The Abbey with Cormal and Madoc at my side, bitterness and anger warring inside me. Not for the crown I willingly gave up, but for the loss of the queen I could finally see when I looked into the mirror.

Arden, Valerian, and Theron greet us, weapons and magic held at the ready. At the sight of Cormal, they relax, only to tense a second later when they see Madoc. Tall, dark, with a menacing scowl on his face, he doesn't appear the least bit friendly.

If this morning's attack was a moment of betrayal, this is a moment of truth. Madoc's agenda might align with ours, but it doesn't mean he's with us. He has gone out of his way to save me... three times. The wendigo, Denir, and Camon. And he even helped me defeat Hyne, the kraken. But do I trust him? That's the important question.

I look up and find his predatory stare locked on the three in front of him. He must sense my gaze because his eyes swing down to mine. Wariness changes to amusement and his eyes lighten as he senses my dilemma, but not one plea passes his full lips.

His warm, scarred fingers loosen their grip on my hand, as if he's preparing himself for my rejection, but mine automatically tighten. Somewhere along the way, I started to trust him, and I didn't even realize it. Maybe it's because he saved me and asked for nothing in return. I've always dreamed of a knight in shining armor. In Madoc's case, tarnished armor might be more accurate, which I oddly find appealing. Regardless, black and white, good and bad aren't scales I've used in my life, and I don't intend to start now.

Swinging my gaze to Arden, I hold up our linked hands. "Madoc is with us."

Her green eyes return my stare and narrow for a moment, then the prickle of her magic disappears as she slowly pulls in her power. But Valerian and Theron turn toward Cormal for confirmation.

Cormal snorts at my statement. "With you, maybe. I don't trust him."

Madoc, his face stern, nods once. "Good. We share a goal, not a friendship."

His tone is nonchalant, but his muscles are tense as he waits for Cormal to make up his mind.

With gritted teeth, Cormal turns to Arden and her men. "As much as I want to remove him from this world, and from Meri's side, Madoc stays. For now. The enemy of our enemy and all that. A shared purpose, but not a friend."

Theron, violet eyes narrowed, sheaths his swords. Valerian

also relaxes, releasing the magic swirling around him until it dissipates.

Arden rolls her eyes at them all.

I glare at Cormal. "I consider him a friend." Sort of. As much as you can befriend something so wild.

Madoc makes a strangled noise in his throat, and Cormal grunts.

Dismissing them, I reluctantly release both of their hands and walk over to Arden to give her a hug. The familiar smell of strawberries and champagne tickles my nose. "It's good to see you. Solandis?"

The crushing hug I receive in response is almost terrifying in its strength. "She's here. Safe. All because of you. We can never repay you for what you've done." Her green eyes are swimming with tears when she releases me.

"She's family." They all are to some extent. Arden, Vargas, and Callyx. But Solandis' unwavering support and love is everything to me. A crown is nothing compared to her. "Where is she?"

Arden's smile dims. "She's resting right now. Vargas' orders. Although, I think she was relieved to relinquish control for a while. This really took a lot out of her, especially with the pregnancy. Vargas will come get us when she's up for visitors."

I desperately want to see Solandis but I hold off. Her needs come first. At least she's safe and unharmed. I doubt this would have fazed her under normal circumstances, but the baby changes everything.

Arden leans in close and whispers, "Callyx returned to The Underworld to report to Lucifer."

It's clear she doesn't want Madoc to hear her. "I understand."

Arden straightens and waves a hand toward Cormal's bloody shirt. "Do you need healing?"

To my relief, Cormal rubs his hand across his chest and shakes his head. "Now that we're out of Fae lands, it's healing quickly. Thank you." He tilts his head toward me. "The Underworld is Leandra's domain and until we can find the bitch, I want to be sure Meri has a safe haven. Is it okay if she stays here?"

Valerian shares a look with Theron, then they both nod.

Theron turns his gaze toward Madoc, cool violet eyes studying him intently. "I assume you'll be staying too?" When Madoc dips his chin, he warns him. "The Abbey is a sanctuary, and she protects her own."

With that subtle statement, he motions for us to follow him. "I'll show you to your rooms. All common areas are open to you, including the library, rooftop, and training rooms."

As we enter the elevator, Madoc hesitates. "Old magic powers this contraption."

Interest flares in Theron's eyes, and he flicks a questioning glance toward me as he answers him. "Yes. It's a bit uncomfortable for some, but this is the only way to travel around The Abbey. Too much magic in the walls makes the shadows unreliable."

Madoc stiffens and steps inside. He inhales sharply when the doors close and darts a glance at the ceiling, clearly uncomfortable.

I slide closer, letting my body brush against his, hoping it will help. He unclenches his hand, but the moment the elevator begins to move, his hands form fists again, all comfort gone. I hope the ride is short.

My mind lingers on his words. Contraption. Almost as if he's never been in an elevator, which is odd. They're everywhere... in all the lands.

The steel doors slide open, and Theron extends his hand toward the hallway. "This is your floor. Any time you want to leave, just step in. The elevator will take you to your destination with just a thought."

By unanimous agreement, we all decide to let Madoc out first. He steps foot into the hallway and loudly exhales.

Theron brushes past him to lead us to our rooms.

It's the same wing I stayed in the last time I was here, so Cormal and I are already familiar with the layout.

Cormal clasps hands with Theron. "Thank you. I'm in your debt."

Theron's eyes briefly slide to Cormal in acknowledgement, but his attention remains on Madoc. "No debt. Not for family." His violet gaze swings to me and warms before he reenters the elevator.

Madoc enters first and prowls around the room, his eyes darting from one item to another, inspecting everything.

I step into my previous room and see little has changed. Plain white walls. Nearest to the door is a small sitting area with a loveseat and coffee table and in the corner, a dining table with two chairs. On the far wall sits a dresser, a couple of night-stands, and a large bed covered with a fluffy white duvet. Two doors lead to a closet and an attached bathroom.

When Cormal enters behind me, I whirl around, unable to wait a second longer. Lifting his shirt, I trace the wound left by the Killian Blade. Pink puckered skin is all that's left of the gaping hole where it plunged into his heart.

My lips replace my hands, skimming the scar on his chest, grateful that we're both alive to fight another day. I pick up the reassuring sound of his beating heart and tilt my head back to look at him.

"Good thing you're hard to kill."

His eyes are full of bemused wonder, as if seeing my concern is still a surprise. He grabs my hand, presses a kiss to it, then links our fingers together.

Adrenaline clashes with reality, and it suddenly feels like a truck ran over me. With Cormal in tow, I move to the couch to contemplate the magnitude of the events that occurred earlier today.

"That was one hell of a morning. Allandra and Camon dead. Lorn a monster or whatever the hell he turned into. Gone forever, I hope."

An image of his green scales flashes repeatedly in my mind. He had me completely fooled. I never saw it coming. Not once did my intuition or self-preservation pick up on his deception or his other form. Enemy. Monster. Thank goodness we never went further than the briefest of kisses or I'd need therapy.

"And to top it off, I had to give a copy of the peace treaty to Faris, of all people," I say with a disbelieving shake of my head.

At the thought of the treaty, I can't help but think of Rivan and wonder if he made it safely to the Water Fae. *Goddess, please keep him safe.*

"A hybrid of a dryad and some sort of serpent," Madoc says with an odd glint in his eye. I raise an eyebrow, and he clarifies. "Lorn. You couldn't sense his other self when you were around him?"

Defensively, I shrug. "No. Fae were drawn to him, but he didn't seem to affect me as much. Isn't a dryad a type of nymph?" That would explain why the Fae hung on his every word.

"Tree nymph, yes, but as the light Fae queen, you should have been able to sense his true self," he interjects impatiently when it's clear I'm not getting the point.

Gritting my teeth, I reveal the truth about my reign. "When I became queen, an extensive amount of knowledge poured into me, but accessing the threads to the people and the land wasn't possible. It was nothing but a black hole." I lift a shoulder. "Eris, one of the brownies in the palace, told me everything disconnected from Nyssa, and the crown, a long time ago."

Madoc paces, quiet for a moment, then shakes his head. "As their queen, the magic should have reconnected with you, but it could be corrupted. Too many deviations from its true purpose." He eyes Cormal. "Where did you send Lorn?"

Cormal returns his stare. "The Underworld."

When Madoc arches an eyebrow, silently demanding more information, Cormal's only reply is a smirk.

"Does it matter?" I ask Madoc.

He ignores my question and resumes pacing.

With a speculative look, Cormal's gaze turns toward the dark man pacing the room. "Faery fire means you're royal. How do we know *you're* not after the crown?"

Madoc waves a dismissive hand. "The light Fae crown chooses its ruler. When the light and dark Fae were cleaved into two, the light Fae embodied their crown with certain traits like wisdom and foresight to choose the best candidate amongst those with royal blood."

I blink. "Right before I threw it in the air, I told it to pick the best candidate—one who would serve both the aristocratic and Lesser Fae equally. Do you think that's why it didn't choose?"

His brow raised high, Madoc pauses and stares at me. "Maybe. It was a good move. One a queen would make for her people."

For a second, I can't help basking in the rare compliment, especially from someone who rarely gives them out. "Thank you. That means a lot. And the dark Fae crown? Was it also given wisdom and intelligence?"

A hard noise escapes Madoc's throat.

Did he just laugh?

"No. It searches for blood and power," he responds harshly.

Interesting. I turn toward Cormal, who's been strangely silent during the entire interaction. "What's next?"

"We need to find Leandra before King Denir gets to her," Cormal replies, his tone grim. "Whatever he wants can't be good for us. How the hell we're going to locate her, though, I'm not sure. The amulet makes her invisible to her enemies."

Madoc stops pacing and turns to us. "What if we sent a hunter who wasn't her enemy? Someone who knows nothing of her except her scent?"

Cormal jumps up, cursing. "Of course. Why the hell didn't I think of that? But who? Tarquin, one of Lucifer's hellhounds, isn't up for another mission." His fingers tap against his thigh as he thinks about it.

"I know someone," Madoc informs him. "He won't care who she is, nor will he ask questions, which will play in our favor. But he'll need something of hers. Do you have anything?"

Both men turn to me. My nose wrinkles at the thought. "No, but I could take you to some of the places we lived to see if she left anything behind. I must warn you, though; she was paranoid, rarely left items that could be used to trace her."

With as many enemies as she had, she knew one slip up would mean her death. I wish I'd been brave enough to steal something and leave it behind.

"There has to be something," Cormal insists. "Starting tomorrow, we'll check the most likely places." His tone is full of fierce determination.

Madoc raises a demanding finger. "I'm going with you. If we find something, I can immediately take it to my friend and start the hunt." When Cormal nods his agreement, Madoc moves toward the door. "I need to let him know."

He leaves without even saying goodbye.

Cormal stares after him with an incredulous expression on his face.

I can't help but chuckle. "Madoc is… unique. I don't think he's used to being around people." Another odd thing I like about him. He doesn't pander to others.

When Cormal grunts in return, I ask him, "Do you think this will work?"

Cormal nods. "It's a good plan." His words are reassuring,

but his narrowed eyes and set face tell me he's concerned about whether Madoc is going to be a problem.

I slide the tip of my finger across the line in his brow. "Give him a chance."

Cormal compresses his lips, but his hand wraps around the back of my neck, and he drops his face close to mine. "You're my priority. Not him."

They will either work it out or attempt to kill each other. Since they're both immortal, I'm not concerned.

I study the dried blood encrusted on his clothes, and desire and anger mix with the maelstrom of emotions raging within me.

My fingertips tingle. With a flick of my hand, I remove our clothes. Revenge can wait. "I need you. Inside me. Remind me that we're alive and here. Together."

CHAPTER TWO

<u>MERI</u>

His eyes flare with his own deep emotions as he sweeps me into his arms and carries me across the room. "You were magnificent today. Fierce. Queenly." He punctuates each word with a hard kiss on my lips.

Laying me across the bed, he skims his lips across my neck, then continues down to the rest of my body, but there's a frantic urgency to his movements as if he's barely restraining himself.

I throw my arms around his neck and pull him down to me, his weight a physical reminder that he's here with me. "I don't want to play. I need you. Inside me. Now."

My heart stopped the second the blade plunged into him. Logically, I knew it wouldn't kill him, but the idea of him dying was almost my undoing. Thankfully, the fiercest of anger rose, and I was able to stand my ground against our enemies. But now I need the kind of reassurance only he can give.

I wrap my legs tightly around him and brush my body up against his.

He shudders, and with a harsh exhalation, sinks into me. Our bodies fuse together, and he raises his head to stare down at me. "I don't have much control," he warns, his eyes tracing my blank forehead. "You're my fucking queen, and I want to imprint myself until all you know is me. All you feel is me."

He slides out and thrusts into me again. Harder. Deeper. "You're mine." His hips piston in and out as he proclaims his love in a hundred different ways, including the words he knows I need the most.

Life. Heat. Urgency. Him inside me, heart beating, I reach up to pull his face to mine. Capturing his firm lips, I pour everything into him. If our future were to end tomorrow, I want this to be my last memory. The depth and strength of us. I release his lips and gasp at the pleasure rolling over me.

My body trembles on the verge of coming, and he stops, holding still until it subsides.

"I'll tell you when you can come," he growls, the words barely coherent.

Blue eyes turn to black, bleeding out the white as his body grows bigger until he's halfway between man and beast, his body surrounding mine while inside he stretches me completely. My senses see and smell only him. Dark and broody with the hint of The Underworld. My head thrashes from side to side as the heat rises again. I grip his hard muscles, scoring them with my nails and magic, needing to come but not wanting him to let me.

Sharp teeth clamp down on my shoulder, and he stops. My body moves restlessly, and he tightens his bite. I finally find some control, but it's harder than I thought it would be. His cock throbs inside me, wall to wall, hard and pulsing, and it takes every ounce of my will to keep still even as my desire climbs to a peak.

He shifts. A micro movement. Out an inch. In an inch. My entire body shakes against his.

Lifting his mouth from my shoulder, he moves it to my ear. "Don't come."

Everything coalesces into a single moment. Balanced on the knife's edge, close to falling, every stroke of his body connects me to him in a way that goes beyond the physical. Alive, still fighting, here by my side, this man is my forever.

A tear slips down my cheek, and he swipes it with his tongue.

"This. Us. I love you, Cormal."

Breathing harshly, he rasps, "Nobody will ever take you away from me again. If I have to burn every kingdom to the ground to keep you safe, I will." He pauses. "Love is such an insipid word for what I feel for you. It needs no structure or boundaries. It simply is. It exists because you and I exist." He pulls out and thrusts into me. "We're never-ending."

"Never-ending," I repeat, knowing he needs the words, too, even though he would never admit it. "You're mine. Man, beast, and everything in between."

The words spur him faster and faster, and my body flies higher and higher, until I'm again at the edge of the precipice.

"Cormal!" I cry out, unable to hold myself back any longer.

"Come," he orders with a growl.

We fall together, our releases chasing each other, tremors cascading over us both, trapped in a whirlwind of rapture. Time passes slowly as the world around us creeps back into focus, intruding on the bubble we've created. Large hands gently stroke my hair and down my back as he holds me to him, unwilling to let me go even now.

I lean back to stare up at him as his body adjusts to his usual size. "Does it hurt?"

Blue eyes appear, making the black recede. "Sometimes." He

shifts his body into a more comfortable position but remains inside me.

With a shaky exhale, I move my leg, intertwining it with his. "Was it like this before? Between us?" The pieces of the past are still hidden somewhere in my mind, but I can't help but wonder if it always been this intense.

"It was sweeter. More innocent," he reluctantly tells me. His hands still, and he grips me tighter. "I was cocky. Thought we would live happily ever after." A derisive chuckle fills the air. "Losing it for so long changed both of us and the very essence of what's between us. It's sharper, and the innocence is gone, but strangely, there's more depth. And for me, there's an almost feral need to protect it at all costs. To hell with everyone and everything else. Maybe one day, the memories of the days without you will ease, along with the fury, but it will take several lifetimes to soften those edges."

"Pieces are coming back to me," I tell him. "While I don't remember everything, I don't like the thought of you making a pact with her to save me. Although, I know I would do the same for you."

He opens his mouth to say something, but then closes it again.

With a lift of my chin, I claim his lips, trying to reassure him that I'm here and not going anywhere. Rolling him onto his back, I shift until I'm on top. With him still inside me, I rock back and forth, staring into his darkening blue eyes.

"For me, love is a powerful word. Full of possibilities and hope. I love you, Cormal. More importantly, I'll fight for you and us. Against all odds," I promise him.

His mind slides into mine, full of fierce images and emotions I hadn't thought him capable of until recently.

I stare down at this man I've admired and hated, fought against and with, and secretly yearned for all these years. While curious about the past, I can't help but wonder if we could have achieved this equality between us. I remember my younger self being in awe of Cormal, hanging on his every word, but his refusal to save me from Leandra made me resentful, turning all my emotions to anger and ash.

The past wasn't a good place for me. Even if I don't remember us, I remember me. Until recently, I was scared and unsure of myself. Confidence wasn't a word I understood. The only time I stood up for myself was when I was fighting with Cormal. In a way, my anger at him helped me forget the rest of my life. But it was a crutch.

Where would the balance have been between us? It's different now. At some point in the last few months, I came into myself, and strength and confidence are no longer just words to me. Cormal and I match like we were created for each other.

Silence reigns between us. There are no words, only gasps and tiny moans as the pleasure intensifies. His cheeks flush as his fingers tighten on my hips.

My hands slide over his well-defined chest, keeping a consistent pace, pushing him to the edge. I want to see the moment he surrenders to me. Muscles cord in his neck as he thrusts his hips up, driving his cock deeper inside me. He's close. I link our hands and lean over him, picking up the pace until I'm riding him hard. The second he begins to pulse inside me, I take us both over the edge until we're lost to everything else.

Boneless, I fall into his arms, letting the waves crash over me until they get smaller and smaller. Finally, my breathing eases, and a contented sigh escapes.

Magic slides over us, cooling and drying the sweat from our bodies.

He turns and maneuvers us until we're each on our side and facing the other. "I never thought about it from that point of view. You endured so much. To me, you were strong. Fearless. Maybe a little young and naïve, but I cherished those traits because I felt old and jaded."

Startled, I stare at him. "A moment ago, I felt your mind slide into mine, but I didn't realize how much you could see." A blush heats my cheeks. "We fit now. Not just because of the power, although that certainly helps, but I'm confident and capable of accomplishing many things I would never have dreamed possible. Even fighting a Kraken." I grin.

He chuckles and brushes the hair from my face. "I know. It took everything I had to stand on the sidelines." His grin fades. "You're the woman I always knew you to be, but you had to believe it, too."

"I do, but I'm also a starving woman," I say dramatically with my hand on my forehead. "Feed me or lose me forever."

He chuckles and waves his hand, transporting a now dressed me to the couch.

Various food appears on plates, their smells making my stomach rumble, along with a carafe of ice water, and I dive in the second he sits beside me.

"Thank you. I felt like I was going to waste away any minute. Dramatic, I know, but I hate being hungry. It sucks."

His brows crash together. "You'll never go hungry again. I promise you."

Wanting to lighten the mood, I grin. "Mmm, you're right. One little wave of my finger and poof, food appears."

He turns to me with speculation on his face. "How much of your power did you retain?"

Closing my eyes, I dive deep inside. The threads to the Light Fae Kingdom and the black hole inside me are gone, given up with the crown. Some bare bones knowledge remains—the races, land borders, and resources. But the overwhelming buzz of power from the proximity of light Fae and the ability to tap into it has disappeared.

Surprisingly, there's a significant amount of magic left, though. More than I felt before I took the crown, which is odd. Did it leave a residue of power inside me?

"Quite a bit. The power I inherited as Nyssa's daughter and… more. I'm just not sure where the extra is from," I divulge with a shrug. "What do you think?"

Magic is still a new world for me. As someone who picked up powers right and left, Cormal might have more of an idea.

He's silent for a minute. "You regained the ability to mimic when the bond with Leandra broke, which means you might have acquired a few new powers. That could account for the additional magic."

I frown. "I thought those powers would eventually fade or become inaccessible. They did before."

Cormal takes my hand in his. "The original magic allowed the wielder to acquire permanent powers." His stare is intense, as if he's trying to tell me something.

I wait for him to continue, and he slowly raises an eyebrow and tilts his head. Does this mean he can't? Is this part of his pact with Leandra? Original wielder. The ability to acquire powers.

"Were you there when I received this power?" I ask him, wondering if he knows how I got it.

"Are you remembering?" he asks with a hopeful expression on his face.

Taken aback, I stare at him. "You can only tell me if I remember it myself? Unbelievable. Who cares? She can't hurt me now, right? The bond is broken."

When he doesn't say anything, I can only conclude I'm right and wrong. I must remember the past; he can't tell me the details. And Leandra is still a threat to me. Inhaling sharply, I wait for the crippling fear to wash over me, but there isn't any, and I can't hold back the smile that stretches across my face. Since the night of my coronation, I haven't felt that overwhelmingly destructive emotion, and it seems losing the crown doesn't change that for me.

Another thought occurs. "You know because you can wield this power. Did you give it to me?"

CHAPTER THREE

<u>MERI</u>

ormal gives me a smug nod but merely admits, "I do possess a... similar magic. It's how I accumulated so much power."

Floored, I can only stare at him as the knowledge hits me. He helped me. Cormal gave me his magic when I was powerless. The ability to mimic. Emotion clogs my throat, and for a second, I can't speak. All this time I thought him heartless and cruel, but at some point, he shared his magic with me, and to give me a power of that magnitude, he must have cared for me. A lot.

A minute ago, I wasn't sure remembering the past would change how I feel. Suddenly, I want to know every detail. How we met. What we were to each other. Why he gave me magic. I remember having the ability to mimic other's powers, but the magic I picked up from others never stayed with me.

What went wrong? Shadowy images from my dreams slide

through my mind, but I don't know what they mean. The only facts I know about that time came from Rivan. Leandra sent me to him to get a rune. Her original intent was to block my magic, but all he could do was limit my ability to wield it.

Slowly, I reveal my thoughts to Cormal, watching his face for any indication I'm right. Satisfaction replaces his intense look, confirming without words Leandra's involvement. It makes me more determined than ever to remember my dreams. I slide a gaze to the clarity rune on my palm. I wonder if Arden has a spell to enhance it.

Knowing Cormal can't tell me, I decide to ask him about the magic itself. "Can I mimic any power?"

"Not every power is available for me to grab," he informs me with a ghost of a smile on his lips. Apparently, telling me about "his" power helps him get around his agreement with Leandra. "The origin of the power is black magic, and it isn't predictable."

"Black magic, huh?" I look at him speculatively, then I pull my hand from his and reach down to pick up my sandwich. Taking a huge bite, I chew for a minute while I think. "Is this the same magic that got your sister kidnapped?"

He glances away for a minute. "Yes. Ri´ created it."

It sounds like he said "Ree."

"Your sister?" I ask. When he nods, I continue. "Is Ree short for something?"

"Riona," he tells me. "But we always called her Ri´."

Taking advantage of his willingness to talk about her, I continue. "She wielded black magic?"

"Better than me," he admits with a proud smile. "At the time, her magic surpassed mine a hundredfold." Memories shine in the depths of his eyes, along with profound sadness. "It was her best and worst moment. Creating that power is what led to her disappearance. In her absence, I've used it to become more in hopes of finding her."

More? Including his immortality? The past is opening doors

between Cormal and me that I hadn't expected. I open my mouth to ask him another question, but the knob turns and Madoc walks into the room, wearing clean clothes.

Stopping abruptly, his nostrils flare and a low growl slips from his throat. His eyes swing to the bed, and I realize he's probably smelling Cormal and me.

Cormal chuckles beside me, and I glare at him before waving a hand to remove the scent of sex.

Madoc's gaze swivels to lock on me, his stare intense and, shockingly, full of heat. Tension sparks between us. An image of us together on the same bed slips into my mind. His dark tousled hair and muscular, scarred body next to my platinum-blond, petite frame is quite the contrast. Inhaling sharply, I raise an eyebrow at him, wondering if the image is all in my mind or if I accidentally shared it with him like I've been doing with Cormal.

It's not as if I haven't noticed him. I notice every male around me, and I really appreciate the delicious flavor of them all. I silently laugh, thinking of my guards and how I thought of Neapolitan ice cream when I looked at them.

Madoc is different, though. Powerful, but that doesn't mean much to me. Anger and revenge swirl in his eyes and the clench of his fists. There's nothing light about him, which sort of explains why I find myself attracted to him. Dark is catnip to me, and he's got more than his fair share.

His steel-grey stare never wavers from me.

Cormal growls, "Not fucking happening."

When we both swing our gazes to him, there's a huge scowl on his face, but it's his eyes that worry me. They're starting to turn black. Guess passion isn't the only thing that brings the beast to the surface.

The sight of it makes me laugh. "Jealous?"

Madoc snorts. "Settle down, brùid. It's not as if you could stop me. Besides, she can make up her own mind."

The utter confidence in his voice is thrilling and a little scary.

I shiver and put down the sandwich. "Moving on from this rather boring conversation. Did you find your friend?"

Madoc shoves a large hand through his messy black hair. "Yes. He's agreed to do it."

"Leandra has spies everywhere. You trust he won't say anything, right?" Cormal questions. "We can't take a chance she'll find a way to avoid us."

A strangled sound emerges from Madoc's throat as if something caught in it. "He won't say a word. I swear on my life." His arrogant eyebrow lifts. "Have you planned our route? I'd like to know where we're going."

Cormal's smirks in defiance. "Not yet. I've been preoccupied." He reaches out and lays a possessive hand on my leg. "Besides, I'm not sure I want you to know until it's time to leave."

Madoc shakes his head and his jaw clenches, but he says nothing. Probably because he too trusts no one.

"We lived in a lot of places. Mostly warm spots, but there are a few very cold locations, too. Do you have a parka and gloves?" I ask Madoc.

"Why? I can just regulate my temperature," Madoc replies with a raised eyebrow.

Ignoring him, I turn toward Cormal. "We'll need clothes. Can you get those for us?" It's easier to magically dress in clothes already created instead of conjuring them from scratch because the process takes a lot of magic and is too time consuming. "Also, can you find out what happened to Rivan? I'm worried about him."

Madoc steps forward before Cormal can answer. "I'll check on him. Where did you see him last?" He listens as I tell him about the treaties. "The kraken might be the best place to start.

I'll return when I have news." Long legs eat up the distance to the door, and he's gone before I can even reply.

Cormal swiftly stands. "I need to check on The Underworld, grab some warmer clothes, and give Kavi some instructions." He leans down and captures my lips in a swift kiss. "Don't leave The Abbey. Please."

I roll my eyes. "I'm going to check on Solandis and have a chat with Arden."

Satisfied with my answer, he leaves, and I pick up my phone to text Vargas.

> Meri: How is Solandis? Can I come by for a visit?

> Vargas: You better come quick. Ever since she woke up, she's been threatening to make me a eunuch if I don't let her see you.

> Meri: Floor?

> Vargas: Fourth floor. Right above yours.

> Meri: On my way.

Chuckling, I wave a hand to clean up the dishes and head toward the elevator. When the doors open on the fourth floor, Callyx is standing there.

"Hey, how is she?" I ask him, knowing Solandis will try to pretend everything is fine.

"She's shaken up by Lorn's kidnapping. Normally, it would piss her off, but the baby is her biggest concern," he replies in a harsh tone. "She's better here, at The Abbey. Safe."

Guilt weighs heavily on my shoulders. "I wish I had never brought him into our lives. Not once did it occur to me that he wasn't what he portrayed to me—Allandra's brother and a light Fae."

"Solandis isn't sure you would have been able to tell, anyway. Mixed bloods are more difficult to identify as light or dark, and you were just learning how to identify the Fae," he reveals with a shrug. "I've got to leave. Lucifer still has me on the hunt for the monster that escaped."

"Should we be worried?" I ask. One monster is quite enough.

"We're not sure. The Devil didn't leave records of those he incarcerated in The Below. Lucifer only knows he's missing because he recently counted them," he tells me. "Oh. Tell Cormal he's on Lucifer's shit list. Nobody is supposed to have access to The Below but him." Turquoise eyes narrow in speculation.

Is that where Cormal sent Lorn? I hope so. I never want to see him again. "I'll pass it along. Be careful." Kissing his cheek, I slide past him and down the hall.

Vargas opens the door the second I knock. Kaius' tall, lean body, chestnut brown hair and light green eyes are gone, and in its place is the old Vargas, with his massively big, stacked muscular body, shaved head, dark complexion, and pitch-black eyes. I don't know if it's because he could only wear that face for a limited time or if he wanted to make Solandis feel more at ease. I wish he could stay in this form. It's so good to see the old him.

"Get in here." Closing it, he engulfs me in a tight hug. "Thank you." Emotions clog his throat, making his voice tight.

Embarrassed, I return his hug and ease out of his arms. "Where is she?"

I don't want to make a big deal out of the whole crown thing, especially when I'm not sure it was ever mine in the first place. Maybe temporarily, like a guardian. I miss being queen, but the light Fae always felt pretentious and self-serving to me.

Strong, thin arms hug me close. "Meri, Meri. What have you done?" Solandis' turquoise eyes stare at me as two tears roll down her face. "The crown chose you as our queen. Why would you give that up?"

Her face is drawn, and her hand hovers protectively over the slight bump of her stomach. Tension sits in the tightness of her shoulders and lines in her neck, and her eyes shine with both gratitude and guilt.

I refuse to accept the guilt. "Because unlike Nyssa or Leandra, family means more to me than power," I state firmly, tucking a stray blond hair behind her ear. "Besides, Madoc doesn't think it was meant to be mine permanently. He thinks I was chosen as a temporary guardian of it."

A small line appears between her brows. "Why would he say such a thing?"

"It's his best guess since I never received the connection I was supposed to get," I explain, revealing his theory. "How are you feeling? Is the baby okay?"

She sniffs. "You're more like me than Nyssa." Her hand rubs across the slight bump. "We're doing good. He or she has been kicking up a storm, but the activity is reassuring." She doesn't say the words, but the stress of potentially losing the baby took a toll on her. Walking over to a nearby chair, she curls up in the plump cushions.

I swallow the lump in my throat and smile at her. "Good. We need more fighters in this family." I slide a glance at Vargas. "What are your plans?"

He walks over and sits on the arm of the chair, then takes Solandis' hand. "We're staying here until after the baby is born. It's safer for Solandis. The fight for the crown will be brutal, and it's best if she stays hidden."

I didn't even think about that, but I guess we eliminated two of the top contenders, and with Solandis here, essentially removed a third from the board. I nod and tell them what I told the crown.

"Madoc says the light Fae crown was imbued with wisdom and foresight. I'm hoping it finds the best candidate to lead the light Fae."

"Madoc seems to know a lot about the light Fae and our

crown," Solandis murmurs with a hint of worry in her eyes. "Are you sure about him?"

"Honestly, I'm not a hundred percent sure," I admit with a sigh. "He's saved my life several times, though. Right now, I'm giving him the benefit of the doubt, but I also know Cormal is keeping a close eye on him."

Lorn wasn't who I thought him to be. What if Madoc isn't either? But the last thing I want is for her to worry.

Her eyes full of relief, Solandis darts a glance at Vargas. "Lorn told me Nyssa placed a spell over the people to remove their memories of him and his sister because they knew she had a hand in murdering our father. They only came back once she was gone, hoping they might be able to snag the crown for themselves if it rejected you. When it didn't, their plans changed."

That's why Cormal couldn't find much information about them until he started digging into the past. "They must have been overjoyed when Leandra showed up to tell them about my dark Fae heritage." My voice is full of bitterness.

"It would have come out sooner or later," Solandis states with a wave of her hand. "What are you going to do now?"

"We're going hunting," I grimly inform her. "Leandra's days are numbered. It's time to finish her once and for all."

CHAPTER FOUR

<u>CORMAL</u>

Kavi glares at me from across the desk, his massive muscles stuffed into the desk chair, and his ebony skin gleaming in the artificial sun shining in from the fake window behind my desk.

"Do you know how many disputes I've had to settle this morning? Three. And I've only been here an hour. I'm ready to kill a few demons just to get some peace." One large beefy hand spears through his black curly hair in frustration.

I laugh. Chaos demons aren't known for their patience. I'm surprised he hasn't killed at least one. "Leadership sucks. Everyone thinks it's great, but in reality, it's full of petty squabbles and greedy demons." He gets up so I can sit in my chair. "What's the latest in The Underworld?"

His black eyes gleam with knowledge. "Callyx dropped by yesterday. Flashed me a picture of a symbol. Asked if I'd seen any monsters lately."

My neck tingles. One monster is a coincidence but two are rare. "Let Lucifer know I added to his collection in The Below." Pure satisfaction runs through me at the thought of Lorn suffering in that hellhole… forever.

Kavi gives me an incredulous look. "He knows, and he's not happy."

Inwardly, I cringe, but my face is blank as I nod. "I'll stop by and smooth his feathers." It's not as if Lucifer doesn't know I have access to most places. After all, he's banned me from entering his palace via any means except the front door like I'm some run-of-the-mill demon.

Kavi stands, his almost eight foot height towering over everything, and rolls his thick neck. "Anything else?"

"Take a day or two off. I'll leave instructions for your return," I order him.

Once he's gone, I contemplate the look on Madoc's face when he smelled the sex in the room. He feels something for Meri. Hopefully, it's just lust, but the bastard is an enigma, and I don't like it. I'd send Kavi to track him, but he'd likely get caught. Madoc's sharp and would sniff him out in a second. Maybe we could tag him. From his reaction in the elevator, I'm guessing he isn't tech savvy.

I slide open the drawer of my desk and pull out a couple of trackers. Dropping them in my pocket, I finish my paperwork, then head out. First stop: Lucifer's. Better for me to go to him than have him track me down. Bastard has a temper.

When I arrive at the palace, I wave at the guards standing at the front door and walk in. Evren, Lucifer's better half, is in his office when I enter. A tall, fierce red-head and the perfect foil for Lucifer's angelic blond appearance.

A goddess and scientist, she's taken on the task of building The Underworld's first university. It's a monumental project, but she's the most qualified to do it. Her ideas and knowledge will make it first class.

Typically regal in public, today she's leaning over the desk arguing with Lucifer. Her voice is loud and passionate as she basically calls him a cheapskate for not automatically giving her the funding she needs to add another building to the plan.

I smother the laugh threatening to escape my lips. It's not good to piss off a goddess who could end my immortality with a wave of her finger.

Lucifer folds his arms and shakes his head. "I'm not saying you can't have the funding. Finish the plan first, then we can talk about what needs to be added." The stubborn glint in his eyes tells me he's not backing down.

Evren must realize it too, because she flips him off.

Clearing my throat, I ask them, "Should I come back later?"

Evren huffs and turns around. "Hello, Cormal. It's good to see you. Please excuse my bad manners, but I can't stay in the same room with someone who refuses to use his common sense." She strides out of the room, red hair streaming behind her, and slams the door behind her.

I wince. "Why don't you just give her the money?"

Lucifer laughs. "She takes on too much. If I gave her the money, she'd work night and day to get it all done before the semester starts." A wicked smile stretches across his face. "She's magnificent when she's pissed off, isn't she?"

"No comment," I murmur. It's a rhetorical question. "Word on the streets is Callyx is hunting a monster?"

Lucifer smile turns into a scowl. "Damn thing must have escaped when I put Gabriel down there."

Uneasy with the idea of Lorn escaping, I question him. "How? There are no doors."

Dark eyes turn toward me, full of speculation. "Is there any place in my kingdom you haven't been?" A second later, he holds up a hand. "Don't answer that. It would only piss me off. No doors, but there is a long tunnel. It's how we feed them." He heaves an aggravated sigh. "Gabriel came back without his wings. He must have bartered them away."

"The monster flew out?" I ask incredulously. Unbelievable, but at least it means Lorn isn't escaping any time soon. "I know you're aware I added one to your collection."

I give him an overall synopsis of what went happened with the light Fae. "Lorn deserved a punishment befitting his crime against Solandis, and I wanted to be sure Meri would be safe from his retaliation."

"Callyx informed me, or I would've hunted you down and demanded an explanation," Lucifer tells me with a note of warning in his voice. "Next time, I suggest you get here a little faster and tell me yourself."

I give him a curt nod. "Meri's safety comes first, but I'll do my best." It's an easy concession to make to someone who has my respect.

Lucifer leans back in his chair. "What's next?"

"Leandra," I say shortly. "We might have a way to track her."

He pauses, as if waiting for me to explain, but when I say nothing, he nods. "She does seem to have eyes and ears everywhere. Good luck."

Reaching out a hand to shake his, I stand and stride to the door. "I'll keep you informed." I stop and turn. "Do you have a copy of the photograph Callyx is showing everyone? You never know when I might turn up some intel."

He waves a hand, and a photograph appears in front of my face. "We don't have images of the monsters themselves, but this is the brand the Devil put on them when he placed them there."

I pluck it from the air and study it. A pentagram with the devil's pitchfork in the center. Crude, but effective. "Thanks."

Minutes later, I'm back at the market, buying clothes for Meri and Madoc. Part of me wants him to freeze his ass off, but in the end, I grudgingly get him a few items. Only because she asked me to do it.

After shopping, I head back to my office to spend the rest of the day working. With several missions in play, I need to check on their progress. One in particular—a lead on Ri´—has my hopes up. It doesn't matter how many I have to chase down; I refuse to give up on her. Besides, I have the manpower to do it.

Minutes after returning, the demon I sent to follow the latest lead arrives. Over the years, I've sent different demons, typically those who are the fiercest or have the ability to slide into the darkest of places. This time, I sent a demon of greed. I don't know why. Either my seer ability or gut instinct told me he was the one to send.

Tall, with auburn hair, he strides in with a cocky smile on his face. "I believe she's alive." He places a photo on my desk.

Unable to believe it, but unable to stop hoping as well, I slowly pick up the photo. Dark hair, blue eyes the same color as mine, the woman is either Ri´ or her doppelganger. But this woman's spirit is nothing like my sister. Her eyes were always sparkling with life. The ones in the photo are blank. Not dead, but as if hope is lost. Blank like there's nobody inside.

Shoving aside the thought for a second, I quickly realize the photo is of her portrait. A painting. Maybe that is why her eyes are blank. She's sitting, back straight, hands in her lap, with a small smile on her face, and she's dressed in a black silk gown. Something she would never have worn in her previous life. Ri´ loved color.

I open my top drawer and grab my magnifying glass. Holding it over the photo, I focus on the glint of gold around her neck. It's a torque. A clear sign of possession, and given our Druid past, also something she would never willingly wear.

My hand trembles slightly as I set both items on my desk. Cautioning myself not to get too hopeful, I wave a hand at the demon. "Details." I can barely get the word out, but my harsh tone conveys everything.

Lot, the demon, drops his cocky smile. "Someone is

searching for information on her. Background. Powers. Anything. I didn't see the person myself but heard it was a male. I asked the shadow demon if I could have the picture for my boss, but he refused." He shrugs his slim shoulders. "I stole it."

Greed makes a demon do dangerous things. Shadow demons can slip through the smallest of cracks. "What's going to happen when you go back and ask him to set up a meeting with the male?"

Another shrug. "Depends on whether I can use your name or not." He thinks about it for a second. "Probably better if I don't. He'll ask for more than his share. I'm sure I can find out what he wants most in his little world and use it as a bargaining tool." His amber eyes shine with anticipation. "Am I good to move forward?"

"Leave my name out of it," I direct him. Too many times, my name has caused them to clam up. "This could be a hoax or deliberate trap. I wish it was an actual photo instead of a picture of her portrait. It doesn't really confirm whether she's alive or not. In the past, my enemies have tried to use this against me. Proceed with caution. Keep me informed of every movement."

With a nod, he swirls a finger and makes a copy of the photo for himself. "I'll be in touch."

Once he's gone, I can't help but examine every inch of the photo again. If it's her, she's not any older than when she was taken, or like me, she's now immortal, but the somber expression throws me. I'm not sure I ever saw the expression on her face. When our brothers died, her face was full of fury and tears and life. She could be a mannequin for all the emotion in this photo.

Meri: Are you coming back tonight?

Part of me wants to rush back and hold her in my arms,

reassure myself she's alive and still mine but I have a million tasks to do before I leave.

> Cormal: Tomorrow morning. Breakfast. In bed.

The fleeting image of Madoc crawling into her bed almost makes me change my mind, but I force the overwhelming feelings of rage and jealousy away. I told her she could have anyone she wants, but his dark gaze and arrogance sets my teeth on edge. Maybe I can find a way to kill him. That would solve the problem for me.

With a little magic, I prop the image up on the corner of my desk so I can stare at it while I get my work done. It's been so long since I've seen my sister's face. Even this wretched photo gives me peace. If she's alive, I'll mobilize all of hell to save her.

CHAPTER FIVE

<u>MERI</u>

My dreams are dark, full of monsters and death. Lorn is front and center, along with Leandra and Cormal. They hound me until sleep becomes elusive. For the first time in a long time, I wake alone, hours before the sun. Neither Cormal nor Madoc returned last night. Arden and her men were gone as well on a mission for The Abbey.

As queen, I wasn't sure if I'd like having tons of people around me, but I loved it. Too many years spent by myself, longing for family or a friend to stay with me. Sometimes the loneliness became so unbearable, I'd often find myself getting up in the middle of the night to wander the streets of whatever place we were calling home.

The light Fae palace always had aristocratic Fae wandering the halls and servants bustling here and there, producing a constant hum of noise beneath even the smallest amount of silence.

In contrast, The Abbey is a sentinel, standing silent and watchful, filled with magic, and ready to guard its inhabitants. It's too quiet here. Living with Leandra felt like this. Suffocating and lonely. Dark and dangerous. When I stayed here previously, I didn't know anything different. Plus, the warmth of protection and my newfound family distracted me. Now I do.

Cormal strides into the room with a firm expression on his face. Seeing me sitting alone eases the raging storm inside him and the crackling tension he brought with him subsides. "Good morning. You're up early." His lips capture mine.

Normally, his kisses are demanding and full of desire, but the way his lips cling to mine suggests a different type of need.

"Are you okay? Did something happen?"

He looks at me blankly. "No, why?"

Instead of answering, I hand him a cup of coffee, but he shakes his head.

"It took me all night to get through everything. More coffee and I'll be bouncing off the walls," he tells me. "Where's Madoc?"

Maybe his mood is due to his underlying jealousy. "He's not back yet. I spent last night alone." Although I try, I can't quite keep the grumbling note of irritation out of my voice.

His blue eyes sweep across my face. "Bad dreams?"

"Plenty, but I expected them," I tell him as I try to find a way to explain how I'm feeling. I don't want to be a burden to him. The Abbey is the safest place for me. "I'm out of sorts here. Like I don't belong. I wish we could go home."

He grabs a piece of bacon off the plate in front of me and tugs me from the small table to the couch. "Where is home?" His look is contemplative as he waits for my answer.

"The Underworld, I guess," I reply, but even as I say it, I realize it's only partially true. "I don't know. Being with the Fae filled some part of me I didn't know was empty. It's going to take a while to figure out where I belong. Being here doesn't help because it's a place of limbo. Temporary."

Strong arms wrap around my body and pull me close. "I understand. Once we've taken care of Leandra, maybe we can find a place in the Fae world. Hell knows I have enough wealth to do whatever we want."

With his scent and strength wrapped around me, my world settles. I tilt my head back and look up at him. "I like that idea. Did you get us some clothes? The sooner we hunt her down, the better."

He nods, then abruptly turns toward the door.

Madoc strides in with a somber expression on his face. "Rivan's missing. With Fisk dead, the Kraken, Hyne, is leading the Water Fae. He said Rivan dropped off the treaty but couldn't stay because he was returning to you. Did you tell him you were giving up the crown and coming here?"

The words crash into me, and my heart sinks like a stone. I never thought he would actually return to me. His mind was set on leaving the Fae world behind. "I didn't tell him my plans. I thought he would feel obligated to stay, and I didn't want that for him." The last time I saw him was in my room at the palace, swearing to find Camon.

"He swore to hunt down Camon and make him pay for selling out Fisk," Cormal says, jumping up. "We took out Camon." He looks pointedly at Madoc, who severed Camon's head from his body and burned him to ashes with faery fire. "Once Rivan found out about his demise, he likely went after his father."

Dread curls in my stomach, and I get to my feet, needing to stand before I throw up. "Brixton is more likely to kill him than welcome him." Two days have passed... he could have already done it. I shove the thought away. I would know if Rivan was dead. I'd feel it. I don't know how, but I'd know. Right? "We need to find Rivan immediately."

Cormal's blue eyes reflect the same fears as mine. We both know it might be too late. "I'll get my men on it. Someone always knows something. We'll find him. I promise you." His jaw tightens until he's wearing his usual expression of determination. Sheer will is his greatest power.

Madoc steps over to me and adds his own assurances. Grey eyes peer at me from beneath long dark lashes. They should be cold, but all I see is warmth in them. "There isn't an area in the Fae lands I don't know. I'll check the places the Phoenix like to hide first." He turns to Cormal. "How do you want me to send word?"

Cormal conjures a phone for him. "Call me. My number is programmed in there."

Madoc stares at the equipment likes it's a snake waiting to bite him. His eyes dart to mine, and a slight pink hue spreads across his cheeks. "I don't know how to use it. Is there another way?"

He's embarrassed, but he shouldn't be. I didn't have a phone until Cormal gave one to me.

Cormal's gaze sharpens. "Take it. If you need me, press this button." He points to the one labeled contacts. "Then tap on my name. I'm the only one in there." With a couple of taps, he shows him. Cormal's phone rings, and Madoc immediately jumps, then scowls at a smirking Cormal.

"Does it work in the Fae lands?" he asks, reluctantly taking the phone from him.

"Not always," Cormal replies with a sigh. "Here." He hands him a card. "Say the spell on the back. I'll find you, but it will take longer."

Madoc slides the card into his pocket. "Thanks." The grudging tone of his voice tells me he isn't happy having to rely on Cormal.

I grab the phone from Madoc. "Here. I'm adding my number too. In case you can't reach Cormal." *Or you don't want to call him*, but I don't say it. I look over at Cormal, who's now glaring at me.

"Don't call her," he orders Madoc. "She's safe here. If she leaves, Leandra will find her."

I open my mouth to spit something rude back to him, but before I can do so, Madoc is nodding his head in full agreement.

"Her safety is most important," Madoc agrees with a firm nod. "After all, we can't find Leandra without her."

Well, that's a reality check, isn't it? My cheeks burn with anger and embarrassment.

"I'm going to find Arden," I tell them. I stomp past Cormal, but he grabs my wrist and pulls me around to face him. I look up and see his blue eyes burning with intent.

"I mean it, Meri," he says in a stern voice. "Stay here. Promise me."

For a brief second, I press my lips tightly together like the old days, but I quickly push past my initial reaction. Rivan needs us. It goes against every grain in my body to give him a promise, but I do. Besides, I might have power, but my bodyguards are gone, and I don't know where to search for Rivan.

"I promise."

Cormal raises an eyebrow.

Gritting my teeth, I force the words out. "I promise I'll stay here."

Satisfied, he tosses an arrogant glance at Madoc. "If I don't hear from you in a few hours, I'll call and check on you."

Madoc snorts. "Don't bother. Keep yourself safe. Meri would be upset if something happened to you." Without another word, he disappears through the door.

Cormal picks up his phone and taps on it. A dangerous smile slides across his face.

Curious, I peer over his shoulder and see a dot moving on a map. "Did you bug Madoc's phone? What is wrong with you?"

"He's hiding something, and until I know what it is, I'm

going to track his every move," Cormal murmurs. He leans down and gives me a hard kiss. "I'll call you if I hear anything." Then he, too, leaves.

Pacing back and forth, I try to get the image of Rivan hurt and needing help out of my head, but it's almost impossible. Pivoting, I grab my phone and send a text. A second later, the answer comes and I'm out the door.

Arden's in the training room fighting with Vargas when I enter. Theron and Fallon are watching from the sidelines, fists clenched, as if they hate the sight. I slide up next to them.

Theron's eyes never move from the two fighters, but he murmurs a quiet greeting.

Fallon bends over and gives me an awkward hug before resuming his tense position. "Good to see you, Meri."

Astonished, I stare up at the tall Elven prince. "We're hugging now?"

The corner of Fallon's mouth curls in a half-smile. "Apparently. Arden says that's what family does. I mean, mine never did, but my father was an asshole." He shrugs as if it doesn't bother him.

"Arden likes to hug. Solandis, Vargas, and Callyx too," I murmur. "Guess it runs in the family." Besides Cormal and the occasional child, I can't remember hugging anyone before Arden. It still feels odd to me.

Clanging swords and swearing brings my gaze back to the fight. Or the end of it, as Vargas stands there scowling at Arden, his hands empty of the sword he held a moment ago.

Arden's shaking her head at him. "Being a chameleon has made you slow. Or maybe it was living in the Light Fae Kingdom doing nothing but bossing Meri's guards around. You need practice." She tosses his sword to him, then turns to Fallon. "You're up."

An evil grin replaces the smile on Fallon's lips, and he rubs his hands together in anticipation. "Get ready, old man. I've been waiting months to wipe the floor with you." A regal-looking silver sword appears in his large hand, and he springs forward.

Vargas' cups his hand and eggs him forward. "Bring it on, pup."

The two immediately start whirling and slashing until they're a blur to the rest of us.

Arden chuckles. "This is definitely helping to take his mind off Solandis and the baby for a little while. It's not good for them to be holed up in their room."

Remembering her tiredness at the palace, I share my thoughts with Arden. "It's more than caution or fear for her safety. This baby is taking a lot out of her. Physically. She's been exhausted since the moment she became pregnant. All the rest hasn't helped, but I think there's more to it. Has she seen a doctor yet?"

Surprised, Arden stares at me for a second. "She never told me this has been going on for a while. I'll get one here to check her out."

As she calls the doctor, she raises an eyebrow and asks, "Why did you need to see me so urgently? For Solandis?"

I look at the rune on my hand but close my fingers around it. The spell can wait. "Rivan's gone missing. Cormal and Madoc are looking for him, but we think he might have tried to go after Brixton."

Theron turns to face me. "The leader of the Phoenix?"

I forgot he was dark Fae as well as light Fae. "Yes, that's his father." I explain to them both what happened to the original Kaius, Fisk's grandson, and Brixton's role in his death. "You wouldn't know of anyone who could help us search the Dark Fae Kingdom, do you?"

"Search, no, but I know someone who lives in the palace who might be able to pass us information," Theron tells me.

"I don't want Denir to find out we're searching for Rivan," I reply with a frown.

Theron dips his chin in acknowledgement. "My brother, Oryn, owes his allegiance to me, not the king. I'll see if he's heard of anything."

I didn't know Theron had a dark Fae brother. "Thanks, I'd appreciate it."

Theron's hand brushes lightly against Arden's back as he leaves to make the call.

Arden's staring at her feet with a frown on her face when I turn back to her.

"The doctor's on her way. I can't believe I didn't have her checked out when she got here," she says to me. "I did heal all her cuts and bruises, but that's all I could do. She let me think she was just a little tired because of her ordeal."

"She may not realize it's more than that," I say in return. The sounds of fighting ease. "They'll be done soon. Let's get her checked out before they finish."

We head to the lobby to meet the doctor and bring her up to Solandis' room.

Surprisingly, Solandis quickly agrees to let the doctor examine her. When they come back into the room, Vargas is striding through the door. He abruptly halts.

"What the hell is going on?" he bellows when he sees the doctor, rushing over to Solandis. "Are you okay? Is it the baby?"

She places a finger on his lips. "I'm fine. Kind of silly, really. With the blood of a cirein-croin in him or her, we need more than the usual food and nutrients. The doctor is going to create a special diet to make sure we get what we need. It's why I've been exceedingly exhausted."

When Vargas lost his body, he took Kaius', but just like he didn't realize he was a chameleon, he didn't know he was Fisk's grandson. And Fisk was pure cirein-croin, a legendary sea monster and one of the most badass Water Fae I've ever met. Their unborn child carries all this heritage in his blood.

He heaves a sigh of relief. "Good. I hate seeing you so damn tired all the time." Pulling her closer to him, he kisses her softly. "So, the doctor is sure about the cirein-croin?"

Her lips curve in a tremulous smile. "Looks like this baby is all Fae. Are you okay with that?" Her tone is soft, but I can tell she's worried he'll be upset that their child won't have demon blood in them.

"They'll have a demon heart," he assures her.

Arden and I glance at the doctor, and she gives a slight nod. We leave them to the rest of it. Arms around each other, we unanimously turn toward the elevator.

"I need a drink," Arden says, dropping her head back against the wall. "Join me?"

If I go back to my room, all I'll do is pace until I hear from Cormal. Plus, maybe Theron will come back with something sooner. I hope so. The thought of Rivan being held somewhere by his father makes my blood boil. After everything he sacrificed for the Fire Fae, and in particular, the Phoenix, he deserves more, especially from his family. And from me.

"I could use a strong drink."

CHAPTER SIX

CORMAL

Sika, the half selkie, races off the minute I've given him the information. It takes a while to track down Ren, a merman and one of my best light Fae spies. Apparently, he's been helping the Water Fae prepare for war. Once he knows it's Rivan, he mobilizes his entire family to help search.

I sent word to Tarquin, the hellhound, but he wanted nothing to do with the Phoenix. Can't say I blame him after what happened between him and Brixton. So, I send out runners to my Fae contacts, both light and dark, to ask if they've seen Brixton. It's better if they don't know I'm actually searching for Rivan.

The dot on the map moves again. I've been watching it disappear and reappear all over the Fae lands for the last hour. Madoc moves quick. It's quite impressive, but also worrisome, because we know very little about him.

Kavi walks in and folds his arms across his chest. "I don't like it when you go on a mission alone. At least take one of the other chaos demons with you. In case you need back-up."

The dot jumps and lands… in the Wilds. I wait for it to move, but when it doesn't, I flash a grim look at Kavi. "I'll take Lux with me."

Very little throws Kavi, but my request for the unstable shadow demon definitely makes him uneasy. He knows better than to argue, though. Grimacing, he waves a hand and Lux appears in my office. Dark as the shadows themselves except for his red eyes, and standing three feet tall, he doesn't look like a threat.

"He has a job for you. Don't fuck it up."

The small demon laughs and swirls his finger across a nearby shadow. "Where are we going?" he asks in an excited, high-pitched voice.

Shaping my own shadow into a noose, I toss it over him and pull him close. "If you don't do exactly as I say, I'll throw you in the Flames of Hell. Got it?" The eternal flames cast no shadows, offering only permanent death to his kind.

He gulps and repeats, "Do what you say. Got it."

"You'll stay in the shadow of the trees, alerting me to any threat that approaches. That's it," I tell him, deliberately using the word alert instead of guard. Off his leash, this small demon can rip the world to shreds using only the shadows around him.

He looks disappointed, but when I tighten the noose, he swears to follow my orders.

"If I'm not back in two hours, come find me," I order Kavi. "We're headed to the Wilds."

Kavi looks ill at the mention of our location, but Lux perks up. "I like the Wilds."

"You would," I tell him wryly. "Let's go." Using my own shadow network, we travel to the portal, then cross over to the Fae lands. In minutes, we're standing outside the Wilds.

I check my phone. The dot is still here, which means Madoc

hasn't moved. What in the hell could he want in here? Does he think Brixton would dare enter this sacred wood? Not likely. The Fae who live here are unlike any other. Twisted and dark, they have little allegiance to anything and a penchant for killing. Kind of like Lux.

At the boundary of the woods, old, gnarled trees block the entrance. An innocent barrier that turns deadly if you try to cross without their permission. I stand and wait. Surprisingly, Lux also stands utterly still at my side. Makes me wonder how many times he's been here.

Twisted branches move, snaking in and out, until the entrance is clear. We have their permission. I step through, Lux right behind me, and when we pass the last root, the branches close, locking us in.

Not far from the entrance, we come to a small mountain. This is the location. I glance around the base, but there's no sign of Madoc. Sensing magic above me, I look up. Halfway up the side is a cave, firelight rippling across its stone mouth.

I look at Lux. "Stay here. Alert only. Understood?" My voice is barely a whisper, but he nods his head several times.

Scampering into the nearest shadow, he settles in. Eyes peeled for danger, he doesn't even blink. Maybe I should consider taking him on more missions.

With a boost of magic, I step to the entrance of the cave, only to find a knife at my throat. I raise my eyebrow in disbelief at his choice of weapon. With all the magic at his disposal, his choice is primitive, but says a lot about his confidence.

He clucks his tongue in irritation. "What are you doing here?" Crossing to the fireplace, he sits down and resumes eating, but his predatory gaze never leaves me despite his nonchalant demeanor.

"Are you really trying to convince me you're camping in the Wilds?" I ask derisively. Does he think I'm stupid? I cast my magic to the corners of the room as I take a deep breath. Mmm. The saturated tones of dark magic.

He smirks at me. "It's safe enough. Better than getting caught between the Lesser and aristocratic light Fae." A weary look crosses his scruffy face. His dusty clothes reflect the amount of traveling he's done today. "I haven't caught one whiff of Brixton or Rivan. Or any Phoenix, for that matter. It's as if they've disappeared from the Fae lands."

I say nothing, concentrating only on finding the source of the disturbance I sense in the air. Magic ripples in the corner, and I send mine to intercept. Camouflaged, the huge creature moves forward, magic pulsing in my direction, but Madoc jumps between us and blocks it.

"Stop!" he shouts at the semi-transparent... thing. "He isn't here to harm us. Friend. Friend."

His words reverberate off the stone walls, but they have the desired effect. The creature solidifies in front of us.

"Friend?" it asks. Head brushing the ceiling, the... monster... stares down at me with pitch black eyes as if he's contemplating my demise.

"Friend," Madoc confirms with a snort. "Don't take this to heart, Cormal. Our relationship will be as brief as your time in this cave."

Wiry hair covers a rough, textured body. Long, dark hair cascades down from a face that is decidedly not human in structure. Demon origin, maybe. Thick protruding brow. Mouth full of sharp, pointed teeth. Five-inch claws at the end of each of its fingers. Bow-legged, it stands at an awkward angle.

"He grows, doesn't he?" I ask Madoc, eyeing the muscles stacked on top of each other. "How tall?"

Madoc grunts. "He could grow as tall as the mountain around us if he wished, but it would take him a while to shrink again. The process is painful too. This is his preferred size." With a swipe of his tongue, he licks his finger and tosses the large bone to the creature who catches it in a lightning fast move.

"Is this the monster Callyx is hunting for Lucifer?" I ask, my gaze catching on the brand on the monster's hip. It's the devil's mark.

Silence reigns for several minutes. "Does it matter? He only hurt one person his whole life. Granted, it was a demon prince, which is why he landed where he did. But if we were counting kills, I'm sure you and I would surpass his record by at least a few hundred."

"It must have been a long time ago," I say slowly, trying to figure out when the last prince died. At least a couple of thousand years ago. Way before my time. "It's odd that nobody has ever talked about it." Demons love to gossip, and time has no meaning to them. They're just as likely to talk about a prince dying today as they did yesterday.

"That's because it was the devil's own brother." Madoc sneers. "He was sent to The Below for one lapse in judgement." Anger sets in the line of his jaw. "An entire life ruined because of who he killed." Bitterness seeps from his lips.

"How did you two meet? If he was in The Below all this time?"

"Because I was there, too," he reveals. "For some reason, Aamon chose to protect me. Now, I do the same for him."

Shock renders me speechless. Of all the secrets I thought he might be hiding, none of them came close to the truth. "How the hell did you get out? There's only one tunnel in and out, and it's a maze of deadly traps."

"Would you believe me if I said an angel?" He shakes his head as if he still can't believe it.

The creature must decide I'm not a threat because he plops down beside Madoc and reaches for the bone in his hand. Quicker than I can see, Madoc cuts his hand. Roaring, he jumps to his feet and towers over Madoc, who does nothing.

"You already had your share. I told you I was hungry," Madoc explains to him as if he's a child. "I'll give you what's left when I'm finished."

Huffing and stomping his feet, he circles around and lies down with his back to Madoc.

"As you can see, he's like a child. Something happened in his development, and he never matured into an adult," Madoc explains to me as he finishes his meal.

Similar to Lux.

"Gabriel," I state confidently. Lucifer sent him there to cool off. When he retrieved him, his wings had been cut off. "How did you get him to give up his wings?"

"The Below has a way of stripping you bare. Gabriel thought he was strong until he faced the true monsters of the deep. One monster's favorite torture tool is the mirror. It's spelled to display only the darkest truths about yourself, the ones buried deep inside that you never let out. After a while, he broke. Begged us to protect him. Our price was his wings," Madoc reveals, his voice full of satisfaction.

"When Lucifer retrieved Gabriel, we took a chance and flew out before Lucifer shut the door, so to speak," Madoc says, flicking a glance at me. "I've been hiding him ever since, but it's driving him crazy. He wants to roam and be free. At least the hunt for Leandra will distract him."

Any thought of turning him into Lucifer or Callyx died the instant he said those words, and by the smirk on his face, he knew it. "Damn you." My mind considers and rejects several options. "This is going to put me in a hell of a bad spot with Lucifer."

Callyx is also going to be pissed. Wait. "Why is Callyx only after him?"

"Nobody but Leandra knew I was down there. She couldn't kill me, but she needed me in a place I couldn't escape," he growls, barely able to contain his fury. "She made a deal with someone, and the next thing I knew, I was fodder for the monsters." He shudders. "I'm damn lucky Aamon befriended me."

The monster rolls over and snorts. "Not my friend."

Madoc quips. "Too bad. You're stuck with me."

Aamon bares his teeth in what I think is a grotesque smile. "Maybe."

The bond between the two of them runs deep, but that's not a surprise. Surviving the atrocities in The Below would forge an unbreakable alliance.

"This is the reason you want to find Leandra, isn't it?" I ask, knowing I'm going to have to trust him. His motive for revenge is the strongest I've seen.

"She stole my future from me," Madoc spits out. "And some of my power. I want it back. All of it. But I'll settle for her death first."

"That's her special parlor trick. Stealing someone's future," I say, sharing in his bitterness for a moment. "Her death is the only thing that will protect Meri."

"Why does she want Meri so badly?" Madoc hands the rest of his food to Aamon, who greedily gulps it down.

I explain to Madoc how Leandra created Meri from the essence of Nyssa and Denir.

He pales. "If she created her, she could also unmake her, right?"

Madoc's quick. "Meri hasn't even thought of the possibility. But I have. A thousand times a thousand to infinity. For a long time, I was forced to protect Leandra, but not anymore. I don't know what she wants with Meri, but with Denir hunting her too, we can't afford to get caught between them."

"Denir." Madoc curls his lip as his face hardens with hatred. "He was Leandra's co-conspirator. Once I have what I need from Leandra, he's next on my list."

Madoc's voice is full of power and magic. He hardly seems

diminished by whatever Leandra took, which means she must have taken something specific.

He tilts his head. "How are you going to prevent her from unmaking Meri with her dying breath?"

"The Phoenix can resurrect the dead," I reveal. It's the key to my plan. "I'm hoping Rivan will revive her. Once we find him." I can tell by the look on his face he isn't quite as confident it will work. "I need a back-up plan, I know. If I only knew what they both wanted from her, it would be easier."

Madoc frowns. "You know this means we need to capture Leandra instead of killing her on sight?" Disappointment crosses his face. "Fuck me." He sits there thinking about it for a minute, then his scowl lightens. "I guess this means we'll need to torture her to get answers."

"Sounds good to me, but first we need to find Rivan," I remind him.

CHAPTER SEVEN

<u>MERI</u>

Blowing off steam for the first time in forever felt good. I hadn't realized how much I'd been carrying on my shoulders, but Arden heard it all last night—my feelings about being queen and how it felt to go from floundering to finding my stride, the difficulty of navigating the intricacies of the court and how the revolution began to impact my reign. I gleefully boasted about winning against a kraken, and of course, Arden wanted to hear every detail of our battle. I told her about the evolution of my relationship with Cormal, which she felt was long overdue. All the people I had met and the ones, like Eris, who I missed the most. It took me hours, lots of tears, and several bottles of wine, to tell it all, but in the end, it felt good. Cathartic.

Enlightening, too. When Arden teased me about Madoc, my trainer and savior, I didn't know what to say. I explained how arrogant and annoying he was in training. How, like Cormal, he pushed me to save myself. Protect myself. But then he saved me... a few times. Toward the end, when things were falling apart and I couldn't find him, I worried about him. Arden laughed and promptly informed me that I liked him. Kind of threw me for a loop, but the more I thought about it and the more wine I drank, I had to admit she was right. Not only do I trust him, I like him.

Bleary-eyed, I wake and glance at my phone. Cormal sent a text early this morning. They're still searching for Rivan. The urge to bury my head in the pillow is so strong, I almost whimper, but I refuse to lie here when I could be doing something to help.

Holding my head, I ease into a sitting position. As I do, I notice a note on the nightstand beside a small bottle.

It's disgusting, but it works. Drink it all.
Arden XX

A potion. Thank you, Arden. Unstopping the cork, I get a whiff of the nasty smell but down it in one gulp. Thick and slightly slimy, the drink tastes like sludge and dirt. For a second, I think it's going to come back up, but it settles in the pit of my stomach and starts to work its magic.

Twenty minutes later, I'm scarfing down food while I text Madoc and Cormal.

> Cormal: We're on our way to meet up with Sika
> and Ren. No news yet.

> Meri: How is that possible? Did you check the
> underground city where they were living?

> Cormal: They're not there. Holed up
> somewhere else.

Meri: I haven't heard from Madoc. Is he okay?

It occurs to me that I'm worrying about two of the most dangerous men I know, and all I can do is shake my head, but just because they're powerful doesn't mean they're invincible.

Cormal: He doesn't know how to text. He's here with me.

My eyebrows rise. I wonder if they tried to kill each other.

Meri: ...

Meri: Do I need to get a healer?

Cormal: That's been resolved. Peacefully. He'll explain. Have to go. Stay at The Abbey.

Resolved. Whatever Madoc told Cormal, it completely eased his mind, which intrigues me. He was dead set against him, and it takes a lot to satisfy his cynical mind. I can't wait to hear what Madoc has to say.

I tap my finger on my lip. Where the hell could the Phoenix have gone? I try to remember all the bits and pieces I heard, but it's not much.

Theron was able to reach Oryn last night, but he wasn't at the dark Fae palace. He promised to ask around when he got back. I nodded my thanks, but I'm concerned it will be too late for Rivan.

I did notice Oryn's reply rattled Theron. He doesn't show much emotion, but he kept tapping his fingers on his thigh. Arden asked him if he was okay, and he told her Oryn was hunting down information but wouldn't say anything else over the phone. It's unlike Oryn to care about anything enough to make an effort.

The rune on my hand pulses. Arden added a spell to temporarily enhance it but said only I would be able to tell if it works. I peer down at the tattoo on my palm. Flames with a heart in it and the clarity rune inside the heart. Every time I look at it, it reminds me of Rivan and the time we spent together. I clench it tight. We need to find him.

> Cormal: Madoc is on his way back. Tell him Ren
> has a lead. Mer people chattering about activity
> in the Forbidden Sea. Going to check it out.

Where is the Forbidden Sea? I close my eyes and try to visualize a map of the Light Fae Kingdom. I can see the land but can't recall the waters around it.

> Meri: Is Solandis up for a visitor? I need
> information.
>
> Vargas: Yes, she's much better, thanks to the
> doctor.
>
> Meri: On my way.

Minutes later, I'm at their door. When I walk in, Solandis is eating breakfast and does indeed look a million times better. She's dressed to perfection and smiling again.

I lean down and kiss her cheek. "You look fabulous. Feel better?"

She pats the chair beside her. "Like a princess. Vargas tells me you need information?" Her turquoise eyes are clear and bright this morning.

"Do you have a map of the Light Fae Kingdom? Cormal said there is activity in the Forbidden Sea, and I can't quite remember where it is," I tell her, snatching up a strawberry from the bowl in front of her.

"That's because we removed it from most of the maps a long time ago," she replies in a serious tone. "Are you quite sure that's the location?"

With a frown, I show her Cormal's text. "Why? What's there?"

She leans forward. "Call Cormal right now. Tell him to pull his men back from there. It's not safe." Her tone is unusually sharp.

I immediately call Cormal, but he doesn't answer. "It's going to voicemail."

Someone knocks at the door, and Vargas opens it to find Madoc.

Instead of his usual ferocious scowl, Madoc's face goes blank when he sees Vargas. "I'll wait for you in your room, Meri."

I jump up. "No, wait. Cormal's in danger. Where did you leave him?"

He stops on the edge of the threshold. "On the shore of the Caraway River. He was speaking with his men. What kind of danger?"

I look over at Solandis, who's staring at Madoc with a peculiar look on her face.

"He's on his way to the Forbidden Sea. We need to stop him," she says emphatically.

Madoc curses. "I'll go. Stay here."

I rush to the door to go with him, but he's already gone. "Damn it. When are those men going to realize I'm not helpless?"

Vargas pats me on the back. "Hopefully never."

I swivel around to Solandis. "What's in the Forbidden Sea?"

She swallows. "The Isle of Avalon. It's a dangerous place. The Fae who lived there long ago died out, but their magic still protects the island. Unless you know its secrets, navigating it can be treacherous."

Avalon. "Rivan's mother came from there."

Solandis' eyes widen. "If he's there, his mixed blood could be a point in his favor. Goddess help us if Brixton stirs up the old magic. All of the light Fae will be in danger."

There's another knock at the door, and Vargas opens it to find Theron standing there in an impeccable pinstriped navy-blue suit. With elegant strides, he walks in and kisses Solandis on the cheek before turning to me.

"Oryn returned to the palace. He confirmed King Denir is in communication with Brixton. The Phoenix have taken to the seas. They're setting traps for the Water Fae along the shores," he informs us. "Unfortunately, he can't tell us where they are at this exact moment."

"The Forbidden Sea," Solandis reveals with a heavy sigh. "Madoc went to intercept Cormal and his men."

"Damn. That's not good. Do you trust Madoc?" Theron asks, his gaze intent. "He's not working for Denir, is he?"

"Yes. I think so. Why would you say that?" I stammer.

"He's dark Fae royalty," Theron states matter-of-factly. "Didn't you know? I thought it was odd he was by your side but it wasn't my place to question you."

Dark Fae? A shiver runs down my spine. "No, I didn't. Did you?" I turn toward Vargas and Solandis.

Vargas shuffles restlessly. "The soldiers talked about him possibly having mixed blood, but I didn't think it was important. There were a lot of mixed blood amongst the soldiers. Tiernan, for example."

Solandis looks at me in surprise. "The second I met him. Today."

Madoc and Solandis never met? The entire time I was queen. I try to recall them together but can't. "Shit. I didn't realize you hadn't met." I wince. "He doesn't feel any different to me than the light Fae."

Both Theron and Solandis look surprised by my statement. "Light Fae are like the sun, all bright and warm. Dark Fae feel cool and aloof. It's how we identify each other."

"Madoc feels dark but so does Cormal. Rivan's the only one who feels warm to me," I explain with a shrug. "Madoc thought

I should have been able to tell Lorn was mixed blood, but I couldn't. At the time, I thought it was because I was missing the connection with the Light Fae Kingdom, but maybe it's me. The way Leandra made me." My voice breaks a little at the thought of being so different from other Fae.

Solandis' arms wrap around me tightly. "You're unique. Don't let this anomaly take away your birthright."

Held in her arms, Solandis' delicate floral perfume calms me. She's right. I've always been different, and when I was queen, it turned out to be an asset. For some reason, The Abbey is stifling my newfound confidence. I need to get out of here and do something.

"Thank you. You're right. And regarding Madoc, I trust Cormal, and he says the matter is resolved. I have to believe he's on our side," I tell them.

Solandis rubs her hands down my shoulders. "We trust you and Cormal, and we'll extend the same to Madoc." Her eyes lock with Vargas, and he dips his chin in agreement.

"Honestly, sometimes I thought he smelled like a demon," Vargas interjects with a laugh. "Weird, huh?"

Uneasy with Madoc coming back to Solandis' room, I give her a squeeze. "Do you happen to have an old map with the Forbidden Sea? I'd like to know where it is."

Solandis closes her eyes and holds out an elegant hand. The map appears, and she gives it to me. "There you go. You know, you should still be able to access the light Fae library if you need anything. It's open to all light Fae royalty."

"Really? That's good to know, thanks," I throw over my shoulder as I head out the door. Centuries of information might come in handy.

Back in the room, I spread the rough edges of the old map on the table and secure it with a couple of books. Leaning over, I visually follow the edges of the land to the water, then search for the Forbidden Sea. I don't see it. I search a second time.

Nothing. I frown. Solandis wouldn't have given me the wrong map.

Using my fingers, I trace the border of the land. As I near a particular spot, my palm heats up, and I stop. There it is. Forbidden Sea. The letters identifying it are smaller than the other bodies of water around it. Maybe that's why I kept missing it… or maybe not. I flip my hand over and gaze at my palm. Did the rune help me, or did I imagine that?

Craggy and tall, the island sits regally at the far end of the sea. There's nothing between it and the mainland but water. Tiny depictions of waterfalls and forests dot its surface along with several small towns. At its pinnacle sits an enormous white castle. Beautiful. Treacherous. Old, wild magic. My heart thumps just looking at it on the map.

Madoc strides into the room with Cormal behind him.

Relieved to see them both, I automatically reach out and hug the closest one. Madoc's hard body stiffens in my arms, but he doesn't pull away. His head bends down close to mine and a large hand presses firmly against my back. I inhale his delicious dark scent and shiver. Embarrassed, I pivot away from him and crash against Cormal.

Cormal's arms wrap around me tightly and his low chuckle fills my ear. "Give him time. He's slowly acclimating to the real world."

I pull back my head and look up into Cormal's blue eyes. Guess he knows more about Madoc's past. "I'm glad he found you in time. If I hadn't gone to see Solandis, we wouldn't have known about Avalon and its dangers. What happened?"

"The Forbidden Sea is full of ships filled with Phoenix. From what we've gathered, they've been making their way along the shores, setting traps for the Water Fae. They stopped moving a couple of nights ago and have been there ever since," Cormal informs me, easing from my arms.

"Why would they think the Water Fae is the biggest threat?" I ask, biting my lip. "Do you think this is because of the treaty?"

"It's likely," Madoc interjects. "As I searched for Rivan, I heard quite a bit about the revolution. The Lesser Fae are torn between the peace and rights promised by the Water Fae and the righteous anger of the Fire Fae. To win against the aristocratic light Fae, Brixton needs a larger army, so he's trying to recruit the Water Fae and simultaneously eliminate any opposition."

That was the whole point of the treaty. It's working, but at what cost? "Did you send word to Hyne?"

Cormal thrusts a hand through his hair. "I did. He's aware of their tactics and is planning a few nasty surprises for them." He turns and faces me. "Unfortunately, the Water Fae's resources are limited, and I'm not sure how much manpower they have in that area."

"Whereas the Fire Fae receive support from the dark Fae and Denir," I say in an irritated tone. "Why have they stopped at Avalon?"

Cormal rolls his shoulders. "Rivan's being held in the castle on Avalon."

Madoc rubs the scruff on his jaw. "The Forbidden Sea, Phoenix, Avalon. Brixton picked the perfect trifecta. How the hell are we going to save Rivan?"

We. Huge step for Madoc. A warm, fuzzy feeling engulfs me.

Cormal throws him a broad grin. "We make a plan."

He loves nothing more than planning and strategizing. Getting the drop on his enemies or pulling off a heist is his nirvana.

Madoc gives him a dirty look, but Cormal doesn't even notice.

"The Phoenix are our first priority," Cormal begins. Conjuring a pad of paper and a pencil, he immediately writes down the first objective. "We need a diversion large enough to pull the entire fleet out of that sea. We need the Water Fae."

"The last thing we want to do is light the fuse between those two armies," Madoc retorts, his jaw clenching in anger.

"You said the Water Fae need resources. You mean weapons?" I ask him, my mind latching on to the first thing he brought up. "Like the weapons you stored in the light Fae palace?" I try to think of the ramifications of giving them those weapons, but I'd rather they go to the Water Fae than any other group. "They were originally going to them. Who's to say Brina didn't find them and confiscate them for the Water Fae after Camon's death?"

Cormal's blue eyes light up. "Brilliant. With those resources, they can create a diversion to distract the Fire Fae." It's the catalyst he needs to focus.

Tilting his head, he studies the expanse of sea between the mainland and the island. "Any portal on the island is likely to be guarded. So, we need a way to get on the island undetected. Flying, maybe?"

Madoc shakes his head. "Anything large enough to carry us all would easily be seen. The portal might be the best way in, but it would be better if we didn't have to fight our way through the guards. We need a reason."

"Hyne could ask for a meeting with Brixton," I say. "Offer to show him the treaty and discuss an alliance."

"I doubt he'd fall for it," Cormal states with a frown.

"He won't, but if your greatest enemy offered to meet with you, you'd do it," I say confidently. "Brixton isn't honorable. He'll take the opportunity to kill Hyne."

Madoc snorts. "Hyne isn't stupid. I doubt he would do it."

I smile. "Let's ask him."

CHAPTER EIGHT

<u>MERI</u>

Unwilling to jeopardize Hyne's standing with the Water Fae, we send a request to meet with him in a private location. He agrees with one caveat—mutual risk—I must be at the meeting. Based on their fierce expressions, neither Cormal nor Madoc like Hyne's demand, but they know he won't back down either.

Dark and musty, the basement of an old pub where the mouth of the Caraway River meets the Vasser Sea clearly gives the kraken a huge advantage. I snicker at the amount of water surrounding us at the moment.

The giant Fae with long shaggy brown hair the color of mud and a massive beard slips quietly into the basement. Dark, fathomless eyes peer intently at the three of us before he sits. Unlike the last time we met, his charming demeanor has been replaced with a somberness that is startling.

I raise an eyebrow. "Lot of water outside. You're not scared of little old me, are you?" I'm the last worry on his mind, but the teasing nature of my tone settles his nerves.

A quiet, but hearty, laugh slips from his lips. "I am. You cheat." With a sigh, he runs a hand down his thick beard. "The world is upside down and inside out. Lesser Fae fighting and murdering each other. Aristocratic Fae hiding behind their walls. The land is in chaos, and hope has vanished."

He stares at my blank forehead. "And we have no queen to lead us." He props his fist on his knee and motions to Madoc. "Who is he?"

"A friend."

"Dark Fae," he notes, raising an eyebrow. "Royalty."

Madoc scowls at his words. "Don't get your tentacles in a twist. I'm only here to help Meri and save Rivan."

Hyne briefly switches his attention from me to him. "The one thing that would unite all of the light Fae is the dark Fae invading our land. You better be telling the truth." From the depths of his dark eyes, a coldness rises that sends a chill down my spine.

"We need a diversion to draw the Phoenix from the Forbidden Sea," I interject, bringing his attention from Madoc back to me. "Without inciting a war between the Water and Fire Fae."

Before I've even finished, he's already shaking his head. "We don't have the resources or manpower to pull off something of that magnitude. Last count, there were seventeen ships in the Forbidden Sea. They would annihilate us."

That's the last thing I want. Maybe we need a way to set them off without involving the Water Fae.

"Fire Fae have already laid traps along the shores, right?" I ask, biting the inside of my cheek. "What if we simply set them off?" I look at Cormal. "Discreetly."

He ponders my question for a second. "I might have a solution. He's an extreme wild card, though, and needs supervision."

Madoc tilts his head. "Are you talking about the small shadow demon?"

"Lux," Cormal informs him, nodding his head. "Would your friend be willing to supervise?"

Both Hyne and I are swiveling our heads back and forth between the two.

"He needs that much supervision?" Madoc asks, raising an eyebrow.

Cormal grimaces. "He's like a small child. Doesn't know when to stop. Would destroy the world if I let him."

An expression of alarm slides across Hyne's face. "You want to let a psychotic shadow demon loose on the Fae? Are you crazy?"

"Possibly," Cormal confirms. "Desperate times and all that." He turns back to Madoc. "Once the Phoenix land, he'll run. He isn't a fan of fire."

"Aamon will do it," Madoc assures him. "If only to leave the Wilds."

At the mention of the infamous territory, Hyne jumps up and plants his fists on his hips. "Not only do you want to unleash a shadow demon, but you're planning on bringing a creature from the Wilds to supervise him?"

Madoc rolls his eyes. "Technically, he's a monster from The Underworld. And likely the only one strong enough to supervise Cormal's little demon."

"No, no, no," Hyne repeats emphatically, his voice strained as if is barely able to refrain from shouting. "There won't be a world left for us to live in. Find another solution." Water seeps from the cracks in the walls and starts pooling in the corners of the room.

I flash a "hurry up" look at Cormal.

Cormal draws a wavy magic line on the dirty stone floor. "This is the shoreline. If Lux sets off the traps, he can contain the damage, then leave when it's done. We need to decide what to do once the Phoenix are on land. In order to save Rivan, we need time. Can the Water Fae set traps to draw them inland and keep them busy?"

Hyne looks down at the floor. "It would take all of us, but we could do it. The problem is… we need a way to defend ourselves if caught, and I don't have access to all the weapons Fisk collected. Brixton laid siege to several stashes and confiscated them for his army." His dark eyes are full of deep-seated anger toward the leader of the Phoenix.

Cormal flashes him a smile. "Luckily, we have access to a large shipment. Once we retrieve them, they're all yours." He proceeds to give Hyne a detailed list. "Will that help?"

Something shifts in Hyne's demeanor. "It would. What do you want in return?"

Cormal waves a hand in my direction.

Hyne warily turns me, and I smile broadly. "I could lie and say it's not much, but it's a huge ask. You could even die. On the positive side, you'll have the chance to look Brixton in the eye and tell him what a piece of shit he is for betraying the Water Fae and murdering Fisk."

His jaw drops. "You want me to request a meeting with Brixton? Why?"

"They're holding Rivan on Avalon. Apparently, it's full of traps and old magic that shouldn't be disturbed. We need a way in," I reveal with a nonchalant shrug. "Brixton needs the Water Fae, but to get them, he needs you out of the way. It would be the perfect opportunity for him. How could he resist?"

Hyne stands there staring at me, silence filling the room around us until my nerves are at a screaming point. Then, suddenly, he doubles over and roars with laughter.

At the sound, Cormal and Madoc stand, hands on weapons and move closer, ready to protect me from the crazed kraken.

Hyne takes a deep breath and the laughter ceases. "I haven't laughed that hard in a long time." He straightens and rolls his eyes at the two men. "Please. Like I would hurt her. Although, come to think of it, it's probably good you had her ask for the favor."

Hope begins to bloom in my chest. "You'll do it?"

"Damn right I will. Fisk saved my ass more times than I can recall," he says with a fierce look in his eye. "Confronting his killer and, hopefully, avenging his death will be an honor."

He points a finger at Cormal. "I want you to create a detailed plan of action I can take to my second in command."

His hand moves to Madoc. "I don't know who you are or what your role is here, but you look like you can handle yourself. You'll go with me as my second. It will throw Brixton off his stride, and we need all the advantages we can get."

Instead of arguing, Madoc arrogantly dips his head in agreement.

Cormal creates a map and starts marking it up. Minutes later, he's done. With a wave of his hand, he creates a copy and hands it to Hyne. "Show this to your men and let me know if they want any changes."

Hyne takes it from him. "The weapons?"

"Where do you want them delivered?" I ask him, brushing the hair back from my clammy neck. The damp air in this basement is making me nauseous.

"There is a ship in this port called the Blue Chameleon," Hyne informs us. "It will hold them. Send me word, and I'll have men meet you. Once the weapons are in our hands, I'll contact Brixton."

He takes a deep breath. "This will either be our beginning or our end. Regardless, we can't sit in the middle forever. See you soon." Taking the stairs, he leaves the same way he entered.

Relieved to get out of here, I follow Cormal into the shadows while Madoc protects the rear. Breathing deeply as I step out into the meadow, I take a moment to fill my lungs with clean air. "All right. Who the hell are Lux and Aamon?"

Cormal chuckles. "Lux is a shadow demon in my employ. You haven't met him because he's a bit—what was the word Hyne used?—psychotic. Only to be used in extreme emergencies."

Sounds lovely. Where does Cormal find these demons? I turn to Madoc. "And Aamon?"

Tensing, he explains his friend and how they met.

Eyes round, the first thing that hits me is how much Leandra has wronged Madoc. She took everything from him, then left him in The Below. An unending pit of darkness with no way to escape. It's so black there are no shadows. It makes The Pit look like a holiday.

I shudder. His willingness to stick around suddenly makes sense. He'll do anything to end her existence. No wonder Cormal changed his mind about trusting him. What is surprising is Madoc's willingness to suspend his search to help us save Rivan.

"Honestly, I can't even imagine what you've been through. Once we've saved Rivan, we'll switch all of our attention to finding Leandra. I promise you." I lay a hand on his arm and squeeze.

He stares at me, then lays his hand on top of mine. A ghost of a smile appears. "Honestly, I thought you'd lose your mind about the monster."

"It's nice to hear you have friends. Besides me, of course," I tease him. "But I'd hate to be you when Callyx and Lucifer find out." My voice might be a tad too gleeful, because I hear Cormal snort loudly behind me. "Now, let's go get those weapons."

CHAPTER NINE

MADOC

Cormal is a force of nature with his unrelenting will and sheer determination. I prop a foot behind me and lean against the wall of his office while I watch him assemble a plan to get the weapons for the Water Fae. I study the faces of his men, noting both their respect and concentration on the task. He respects them equally, answering their questions, and changing the plan when they don't believe a particular piece will work.

Dark power seeps from his pores, saturating the air around him. With its seductive quality, it draws his men closer. The essence of his power is unnatural and an abomination to the natural order of things. A mish mash of magic from various races, it's chaotic and raw. It should be destroying him from the inside out, but somehow, he's able to contain and harness it for his purpose.

A human who found the power to become immortal without

becoming a vampire or shifter. Who knew it could be done? I wonder how he achieved the impossible. I know he gained the ability to wield magic by drinking his father's blood, which also turned him into a beast, or a brùid. Neither of those things would give him immortality. Is this the power he gave to Meri? Her ability to mimic isn't Fae in origin.

My gaze turns toward the beautiful woman in the corner watching his every move, her turquoise eyes glaring at him in irritation. Magic sparks from her fingertips, but not once does she interrupt. Afterward… she'll give him hell. For the first time in eons, I have to smother the laugh threatening to escape.

Another abomination. Made not born. Equal parts light and dark Fae with a touch of dark magic in her. Not solely from the power Cormal shared with her, but something else hidden deep inside I can't quite put my finger on. I doubt she's aware it's there, but it's what drew me to the Light Fae Kingdom and to her.

Flawless perfection on the outside, I was so fucking irritated at the first sight of her. Queen of the Light Fae. She fit the golden image of goodness and light with her platinum hair and trademark turquoise eyes, but her small stature gave me the first clue to her difference. Most light Fae royalty, like Solandis, are tall but not her.

Unable to find Leandra and needing to lie low, I used those excuses to stay, but I'm not sure I would've been able to resist the call of her. Or the darkness within. When I found out she was to train with one of her soldiers, I eliminated him. Took his place. The moment I stepped into the training room with her standing there, the pull became stronger. But it was her reaction to the knife coming at her that intrigued me. A Fae would have thrown magic at it. Balancing on the balls of her feet, she prepared to duck as if she'd been doing it her whole life.

Training her was an exercise in patience. At first, it was her inability to wield her magic, but she managed to overcome that hindrance. Later, it was my inability to keep my distance. Our short sessions weren't enough to satisfy my curiosity. I started following her around, watching from the shadows, even when she left the palace to go on her dates with Lorn. I was there trying to figure out why I was drawn to her. The only time I took a break was to check on Aamon. Every time I saved her, whether it was from the wendigo, Denir, or her own court, my obsession deepened.

Emotionally, I've done my damndest to stay away from her. The light Fae queen is the last Fae I wanted in my life, but she continued to chip away at my walls, breaking down the barriers between us. Her irreverent disregard for royalty protocols and proper aloofness was astonishing. She makes friends regardless of status. I'm her friend, yet she doesn't know who I am. None of them do. And I know the time to tell them is coming closer and closer.

She steps out of the shadows next to me, making me jump. "Can you believe him?" Her small hand waves elegantly at Cormal. "Not once has he mentioned me in this plan, but if he thinks I'll stand on the sidelines or go back to The Abbey, he's lost his mind. This is my fight more than it is his. He's not even Fae."

The thought of her returning to the light Fae palace makes my blood churn. They would love nothing better than to blame this whole revolution on her. "Maybe you should join us after we have the weapons." Seconds after the words leave my lips, I almost smile, knowing her reaction will be fierce.

Anger surges across her delicate face. "He didn't mention you either," she spits out, lifting a taunting eyebrow in my direction. "Are you sitting this one out?"

Normally, I'd be pissed off at the thought, but the glee in her voice only makes me want to chuckle. A common occurrence around her. Nobody else makes me want to shed the armor I created so long ago.

Her scent is alluring, a mix of orange blossoms and jasmine with an underlying earthy note of musk and amber. It teases me, pulling me in closer. For a second, I fight it, not sure if she's ready to know how she tempts me, but my hesitation almost immediately slips away. I lower my head, inhaling her sweet perfume, and picture the two of us in her bed as I dip my tongue into the honey sweet nectar between her legs.

I let the image play out—my dark head between her creamy thighs, doing all the wicked things I've dreamed of since the moment I felt her body beneath mine on that mat. My cock hardens at the tantalizing sight of her writhing on the bed, sheets clenched in her hands, as her head tosses from side to side.

She gasps, and I draw my head back to stare into her desire drenched eyes. "Stop it!" Her gaze darts to Cormal, then back to me. "You don't even like me, remember?"

I didn't realize she could see the images in my head, but I can't say I mind either. All it does it make me loosen the control I've held onto for ages.

"Like is weak. Do I have to like you to want you beneath me?" I ask, pressing up against her until she can feel every inch of me. Her scent deepens as her body drenches itself in anticipation. The pulse at her throat flutters rapidly. "Does liking me make you want to spread your legs and surrender to my every whim? Mmm. Tell me."

She tilts her head, searching my face to see if I'm serious. "I like you better when you're mean."

Ouch. "No, you don't. It's just easier to keep the wall up between us." Giving up her crown opened a door. One she doesn't understand now, but she will. "Shall we spar and find out? I'm sure you can use the practice."

Her ire cools instantly. "Keep your hands to yourself. I spent too many years letting Cormal's hot and cold routine spin me into knots." Her bright eyes search mine as if she's looking for answers.

"Mmm. You'll still be my friend, though, right?" I tease her, unable to help myself.

She scoffs. "Now you want to be friends." She turns away before answering me. "Yes, but only because I think you really need them."

Like a burr, her words burrow under my skin. The truth sucks.

NORMALLY, when a portal is accessed by a non-Fae, an alarm goes off, but Cormal changed a few things when he fixed the alarm for Meri, including the ability to bypass the system and enter the kingdom without alerting anyone. Same goes for the palace when we arrive. Positioning his men, Cormal slips through a door in the basement, then opens it for the rest of them. Meri stands near the truck to direct the loading of the shipment while I patrol the area.

Unwilling to risk the use of magic, we're doing this the old-fashioned way. A thirty-man team with each man physically carrying out a crate and loading it onto an old-fashioned truck. Once we're done, we'll drive it from one portal to another near the ship.

With this many men, it doesn't take long. As I'm closing the back doors of the truck, I hear a whistling noise behind me. I swivel around to find a guard holding a knife to Meri's throat. She must have walked off to find Cormal. *Damn it.* A bead of blood trickles down her neck.

Fury rises. "How many damn times have I told you to keep your shield up?" Stalking toward the two of them, the guard shouts for me to stop, but I ignore him. "Your enemies are ten times more powerful than the weasel holding you. If they catch you, they will kill you. Do you not understand that?!"

"I will kill her!" the guard shouts at me. "Move back!"

I'm fucking pissed at her right now. "Are you going to take care of him, or do I need to save you?"

The guard sputters obscenities.

Infuriated, her bright eyes flash in return, and in a single move she unarms and kills him. "There. Happy now?"

"It shouldn't have happened in the first place," I snarl at her.

"It's not like my enemies know I'm here tonight," she protests, her jaw locked in anger.

"The night Leandra found me, I was relaxing with a friend in his home. A place that should have been safe. By the time I thought to raise my shield, she'd immobilized me and killed him," I bite out furiously. The memory is as fresh in my mind as if it was yesterday instead of three thousand years ago. "The location doesn't matter. Your ability to wield magic may or may not be greater than hers, but in the end, if she slips through your shield, it doesn't matter. Same for Denir. Wrap your fucking shield around you and make it impenetrable."

I brush past Cormal, who's eyeing the dead guard with a murderous look on his face, and finish closing the doors. "We need to go. Now."

At the port, we quickly load the weapons.

Once he's confirmed they're all there, Hyne shakes the hand of his second in command and orders him to watch his back. With a swift move, he vaults over the railing and lands on the dock next to us. The ship begins to move behind him, leaving the port with its precious cargo.

"Everything okay?" He glances between Meri and me, but when we don't answer, he glares at us. "Whatever it is. Get over it. Brixton's an asshole, but he's sharp. The meeting is set for tomorrow evening, which means our diversion needs to happen tonight. We need to trigger the traps to draw the Phoenix from the Forbidden Sea. Once on land, they'll be able to follow the blatant trail left by my men. To keep them occupied, we added surprises along the way. Hopefully, it's enough to give us the time we need to meet with Brixton and save Rivan."

Cormal curses and picks up his phone. "Kavi, get Lux and meet me at the rendezvous point. Fifteen minutes."

I immediately slip into the shadows. Thankfully, Aamon's still in the Wilds, which isn't far from here.

CHAPTER TEN

<u>CORMAL</u>

Hyne, Meri, and I get to the rendezvous point first. The Phoenix laid traps along the shore, hoping to catch the Water Fae. We're going to use all their hard work to trick them into thinking it worked and draw them away from the island.

Kavi appears with Lux. Hyne mutters furiously under his breath when he sees the dark little monster. Bristling, I turn toward him and shake my head. "He's harder to control when he's pissed off. Shut the fuck up."

Hyne chokes at the tone in my voice, but an unhappy Lux is like a destructive genie, and damn near impossible to put back in the fucking bottle. I watch the dark demon skip over to us.

He stops and looks at Meri. "You're pretty. Are you my friend?"

I flick a warning glance at Meri, but she's already bending

down to his level. She studies his face for a minute. "Do you want us to be friends? It's a big question, so make sure you think about it. Friends are there for each other and enjoy spending time together. We support and trust each other. Still want to be friends?"

His small face is serious as he considers her words. "What if I make a mistake? Or do something bad?"

"It depends," she replies with a rueful look on her face. "Sometimes it's easy to forgive each other and sometimes the hurt goes too deep." When his shoulders drop, she takes his hand. "We can try, though, can't we?"

Staring at him and Meri in disbelief, I realize I'm never getting rid of Lux now. I put my hands on my hips and glower at her.

Standing, she raises their clasped hands. "Friends?"

With a dark grin, he nods. "Friends."

"We need to get a move on," I snarl, irritated beyond belief.

I look around and spot Madoc and Aamon behind me. The look on their faces as they stare at Lux and Meri makes me want to bang my head into the nearest tree. Two more conquests, although I suspect Madoc's been teetering on the edge for a while.

Because of the pact with Leandra, I couldn't spend too much time around Meri, but I had men watching her. Report after report would come in, telling me about her strays. Beasts, demons, people, kids, lost souls, it didn't matter. Her loneliness created a hole inside her, and the only way she knew to fill it up was to befriend another. I used to worry they would get her in trouble, but if anything, they often deflected Leandra's wrath.

"Lux," I say quietly, motioning Madoc and Aamon forward. "This is Aamon. He's going to stay here with you and make sure you do exactly what I tell you. He'll let you know when it's time to leave, okay?"

Lux's red eyes assess the monster before him. "You're like me, aren't you? Never grew up."

Aamon considers his words, then shrugs. "Sort of. It's okay."

Lux turns to me and smiles. "I like Meri. And him."

Thank hell for small favors.

Before he can turn his attention to Madoc or Hyne, I direct him to the map. With my finger, I trace each line from the shore to the trap, then I show him how to set one off. When the first one explodes in a geyser of water and fire, he jumps back and squeals in delight.

He sets the next one off and once the dust settles, I pat him on the back. "Good job. The rest of the traps are laid out on the map. Follow it to the end, setting them off along the way. Then Aamon will take you with him to the Wilds, okay?"

He claps his hands and jumps up and down with excitement. "Got it. This is fun!"

"We've got to go to a meeting," I explain to him. "Kavi will meet you at the edge of the Wilds tomorrow morning to take you home."

Lux is barely listening to anything as his eyes dart from the map to the next target. I hope this works. He gets so caught up in causing destruction, he doesn't know when to stop.

"Bye, Lux," Meri calls out.

He whirls around and waves his leathery hand. "Bye, friend!" Then he dashes off with Aamon on his heels.

"Keepers help us all," Hyne pleads in a gruff voice. "This better work."

After waving goodbye to Kavi, the four of us move to a little stone cottage on a seaside cliff. Warded by Kavi earlier, it provides us with the perfect view of the sea and Avalon. From here, the ancient island is shrouded in fog, with only the mountain peak visible, but we can clearly see the ships in the sea below.

"Sneaky," Hyne rumbles behind me, his eyes on the seventeen ships unfurling their masts. Phone in hand, he texts his second command to let him know the Phoenix are coming.

Seconds later, they sail off, using magic to whip the wind and get there faster. "They should arrive when the last charge goes off. Hopefully, they'll chase their prey inland instead of returning here."

Covering the windows with the darkest of shadows, I light the fireplace and sit at the table, Solandis' map of Avalon before me.

Meri frowns for a second, then closes her eyes. Her brow crinkles with concentration, then she holds out her hand. A rolled parchment appears, and she hands it to me.

"It's a map of Avalon's castle," she says nonchalantly, but the smirk on her face tells me I should have asked her for this earlier.

She's right, I should have. Just like I should have included her and Madoc in the debriefing for the weapons cache. She gave me hell for that one, too.

I lean over and kiss her pink lips. "Thank you. This helps tremendously."

Rolling it out, I secure the corners, then we all stand to look at the massive castle. Bailey, outer courtyard, battlements, outer gatehouse, portal, and all the usual rooms and layout you expect to see in a castle as well as a few unknown areas.

"You'll enter here." I tap the arch in the portal. It stands in the outer courtyard. "We need to find a way to shield you from the battlements."

Hyne shakes his head. "Brixton won't kill me right away. Most of the Lesser Fae like me." He pauses for a second. "Well, they did before my mate passed. Anyway, the point is, he won't want too many witnesses. It could make me a martyr. That's the last thing he needs if he's going to convince the Water Fae to join him when I'm gone."

His dark eyes scan the castle from head to toe. He taps his finger on a rough area depicted by rocks and water. "There. If I die in the water, I won't surface. Everyone knows krakens return to the deep."

I bend over to read the small type. "Grotto." Moving my finger to the rear, I follow a long hallway. Along the way, small rectangular rooms catch my eye. "Dungeons."

Meri taps her finger on one. "Do you think that's where he's holding Rivan?"

"I'm not sure. Maybe," I murmur, skimming the rest of the map. "There aren't that many secure rooms. Most are open to the next. It's either one of the bedrooms or the dungeons."

Hyne snorts. "Brixton hates Rivan for surrendering. It would have been better if he'd have died with his men. He'll hold him in the worst place possible." The blunt tip of his finger taps the dungeons.

Meri's face lights up with anger, but she looks away before anyone else can see it.

Madoc's hand rises and hovers over her shoulder for a second, as if he intends to comfort her, but he drops it when she lifts her head. His dark eyes meet mine, and his face resets into his usual scowl.

Something to deal with later. "You know Brixton better than us. What do you think he'll do first?"

Hyne chuckles. "Invite us in for a drink. He pretends to be very civilized until the knife is slicing across your throat."

I trace a line from the portal to the great hall. "Ok, he brings you two here. Offers you a drink. How many guards will he have with him?"

"At least twenty," Hyne replies with a broad grin. "Any less would be insulting to me. More and he'll open himself up to my insults."

"That's good. We can use that to buy us some time. Ask him questions about the real Kaius and Fisk, his plans, and whatever else you think will make him talk. A lot," I tell him. "Madoc will refuse the drink, stand by your side, and hold a shield around the two of you."

Hyne raises an eyebrow at Madoc. "A dark Fae with scars for days. He might be too much of a threat. We'll need to tone him down and make Brixton think there's nothing out of the ordinary about him."

Meri studies him for a second, then waves her hand. Glasses appear, along with a navy shirt instead of his usual black. She adds jeans and a simple fisherman's cap. "Will that work?"

"Give him blue hair, similar to Fisk," I add. "He can be a mix of dark Fae and Water Fae."

"Good idea," Madoc inserts, adding a hint of scales along his forearms while Meri changes his hair to a deep blue.

Both Hyne and I nod at the same time. "Perfect."

"We need a way to get Meri and me into the castle," I murmur, studying the expanse of sea between the two. "Can we go by boat to the grotto? It would put us in position for both Rivan and you two."

Hyne's large shoulder lifts. "I need to go down and read the sea."

When we all look at him in confusion, he rolls his eyes. "I need to get in the water. It will tell me about the inhabitants and any obstructions along the way."

The sun is barely cresting the horizon. "Dawn is coming. You might want to go now. We'll cover you from above."

Bitter wind whips around the cliffs in front of the little cottage, but a little magic creates a buffer from it. We stand and watch as Hyne takes a running jump off the cliff and dives into the sea below.

Meri moves in closer to me. "Do you think this is going to work?" Her eyes are full of worry. "What about the old magic?"

That's the biggest unknown. I couldn't find anything to

protect us. "All we can do is keep our shields up and hope nothing wakes."

Madoc looks pointedly at Meri. "A shield. Did you hear him?"

She scowls. "I heard. I will. I know I forgot earlier, but it was one lapse." Her voice has an edge that makes me shake my head at Madoc.

He heaves a sigh but relents. One step brings him closer to her. "Thank you."

She says nothing, but the tension eases from her shoulders.

Madoc suddenly whips a hand across her eyes, and she laughs. I look down and see a very large and very naked Hyne strolling out of the sea.

"Clothes," I tell Hyne, who looks at me as if I'm crazy.

He darts a glance at Meri, whose eyes are still covered, and chuckles. "I see. Done." Tailored black pants and a button-down shirt cover his body.

Madoc removes his hand, and Meri winks at Hyne. "I'm sure you had all the ladies once."

Hyne preens and winks back. "Krakens are big and known for their longevity."

Madoc and I groan in unison. "Stop."

Hyne motions to the water behind him. "There are creatures in the sea I haven't seen in at least a thousand years. And there are a couple of unknowns, too. Most of them seem benevolent, but it's hard to tell."

Tying his wet hair back, he continues. "I can get you across in a boat in five minutes, but there are traps in front of the grotto you'll have to unravel. The sea had very little information on them, except their presence."

"Ok, creatures, unknown traps, five minutes," I say, contemplating the worst that can happen. "We'll make it work."

The sky lightens further. "Let's get back inside before someone sees us out here."

For the rest of the day, we study the castle, especially the exits. There are a few places marked with a door, but I don't see their origin. Probably best to stay away from those.

Madoc slips away to confirm Aamon and Lux made it back to the Wilds.

As the sky darkens, I hear Meri say quietly, "We're coming for you, Rivan. Hold on."

CHAPTER ELEVEN

<u>MERI</u>

A disguised Madoc stands in front of the cottage, waiting for Hyne to join him. They'll take the shadows back to the port and enter the portal there in case Brixton has spies.

"You look good with blue hair," I tell him, smoothing it behind his ears as I place the cap on. "There." Tilting my head, I consider the full picture. "Definitely more approachable." My fingertips tingle from touching him, and I press them into my thigh.

Madoc stares down at me with an unreadable expression on his face.

It's completely unnerving. "Try to keep your eyes down or at least away from Brixton. You'll ruin the whole effect with that fierce predator look on your face."

A wolfish gleam enters his eyes, and he leans in close to whisper, "Guess I'll have to find some prey."

Him breathing hard against the back of my neck, stalking me in the dark, makes me want to run… so he can catch me. *What is wrong with me?* Maybe all this time we're spending together is addling my brain.

Swallowing hard at the slew of images, I take a step back. "Be careful. Try not to kill anyone until it's time."

His look hardens. "Keep your damn shield up."

Instead of answering, I return his black look and stroll over to Cormal and Hyne, who are stepping out of the cottage.

"Have you heard from your men?" Cormal asks Hyne.

"They were able to lead the Phoenix a fair distance inland to a lake," he replies. "They've taken to the underwater caves as the Phoenix search for them."

Cormal hands them both a tracker and an earpiece. "Good. That should give us time. Here. Hide the tracker. Wait to put the earpiece in until you're sure Brixton won't see it. Follow the plan."

When they're gone, Cormal erases every trace of our presence from the one-room cottage. Dressed in dark clothing, thick jackets, and boots, we head down to the shore and take a seat in the boat, facing each other. Small and wooden, the little boat rocks back and forth, bobbing on the rough waves. Nervously, I grip the sides, praying it doesn't tip over.

Once we're sitting, Cormal uses magic to cloak us from anyone's sight. Wind slices through the water around us, stirring the waves higher, but we sit and wait. My foot taps restlessly against the bottom of the boat.

Drawn to Cormal, I stare at the dark man across from me, still amazed we're together. Cormal's eyes are glued to the trackers moving on his phone. Water splashes on his face, but his concentration never wavers.

For years, all I saw was his ruthless, selfish side. It's still there. He hasn't turned into a saint but watching him do everything to save Rivan... it means more to me than if he had told me he loved me.

I lift my gaze from him and find the island across the sea.

We're coming, Rivan.

Hurry.

I gasp at hearing the reply in my head, and Cormal looks at me sharply.

In a stammer, I explain. "I don't know if it was Rivan's voice or another's, but we need to hurry."

He looks down at the phone. "They're on the island." Waves crash against the shore behind us. For several minutes, he stares at the phone. Dark brows pull together. He holds the phone up higher. "Either the technology isn't working or something is wrong. The trackers haven't moved away from the portal."

Heart racing, I can barely breathe.

Cormal curses.

The cry of a bird startles me, and I look up to see it fly past.

"They're moving... into the bailey," Cormal says with a frown still on his face. "They've stopped again. Their progress is too slow. My gut says they're in trouble." He looks up at the cliffs fading above us as day turns to night. "Can you get back to the cliffs? I want to check it out, and it will be easier if I'm alone."

Mulishly, I shake my head. "No, we're going together." Lifting my arms, I channel the wind into a single stream and send the boat farther into the sea. Then I lift up a hand behind me and motion to the water. A wave forms, pushing the boat forward as I use the wind to keep us straight.

"Damn it, Meri!" Cormal yells across the boat. "Who the hell is going to save us if we head straight into a trap?"

I think about it for a second. "Kavi. You told him what we were doing, right? He can grab Lux, Aamon, and whoever else he needs. Callyx. Vargas. Arden and her cadre. We have people to save us. Rivan has nobody."

Cormal thought about bringing the others to save Rivan, but the balance between the Fae and The Underworld is delicate. The only reason Vargas and Callyx were there when I gave up the crown was because a Fae had kidnapped Solandis.

He runs a hand down his face. "Drop me off at the opening. I'll unravel the traps, then head inland. You'll continue into the grotto by boat. If we split up, they may not catch us both."

Fierce determination settles on his face, and the sight of it eases my fears. It's his best look. The one that says his will is stronger than our enemies.

Unlike Hyne, it takes me closer to twenty minutes to get us across. From the water, large boulders block our view of the island, but that's good because it means the remaining Phoenix likely can't see us either, unless they're in the air. I look up and see a perfectly blue sky. Maneuvering the boat close to the craggy shore, I hold it still.

Cormal smashes his lips against mine. "They're not fucking around. Take no prisoners. Kill them first. Got it?" He jumps out of the boat and onto the rocks. "And as Madoc would say, keep your damn shield up."

Great, now he's got Cormal saying it. "Don't have too much fun!"

Magic slips from his hands and hovers over the mouth of the cave. Mouthing words I can't hear, his fingers dip in and out as he unravels the traps. Once he's done, he signals to me, then disappears into the shadows. I say a little prayer to the keepers to keep him safe. Although he has an uncanny knack for coming out on top, luck only goes so far.

I maneuver the boat into the grotto's entrance and spot a hook on a rope suspended above me. With a twirl of my finger, I pull it down and loop it around the slats in my seat. Once the boat is secure, I put my palm on a nearby boulder to steady myself.

My palm heats the second it touches the rock, and I barely

refrain from hissing. Shoving aside the pain, I step out of the boat and onto the rocks. Heat sears my hip, and I bite the inside of my cheek to stop from crying out.

What the hell?

Voices echo across the cave. Loud curses bounce off the surrounding stone walls, Hyne's booming voice easily recognizable. Cormal was right. They're in trouble.

I carefully climb up to the top to peer farther into the grotto. Hyne's yelling threats at a tall man in front of him and shaking his cuffed wrists. I've never met him, but Cormal described Brixton as a big man with a warrior's build and flaming red hair. That has to be him.

I move up another inch and find Madoc. Held between two men, with a third behind him, his face is impassive, but his eyes are busy, darting around the cave, likely looking for something to use. His wrists are also bound in gold handcuffs.

The cuffs look remarkably similar to the ones we used at the palace to prevent Estrella from using magic during her interrogation. Would the same key work? Solandis said I still had access to the library but does that extend to other areas of the palace? I close my eyes and concentrate until I can see the interrogation room. Gold cuffs hang on the wall near the door with the key in the lock.

Opening my eyes a second later, I sway. I must have used more magic than I thought. A large hand reaches out and yanks me to my feet.

"A Phoenix can sense power, didn't you know?" a smooth voice chides me.

I straighten and jerk my arm from his hold. "I did, actually, but thanks for the reminder. You must be Brixton."

A line appears between his brows. "And you are?" He holds up a hand. "Wait, don't tell me. The light Fae's former queen, Meri, right? Wow. You certainly didn't get the height, did you?"

He throws his head back and laughs loudly. His men join in his mirth until the entire cave rings with their laughter.

Thanks to Theron and the information his brother, Oryn, gave us, I know Brixton's working for Denir, or at least, with his support. I smile at him. "No, maybe I take after my father… King Denir. You know him, don't you?"

His laughter stops, and he shakes his head. "Denir has no children."

"Oh, but he does. And even now, he's turning over every stone to find me." My voice rings with truth. Granted, it's not in the way I've implied, but sometimes the truth is nothing but simple words spoken out loud. They have no meaning until you give it to them.

Power ripples over me, and he flashes a thunderous scowl. "Dark Fae royalty. Light Fae royalty. How is that possible?"

"If I told you, he'd kill you," I tell him. Also, true. Like Nyssa, the last thing Denir wants people to know is how I was created.

He shoves me toward the cave's entrance and his other two prisoners. Stumbling on some rocks at the last minute, I fly forward, letting the momentum carry me into Madoc. My hands brush his for a brief second. One of the guards jerks me away and shoves me back toward Brixton.

Madoc's elbow whips up and catches him in the throat. "Don't you fucking touch her."

The guard bends over, coughing, and Madoc whips the cuffs over his head and chokes him to death.

Brixton laughs. "He's going to be pissed when he regenerates."

Madoc snarls back at him. "He shouldn't touch what isn't his."

Impulsively, I swipe my foot across the ashes, sending them into the water beside us, then use the wind to send the rest out of the mouth of the cave. "It might take him a while."

"Bitch," Brixton snarls, back handing me across the face.

"We'll make sure to scatter your ashes to the four corners. See if Denir can track you there."

I spit out the blood in my mouth. "Weak. Leandra hit harder than you."

Leandra's name does what Denir's didn't, and a sliver of fear crosses Brixton's face. "How do you know that old hag?"

I snort. "Say it louder. She's got ears everywhere. The last person to call her a hag ended up in The Pit."

Yep, that was me. It was literally the last word I threw at her before she sent me into the depths of hell. This is fun. Who knew the truth could be so freeing?

His lips clamp together as he contemplates me. He motions to one of Madoc's guards. "Lock her up. Send Nya to Denir to ask about her."

Saved from instant death, at least. My eyes meet Madoc's, and he nods. When the guard steps away from him to grab me, Madoc slams into Hyne, knocking him into the sea.

Brixton chortles and grabs for Madoc only to rear back in astonishment, gold handcuffs clamped around his wrists.

Something tickles my side, and I turn to find the guard trying to stab through my shield. I open my hand, hoping the Killian blade will appear but nothing happens. The next time he thrusts it forward, I change it to a feather.

"Sorry, not ticklish." I sneer, then add power to my fists. With a right cross and left hook, I hit him hard enough to knock him backward.

In response, he gives me a maniacal grin and rushes forward, tackling me to the ground, but instead of attacking me, he raises the knife and slices across his throat. Faery fire erupts across his body, and I hear Madoc yelling behind me. Unable to do anything, I hold my palms up and throw everything into my shield. A thin, silver stream appears between the two of us, then wraps itself around him. His mouth opens in a silent scream as he turns to ash.

Coughing from the dust, I scramble away from his remains and stand. Eyes glued to the ground, I plant my feet and wait for him to regenerate.

Grunts behind me has me shuffling to the side until I can see Madoc. The first guard, whose ashes I swept into the water, finally regenerated and made it back. Madoc is fighting fiercely, but every time he kills one, the other keeps him busy until his friend regenerates.

Brixton erupts into flames, killing himself, and the cuffs drop to the floor. Madoc shifts until his back is to the wall and continues fighting. Brixton's ashes swirl in a tornado like wind and begin to reform.

Damn, that's fast.

I swivel around to the one I somehow killed a moment ago, but he hasn't regenerated. Puzzled, I step closer. There's a silver sheen laying across the ashes. Is that preventing him from returning?

Desperate, I replay the scene in my head. All I did was raise my palms. I hold them up toward the guards fighting with Madoc, but nothing happens. I turn further and hold them out toward Brixton's ashes, but they continue to swirl and reform.

I step toward one of the guards battling Madoc and tap him on the shoulder. He turns and throws his hand out, but I duck and punch him in the balls. His face scrunches up in pain, but it doesn't slow him down. Fire balls don't deter him either. A large fist connects with my head, and pain explodes across my temple. It recedes a second later.

Harnessing the wind, I wrap it around him and let it carry him out, but large fiery gold wings snap out, and he stops himself. No wonder the war went on for so long. Phoenix are damn hard to defeat.

Cormal emerges from the shadows at the mouth of the sea and binds him with magic, then hangs him from the hook I saw earlier.

Two massive blue serpents rise out of the sea, teeth snapping, and grab him. With a single jerk of their heads, his body tears in two, each of them swallowing their half before disappearing again beneath the surface.

Cormal puts his back to Madoc's. Dividing the final two guards, they quickly eliminate them. This time, they're able to cast magic against them regenerating. Separating, they both turn to face Brixton.

Fire and magic rip through the cave as the battle starts.

Suddenly, a massive plume of water shoots out of the sea like a geyser, and Hyne comes surging up with it in kraken form. Eyes the blackest of black stare down at all of us in one of the most terrifying sights I've ever seen. No wonder Fisk thought I'd be afraid to fight Hyne. If I had seen him in this form, I would have peed my pants and begged for mercy.

In a flash of light, Hyne's human form emerges, and he throws the gold cuffs on the ground. "Bastard. Don't kill him until I get a piece." A spear of water forms in his hands.

Hurry.

It has to be Rivan's voice. I rush toward the entrance, careful to step over the ashes from the guard I fought. When I do, I see the silver is spreading across the surface of the cave.

"Cormal!" I yell, pointing to it. "I don't know what it is, but I wouldn't step in it."

Brixton roars in disbelief. "No! Somehow you've woken the island." He scrambles backward. The serpents appear beside him, heads swaying like a snake eyeing a snack.

"Fuck!" In a flash of wings and fire, Brixton flies out of the cave, leaving the island and us behind.

Hyne curses. "Bastard escaped. Damn it. I was this fucking close to ending him for good."

Cormal waves a hand in Hyne's direction immediately clothing him. "Another time. We need to find Rivan and get out of here." He eyes the small boat beyond the serpents. "Can you control them?"

Hyne scoffs. "Only the island controls the creatures around here. I'm thankful they respected me enough to leave me alone while I got out of the cuffs. Took me a while. Dropped the damn key." He looks at Madoc. "Thanks, quick thinking."

Madoc joins us. "I knew you wouldn't drown. Better than letting Brixton kill you."

Cormal steps over the silver stream of magic or whatever it is. "There's a couple of ships berthed at the harbor. We'll have to grab one of them. First, Rivan."

CHAPTER TWELVE

<u>MERI</u>

All of the rooms in the dungeon are empty. Forced to search floor by floor, our progress is slow as we make our way up to the top. Cormal and Madoc send their magic ahead of us to search for any remaining Phoenix, but they've all fled. Brixton must have warned them. Cormal swears the island looks the same as earlier, so we can't be sure if he spoke the truth.

Top floor. "This is it. If he's not here, he isn't in the castle." But where could he be? I refuse to leave without him.

Rivan.

Hurry.

Where?

Hurry.

Every room is empty. There are no more floors above us. I step out onto the balcony to look out across the land. A harbor with a couple of newer ships that must have belonged to the

Phoenix and a few rickety ships bobbing gently in the water. A small, deserted town with a crumbling well and small, worn houses. Drab and dreary-looking bushes, trees, and flowers. The only interesting thing is the roaring waterfall on the mountain behind the castle.

Absolutely no sign of Rivan or any life for that matter.

"There!" Madoc shouts, pointing to the waterfall.

With a frown, I turn and look. White water pours down the side of the mountain from the top. Confused, I turn to look at Madoc again, and see a flash in the corner of my eye. Pivoting, I stare at the water, waiting. High up the mountain, close to where the waterfall starts its descent, red light flares brightly behind the curtain of water.

For a second, I stare at it, not understanding, but then it hits me, and I scream, "Rivan!"

Hyne lifts his hands, parting the waterfall like a curtain, until we can see behind it.

Loud curses fill the air from all three men, but tears slip down my face as I stare at Rivan. Suspended upside down from the mouth of a cave, his ankles and wrists bound by gold cuffs, is Rivan. Naked with no runes left on his body. How many times did he drown and regenerate? A hundred? A thousand?

"Get him down," I demand hoarsely, my voice full of pain and anger.

Cormal's magic holds him up as Madoc's magic releases him from the metal cuffs binding him to the mountain. Carefully, they dress and dry him. Then float him softly down to the outer courtyard. Once I see him pass the balcony, I take off running.

Madoc spits out a curse. "Hyne, follow her."

Racing down the steps and out of the castle with the kraken behind me, I hit the dirt beside Rivan's body. "Rivan. It's me. Meri. Open your eyes."

"Hurry," he whispers over and over. "Hurry."

"You're safe," I reassure him, stroking my hand across his

rune-free body. Regenerating strips him of all his protections. I pick up his hand and clasp it tightly in mine. "Open your eyes. Look at me."

"Not here," he mumbles, turning his head to the side as if he can't bear to look.

Bending down, I carefully grasp his chin and turn him back to me. My lips find his, warmth covering the cold, and I pour all my feelings for him into a long, searching kiss. Pouty lips move gently against mine, slowly coming to life. Tears slide between our lips as my relief overflows.

He surges up, taking my head in his hands, and sweeps his tongue into my mouth. Desperate and urgent, he consumes me, making me a willing prisoner to his need. He pulls his lips from mine for a brief second, his eyes full of desperation.

"Tell me this is real."

Needing more, I bring his lips back to mine, a silent answer to his question. I feel like I've been waiting forever for him. To kiss him without restraint. Hold him tightly in my arms. Run my hands over his lean body.

"I'll go prepare the ship." Madoc's tight voice filters through the haze around me. "Hyne, want to help?"

A hand on my shoulder. "Meri, we need to go. The island is... changing."

Rumbling makes my body sway back and forth, but it's strong enough to make me pull away from Rivan. I look around and see an invisible wave rolling across the island, changing the previously muted land, brightening, and sharpening every tree, flower, and building with color until they're almost blinding in their intensity.

Rivan opens his eyes and stares at me. "You came for me." Amber gold and filled with disbelief, he shakes his head as if he can't believe I'm here.

I place my hands on each side of his head. "I'll always come for you. I promise."

Cormal leans down. "We need to fucking leave. Now." Grasping Rivan's arms, he helps him stand. "Can we ride the shadows?"

Rivan looks around, and his eyes widen. "No, but you're right. We need to get out of here." He takes a few steps forward and stumbles.

Cormal sweeps him up and places his arm around his shoulders. "I've got you." Using magic to help him carry the extra weight, he begins to run, Rivan on one side and me on the other.

We make it to the dock, and I use the wind to bring us on board.

Hyne's standing at the helm, waves held high, and the second our feet touch the wood, he uses the force of water to rapidly propel us away from the island.

I grip the railing and stare back at Avalon. "What's happening?"

Rivan looks at me and raises my hand. "You woke the island with my mother's magic." He taps the rune in the middle of my palm, then dips his head toward my hip. "It's why my father killed me before he took me there. He had to strip the runes from my body first." Dark thoughts twist his features into something almost unrecognizable.

I link our pinkies together. "Why does he hate you?"

Rivan's silent for a few minutes. "He thinks I'm a disgrace for living when the rest of my legion were slaughtered. Maybe he's right. For years, I thought I'd find a way to escape Nyssa, but as time went by, I lost hope. Without hope, I didn't care."

He stares out across the rippling waves. "Fisk's death sparked something in me. A warrior I thought I'd smothered a long time ago." He lets loose a derisive laugh. "Brixton showed me that warrior was weak. It wasn't even much of a fight. He disarmed and killed me in the first minute." The hand on the railing clenches into a fist. "The last five days of torture was simply to teach me a lesson in futility."

Bitterness fills the air, tinged with a darkness I don't usually feel around Rivan. What do I even say to help him? Helpless is a feeling I know too well. A dark hole, it can steal your will to climb out, and overcoming it is tough. All I can do is be here for him.

"Cormal," I say softly. He's been standing on my other side, silently listening to our exchange. "Where are we going?"

His hand sweeps down my back. "To The Abbey. But we start our search for Leandra tomorrow."

I look at him and nod. "Good. We need to finish her so we can figure out how to handle Denir."

"Denir?" Rivan asks with a worried frown. "Why? What's going on?"

For the next hour, I explain everything that happened after I gave him his freedom. "For some reason, Denir thinks I have something of his. Leandra wants to use me as a tool for revenge. Lost love and all that bullshit. We can't continue to dodge them both, so we've decided to hunt her first."

Rivan steps away from me, letting my pinkie drop from his. "Why didn't you tell me?" He sweeps a hand through his hair, the red and black strands showing his dual heritage.

I vehemently shake my head. "At the time, I thought my crown was always going to be between us and the only gift I had to give you was your freedom."

He looks up to the sky as if he's contemplating flying away. "The last time I saw you... when I brought you my copy of the signed treaty, you knew you were going to give up your crown. I told you I was going to give Fisk's copy to the Water Fae, and then I was coming back, but you didn't say anything. You could have told me then. Why didn't you?"

"You gave up so much for the war the first time, I didn't feel it was right to ask you to get involved again," I cry, reaching for his hand. My heart breaks at the look on his face.

Jerking away from me, he looks at Cormal and Madoc. "No. It's because you thought I was fragile. Weak. Just like my father. If you thought I was able to handle it, you would have asked me to stay." Pivoting on his heel, he stalks away, shoulders stiff with hurt pride.

I take a step to go after him, but Madoc stops me. "I'll go. I know a way to help him." With those cryptic words, he follows Rivan below deck.

Crying, I look at Cormal, and he opens his arms. "It will take a while, but he'll come around." He sweeps a lock behind my ear. "But, Meri, you have to stop thinking you know what's best for him. Our damage is ours to overcome. We're stronger for it. Be there for him but let him find his path."

"He has to save himself first," I say softly, realizing for the first time why Cormal was adamant I learn how to save myself.

CHAPTER THIRTEEN

<u>MADOC</u>

Rivan paces back and forth, practically tearing his hair out, as he tries to figure out what to do. I'm probably the only one who knows the crushing weight of being forgotten by a world that left you behind a long time ago. Do you return and fight or find another path? There was a time in the dark when I thought "good riddance," but my fury quickly smashed the defeating thoughts.

"What hurts more—Brixton's words or his sword?" I ask him, curious to know whether he can be honest with himself.

He stops. "What?"

Leaning against the door, I lift a shoulder and answer, "His words bested you before he even lifted his sword. After that, the match was over."

Flames ignite in the depth of his eyes. "My father's never had anything nice to say about anyone but himself. I got used to his abuse a long time ago." His tone is even, but the tic in his jaw gives him away.

A faint smile curves my lips. "My father was the same, but no matter how many times we remind ourselves of that fact, their purposely chosen words always pierce our armor and hit their target, don't they?" My father could give lessons to Brixton. Not all of the scars I wear came from the monsters below.

"After all these years, you're free. It's time for you to choose your path. Figure out who you are and what you stand for without the influence of anyone else," I urge him. "If you want to be known for being kind and selfless, build a school or an orphanage. There is always a need for good deeds and stewards in this world. On your deathbed, people will sing your praises."

The corner of his lip curls, but he says nothing.

"Once you were known to be the fiercest of warriors. Then you selflessly sacrificed your life to save the children of the Fire Fae," I muse, holding both palms up as if the two weigh equally. "Only you can be master of your destiny. Who do you want to be going forward?"

There isn't a wrong choice with either, but he needs to decide for himself.

"I've met you before, haven't I?" he asks out of the blue.

"A long time ago," I reply as I walk away.

It's not the time to delve into the past. I climb the stairs to the deck. Meri turns to me with a question in her eyes, and I shake my head.

"He needs space and time to figure things out."

She flashes me a look of understanding. "It will take us time to find something of Leandra's." That's all she says until we get to the port.

She throws her arms around Hyne. "I can't thank you enough. Today meant the world to me. Are you going to be okay?"

Hyne gives her a determined look. "I'll be fine. I gave him the opportunity to kill me. He won't get another chance. The weapons you gave us will help, and we've got powerful allies."

Meri frowns. "Lady Brina?"

He sighs and shakes his head. "No, she chose the Fire Fae. Better chance of fighting the light Fae who looked down on her at court." He places a large finger against his lips. "Many of the light Fae courts support peace and have pledged to help us uphold the treaty. Once we have a new sovereign on the throne." His look is pointed.

"Good," she replies firmly. "The crown will choose the ruler who is best for both the aristocratic and Lesser Fae."

With a snort of disbelief, he turns to us and says goodbye. When he gets to Rivan, his smile disappears. "It takes great strength to choose peace. At least, that's what Fisk used to tell me. To be honest, I'm finding it takes a hell of a lot of patience. I prefer a good fight myself." He leaps off the ship to land on the dock next to his men. "Until next time, little queen."

Cormal creates a portal right on the deck. "Let's go."

Everyone is waiting for us when we return.

Solandis yanks Meri into her arms. "What were you thinking? The light Fae will kill you if they get the chance. Their world is upside down, and most of them blame you for the revolution."

Her words make Meri pause. "Most? Are you still in touch with any of them?"

"They won't leave her the fuck alone," Vargas grumbles.

She waves a hand to shush him, and understanding crosses Meri's face when she realizes the light Fae have been asking for Solandis to return and be their queen.

Her hand reaches out to grab Solandis'. "Don't worry, the crown will choose the right person. You would be the perfect queen, but we both know your heart isn't in it."

Solandis sags slightly in relief. "It's not. I don't want it to choose me, but who else is left?"

Rivan steps forward, and everyone stops talking.

"This is Rivan, my friend," Meri informs them, looking sadly at Rivan.

He immediately looks away, and it takes everything I have not to knock some sense into him. I glance over at Cormal and see his narrowed eyes locked on Rivan.

Meri darts a glance at Arden.

"Why don't Valerian and I show you around? We've got pretty much anything you need here. Food, fantastic rooftop..." Arden suggests, stepping in to save Meri. Her voice trails off when Rivan lifts a hand.

"Do you have a training facility?" he asks her.

Solandis, along with the rest of the cadre, groan at his question, but Vargas and Arden light up.

"State of the art," Arden says in a singsong voice. "And it changes based on whatever you need. But the best part... it comes with trained warriors who will kick your ass every day." She waves a hand at Vargas, the cadre, and herself. "Want to see it?"

Rivan nods, and Vargas claps him on the back. The three of them head off to see the room that's going to be Rivan's salvation. I eye the glee in Arden's and Vargas' faces. He may regret asking them for help.

Solandis turns back to us. "I heard Brixton escaped and is vowing the usual vengeance."

Cormal rolls his eyes. "Good word travels fast. Your sources didn't happen to say where the bastard is hiding, did they?"

Solandis' twinkling laugh fills the hall. "No, but if I find out, I'll let you know." Surprisingly, there's a murderous glint in her eye that tells me she'd gladly kill him herself. Good. She frowns. "I also heard the island woke up."

I scowl, not liking the fact myself. As if we needed another problem added to our plates. "If I'd have known the origin of

Meri's runes was Avalon, I wouldn't have let her step foot on the land."

The repercussions could be severe. Old magic has a sentience not present in modern magic. My eyes are drawn to the walls of The Abbey, brimming with the magic flowing inside them as if they're alive. Case in point.

Meri's eyes dart between the two of us. "Why does it matter?"

"Old magic doesn't follow the same rules," I explain to her. "It doesn't need someone to wield it. It has a will of its own. But it's wild and untempered by control or a conscience, which means it's omnipotent. Avalon magic only listens to the descendants of Avalon. There are too few of them left to maintain its balance."

Turquoise eyes look at me suspiciously. "You seem to know a lot about it."

"My father told me the stories," I tell Solandis. Needing to get off this subject, I look at Cormal. "Where are we going first?"

He raises an eyebrow at Meri. "Your call."

Her nose scrunches up as she thinks. "Hiemal. We spent an entire winter there. It was wonderful."

Cormal's mouth quirks up as if she said something that pleased him.

"Is it a nice place?" I ask, trying to understand why they're happy.

Meri snorts. "It has subzero temperatures and is covered with ice, but thankfully, Cormal found us some gear."

And she happily lived there an entire winter. Meri rarely talks about her childhood. All I know is she lived in The Underworld with her guardian Leandra. I have a feeling this is going to give me a rare inside look into her past. One she has never let anyone see except Cormal.

CHAPTER FOURTEEN

<u>MERI</u>

Rivan isn't working out, he's punishing himself. At least, that's what it looks like. Sweat pours from him, as his muscles strain to lift yet another set of weights. Not once has he taken a break in the two hours I've been here. Of course, he could be using exercise as an excuse to avoid me, but the gritty determination on his face makes me think he's lost to the destructive thoughts in his head.

Turning away, I slip out and head down to the lobby to meet Cormal and Madoc. Today, we're going to Hiemal. Bitterly cold and practically deserted, it was a haven for me one winter. Through the bond, Leandra often kept me on a tight leash, but with nothing but a frozen tundra outside our door, I could explore to my heart's content.

Madoc's eyeing the parka in his hand with a perplexed look on his face. "Why do I need this? I can regulate my body

102

temperature with ease." He said the same thing about the ski mask and goggles I gave him earlier, but I insisted.

Hiemal is a strange place. Part of The Underworld, it lies in a valley between two mountains, but it existed long before anything else around it was created. A bubble in a time warp, it operates by its own unique set of rules. Time moves incrementally there. A few seconds could mean a day in the outside world. Magic is limited to the most basic of elements like fire, water, and wind. Creatures roam freely across the land. In a way, it's almost like the Wilds or Avalon, with its unpredictability and fickleness.

I roll my eyes. "Take it. If you don't need it, then you don't have to wear it." Cormal holds my own coat as I slip it on and completely button it, then put on thick gloves.

Cormal chuckles. "You'll need it. Are we ready?"

Excited, I take a deep breath and smile. "Let's go."

Ten seconds later, we're exiting the portal and struggling to find our breaths. I motion for Madoc to pull down his mask and cover his eyes. Steel-grey eyes are wide with uncertainty as he does what I tell him. He immediately pulls on the parka and buttons it up, then raises the hood like Cormal and me.

With a huge scowl on his face, he raises his hands and creates a small fireball, but I reach out and smother it.

"We don't want to attract the local wildlife," I tell him. I slip a hand in his coat pocket and pull out the gloves I stashed in there. "Let me help you."

Motioning for him to hold out his hand with his fingers spread, I quickly get the first on, then glance up at him. My mouth twitches at the bundled warrior in front of me, lips compressed and eyes glaring at the landscape around us. It only takes a couple seconds to get the other one on. He flexes his hands and takes a deep breath.

Cormal comes back from scouting and raises an eyebrow. "Are we ready?"

In answer, I pick up my foot and carefully place it flat on the ground, then do the same with the other. Ice requires a sort of march to get across it without falling on your ass. Cormal easily picks up the pattern. I hear a curse and crash behind him and when I turn around, Madoc's sprawled out on the ground. Cormal reaches down and helps him up, then shows him how to walk.

Thankfully, Cormal placed the portal close to the shack where we lived, so we don't have far to walk. My eyes sweep the area around us, easily picking up the changes from the last time I was here. A couple of trees are down. Some creature marked the trees with its claws. The nearby stream is slightly smaller, but it still flows despite the brutally harsh cold.

Following the barely visible path, I round the corner and get my first glimpse of the small wooden structure. Part of the roof is caving in, and the door stands ajar, but it's not too bad considering it's been over nine hundred years since I last visited.

Cormal stops me. "Let me check it out first."

With a nod, I step carefully to the side and let him pass.

Reaching under his parka, he unsheathes a pair of xiphos from his chest and eases the door open. The short, double-edged swords have been a favorite weapon of his for a long time, and he's quite lethal with them. Quiet descends as we listen for any movement. Hearing nothing, he slips inside to search. Moments later, he sticks his head out and motions for us.

I push the roughhewn door open wider and peer inside the place I called home for an entire winter. We could never stay in one place for long, but the natural defenses built into the landscape around us provided Leandra with enough assurance to stay put for a few months.

I pull down my goggles and lift up the mask. Ten by ten, the square room doesn't hold much. Leandra's pallet was in the far corner, but that's long gone. The remnants of one of the two chairs are on the floor next to the rickety table and the fireplace. There are a couple of crooked shelves with dishes still perched on them above a cracked porcelain basin.

Madoc stares around the room in shock. "Where did you sleep?"

I sweep the toe of my boot across the dirt floor. "Here. By the fireplace. We had to keep it lit at all times so we wouldn't freeze." I smile. "First winter I can remember being warm."

Cormal's fist clenches at my statement. "Do you see anything of hers?"

I move to the corner where she slept and pry open one of the boards in the wall. Empty. I glance back at them both and shake my head. "Nothing in the cupboard and the bed she slept in is gone. She burned it before we left."

Madoc tilts his head and asks, "Why?"

He's not talking about the bed. "This was a palace compared to most of the places we lived. Here we had water and heat. A roof over our head," I answer. "And because we were extremely isolated, she had to stock up on food ahead of time, which meant regular meals. But the best part is outside."

I take one last look around at the dingy floor and walls and silently thank them for sheltering me, then I roll down the mask and put on the goggles. Motioning for them to follow me, I step outside and slowly march around to the back. Ice changes to rocks beneath our feet, and I motion for them to climb the small mountain of boulders in front of us.

It takes us about twenty minutes to reach the top. Once we get there, I point to the pool down below. "It's a hot spring." I wave a hand at the forest surrounding us. "Here, she couldn't give me tasks to carry out. So, I spent all day exploring before I came home to a hot bath, dinner, and warm bed. Heaven."

I can't help but glance at Cormal. "He even came to visit me a few times without her knowing." The memory of me staring up at him, hoping he would make a move, with the steam rising around us. "Do you remember?"

Cormal clears his throat and pulls me closer. "Mmm, our first kiss. I'll never forget." His gloved finger traces a soft path across my lips. "One of my top five days ever."

"Mine, too," I admit with a sigh. It was the beginning and end of my memories of us together, but one I treasured for the longest time. After we left Hiemal, things changed between Cormal and me, and all these years later, I'm still trying to find out why.

"We need to go," Cormal says, pointing to the darkening sky.

He begins the descent first, and Madoc and I follow. Unlike our trek here, he moves quickly, heading straight for the portal.

Madoc brushes my arm. "What's the rush?"

"This isn't a place you want to be after dark," I inform him, panting a little from the rushed pace.

Daylight begins to dim, and Cormal picks up the pace. "Hurry!"

"There is no setting of the sun here," I tell Madoc. "Night falls between one breath and the next, and the sky turns black."

A horrifying roar rises behind us, but I don't dare turn to look.

Cormal stands at the edge of the portal, and when I get close, he grabs my coat and pitches me through it. Madoc and Cormal dive through at the same time, and the portal closes behind them.

"That was close," I say, laughing at the three of us lying on the floor of The Abbey.

Arden's head appears above me. "Are you guys okay?"

I raise a hand, and she helps me up. "Peachy." With deft movements, I strip off the gear making me sweat and swipe a hand across my damp forehead.

Cormal and Madoc remove all of their items as well.

"Where to next?" Cormal asks as he gathers up our clothing and magically makes it disappear.

"There are a few places we stayed at for less than a week. In our rush to leave, maybe she left something," I speculate with a shrug. "I'll write down a list."

Madoc hasn't looked at me since we returned. "I need to check on my friend." With a wave of his hand, he strides into the portal without even saying goodbye.

Puzzled, I look at Cormal, but instead of looking confused, there's an odd smile of satisfaction on his face. "I'll check on him, then I need to go to my office for a bit. Will you be okay here?"

"Take me with you," I plead almost desperately. "Your place is as safe as The Abbey."

He shakes his head. "I need to visit Lucifer and bring him up to speed." Pecking me on the lips, he too disappears into the portal.

Irritated, I look at Arden. "Still make those great sandwiches?"

She links her arm in mine. "Yes, and I have wine. Since you have magic now, why don't you get us some cupcakes?"

Brightening, I laugh. "You're right. Who said magic can't make you happy?"

LATER, full of food and wine, I leave Arden downstairs, but instead of finding my room, I make my way to Rivan. Arden told me they had all taken a turn training and sparring with him today, but it wasn't enough, so she created a spell to give him imaginary foes while they all sleep.

I inhale sharply at the fight before me. Alone, he battles, feinting and thrusting, against other warriors. Swords clash and ring loudly in the air. If Arden hadn't told me this was a spell, I'd never believe it wasn't real. Not wanting to interrupt his concentration, I slide down the wall to watch.

His burnished skin is naked, void of all the runes that protect him. I wonder if this is part of his chosen punishment. The first night we met he lay on the floor, his runes near shredded by Nyssa's nails, yet not once did he consider regenerating. He feared losing his protection more than the excruciating pain. And here it's been at least a week without them covering his body.

A knife slashes across his arm, and I wince. Rivan, on the other hand, looks at the wound and flashes a grim look of satisfaction. It hurts to see him like this. Unable to watch anymore, I quietly stand and make my way to my room.

The long day and several glasses of wine help. Falling asleep the second my head hits the pillow, I drop into the memory of Cormal and me at the hot springs.

Luxuriating in the warmth of the water surrounding me, I lie back and float on its surface. Bitter cold air caresses the flashes of skin I expose above the water for the briefest of seconds, but the heat and steam quickly soothe the sting they leave behind.

We've been here for three weeks, and it's been heaven. There are no tasks to hunt down a magical item or deliver a promise of death to one of her many enemies. She rarely even peeks her head out the door to find me. Not wanting to incur her wrath, I get up early in the morning, grab a piece of toast, and head out to explore the frozen tundra around us. I keep waiting for her to tell me to pack up, but every day she doesn't is another day in paradise.

"I didn't know there were sirens in this part of the world," a dark, smoky voice jests from the rocks above me.

I immediately submerge my body and wipe the water from my eyes. It's the man who came to visit Leandra a couple of months before we moved here. The same one who fueled my dreams for week, with his dark hair, blue eyes, and wicked smile.

"Cormal," I stammer. "What are you doing here?" I turn my head to look at the desolate landscape. "How did you even find us?"

He flashes a smile that makes my toes curl. "There are few places I haven't been. Until now, this was one." He looks around. "Dangerous, but the quiet is peaceful."

A vague answer, but I'm not surprised. It's what I'd expect from the king of criminals. "Leandra's in the little house down the path. If you turn around, you should see it from where you're standing."

White teeth flash. "I'm not here to see her." His hands rub up and down his arms. "I'll return tomorrow. Same time and place?"

Days slide by in a spinning wheel of images. Long walks in a white wonderland with equally long discussions about nothing and everything. Innocent dips in the hot springs that slowly become infused with a layer of unfulfilled need.

Like today.

Blue eyes study me intently as he faces me in the water.

My fingers clench with the desire pulsing through me, but I hold them under the water so he can't see. Nervous, I bite my lip, wondering if he wants me the same way I want him, or if this is some long game of torturous friendship.

His large hand reaches out and snags me by the waist. "If you don't want me to kiss you, tell me now."

The huskiness of his voice propels me forward. "That's all I've wanted for weeks. Kiss me, Cormal." I wrap my slim arms around his neck and press my naked body up against his.

He inhales sharply and spears his other hand through my hair. Firm lips softly touch mine like butterfly wings once, twice, three times. When I move restlessly against him, wanting more, he groans, and those same lips harden, ruthlessly devouring everything in their path. His tongue plunges into my mouth, stroking and sucking, and stealing every thought from my head. I moan beneath the onslaught.

Without thinking, I wrap my bare legs around his body, and for a second, the kiss gets even wilder until he suddenly jerks away. Completely.

Startled, I stare at him. "What is it?" My body throbs in all the places it touched his, and all I want is to be in his arms again.

"You're not ready," he tells me.

Bewildered, I frown. "For kissing?"

"For all the things I want to do to you."

It's still dark when I wake, my body throbbing now as it did then. Young and inexperienced, I didn't know what he meant, but I thought I did, and I wanted it with every fiber of my being.

My hands drift down my body, tempted to take care of myself, but I hold off. It's not my fingers I want. It's him. It's always been him.

CHAPTER FIFTEEN

CORMAL

Aamon and Madoc are covered in bruises, welts, and blood when I arrive. Madoc flicks a glance at me, then continues to bloody his fists against his opponent. Neither of them are using magic, only brute force. Aamon pauses every once in a while, but Madoc refuses to let him stop, snarling at him to get back in the fight. This goes on for at least another hour.

Aamon finally folds his arms and shakes his head. "No more."

Madoc flips him off and stalks away. "Fine. I'm going to grab a shower."

I conjure a couple of chairs for Aamon and me. For several minutes, we sit in silence.

"Has he been like this since he returned?" I ask nonchalantly, as if I'm not too invested in his answer.

Aamon eyes me with suspicion but nods. "Upset." He moves restlessly on the chair.

"Here," I say, offering him an orange.

His large hand takes it, but he gives me a confused glance.

Grabbing the other one in my pocket, I peel it, then slip a slice into my mouth. "It's good."

One of his claws slices across the orange, cutting through the peel into the fruit, and juice runs into his hand. He wrinkles his nose and hands it back to me.

Patiently, I peel it and hand him a slice.

Zesty orange flavor hits his tongue, and his face lights up. "More."

Handing him the rest of the slices, I watch him dump them all in his mouth at once. "Good."

"What is he upset about?" I murmur, not wanting Madoc to overhear.

Aamon lifts a shoulder. "Ice. Cold. Leandra." He leans closer. "Meri."

I chuckle. "Good." Aamon's downcast face tells me there's more. "What are you upset about?"

"Want to be free," he says with a sad look on his face. "Madoc say no."

"It's not safe for you to be out there," Madoc spits out as he stalks over to where we're sitting. "What have you been saying to him?" He folds his massive arms across his chest, but it only makes me laugh.

"Intimidation doesn't work on me," I tell him, popping another slice in my mouth. Rancid breath blows across my nose, and I rear back and look at Aamon.

He turns hopeful eyes on me. "More?"

This time, I hold the entire orange out to him. "Carefully peel it. Then eat the inside." Madoc moves to take it from him, but I wave him off. "He can do it."

Aamon's tongue slides out as he concentrates on not

squashing the fruit in his hand. Claws slowly peel off the outer layer. Once it's gone, he turns to me, and I show him how to open it up and take one slice, which he does.

Aamon flashes his gruesome grin at me, then Madoc. "Good. Want?" He offers a piece to Madoc, who takes it and pops it into his mouth.

"What's the point of all this?" he asks me, his voice even as he flashes a quick glance at Aamon.

"How much has he learned since you became friends? Quite a lot, I imagine," I muse. "The traits he's exhibited in the last few minutes tell me everything. He's careful with his strength. He's capable of displaying more complex emotions like empathy and understanding, especially when you're trying to work something out of your system. He learns quickly. Why keep him here?"

Madoc scoffs. "It's not safe for him out there."

"Because he's a danger to those around him?" I deliberately state.

He stalks forward in a cold fury. "Meri's more likely to kill someone than he is. Aamon only wants to live. Enjoy life. He doesn't want to fight." His pointer finger stabs into my chest. "But he would if they provoked him. Then where would he be? Back in The Below. This time forever."

"Or we can help him find his path. Come with me to Lucifer's. Plead his case. Let him assess Aamon himself before Callyx finds him or something bad happens," I urge him. "You know it's the only way."

He jerks away. "No, he'll send him away."

Aamon raises his hand. "Want to."

"You don't understand," Madoc tells him. "What if he sends you back?"

Aamon looks at the cave above us and shrugs one of his large shoulders. "Prison."

Madoc searches his friend's face for several minutes. Whatever he sees makes his shoulders drop in defeat. "We'll give it a try, but if I don't like what I see, I'm sending you somewhere safe."

Aamon flashes his sharp teeth in a semblance of a grin, and it sends a shiver down my back.

"Make sure he doesn't smile when he stands before Lucifer," I snap at Madoc before turning toward the exit. "No time like the present."

Following me, Madoc hisses in a furious voice, "If this doesn't work, I'm adding you to my list."

"There's a long line ahead of you," I jeer. "Although, unlike most of my enemies, you might actually have a chance."

His scowl slips for a second, and the corners of his mouth twitches, but he quickly pastes it back on. "But then I'd have to contend with Meri."

Her name brings me back to the other reason I came to see him. "You left in a hurry. Meri was concerned." She wasn't—this time—but he needs to understand his actions affect her even if she never says anything.

At the reminder, his fists clench and he looks away. "I… her life. That shack. If that was her idea of heaven, hell might kill me." There's a tortured look in his eyes that wasn't there this morning, and it thrills me to see it. He cares for her more than he even realizes.

Stopping before we get to the portal, I turn and level him with one of my darkest looks. "It's going to get worse. Bury those feelings deep inside. Don't let Meri see your pity or disgust. She knows most of the places were shitholes. Hell, a shithole would have been a step up. But in her eyes, this was the life she was dealt, and she's proud of overcoming it."

He inhales, nostrils flaring at the thought, but jerks his head in agreement. "Fine. Let's go see a man about a monster."

Satisfied, I take us to the palace and the meeting I'd already set up with Lucifer. The man doesn't like surprises, and given he's ruler of The Underworld, he isn't someone you want to piss off. Friend or no friend.

Callyx, Evren, and Lucifer are all waiting for us in the throne room. From the edges of the black marble floors, black obsidian walls rise high to the ceiling above, where they meet arches made of real gold encrusted with gems. Huge, elaborate chandeliers made of the same metal cast flickering candlelight across every surface. Nothing in the room is more intimidating though than the throne made of bones from Lucifer's enemies.

Equally fierce is the look on his perfectly sculpted angelic face—the one that says he's contemplating someone's death. Probably mine. I didn't exactly warn him I was dropping the monster he and Callyx have been searching for in his lap.

"Lucifer, this is Madoc," I say, pointing first to the man. "And Aamon, his friend." When I arranged this meeting, I only explained I thought there had been an injustice, and Lucifer should hear the case for himself.

Lucifer's jaw clenches tightly, but he dips his head cordially toward them. Callyx flashes me his "are you fucking kidding me" glare, but I ignore it.

Aamon blinks at Lucifer. "You not devil."

Lucifer tilts his head. "No, I'm not, but I rule this realm now."

Madoc clears his throat and begins, "Aamon was sentenced to The Below by the devil for killing his brother, a prince of Hell. When I woke in that hellhole, I was weak, disoriented. I didn't know where I was. He found me. Protected me from the others. Became my friend." Madoc flashes a rueful grin toward Aamon.

"How did you end up there?" Lucifer questions, darting a look at me.

I hold up my hands. "Not my doing."

"Leandra. She needed to keep me alive, but in a place I couldn't escape. Beyond The Underworld, there are few places that could hold me indefinitely. The Below was the perfect solution for her," Madoc arrogantly informs him.

I secretly smile. Lucifer likes arrogance.

Callyx glances at Lucifer, and he nods.

"You won't find her. Evren's amulet hides her well," I interject before Callyx can leave.

Lucifer shifts in his seat to wink at his beautiful queen, then turns back to Madoc. "Of course it does. Continue."

Madoc's gaze darts between the two. "I heard quite a lot about Evren when Gabriel landed in our laps. It's nice to meet you."

Her mouth twists. "I'm sure whatever he said wasn't the least bit flattering."

Madoc shrugs. "He was an asshole."

Evren smiles in agreement.

"Gabriel?" Lucifer asks, leaning forward. "He spoke to you?"

"More like ordered me to save him," Madoc says derisively. "That was before he met the rest of the inhabitants. The monsters in the dark have a way of stripping you down to your soul. His must have been ugly. It didn't take him long to start begging for our protection. When begging didn't work, he resorted to bargaining. All he had to offer... was his wings."

Lucifer stares at him in silence for a minute, then roars with laughter. "I wondered what happened to them. Hell of a bargain. I assume you used them to fly the two of you out."

When Madoc nods, Lucifer turns to Aamon. "Are you sorry for killing the prince?"

Aamon slowly shakes his head. "He bad. Hurt my friend."

Madoc steps in front of Aamon. "One person isn't worth the sentencing they gave to him. I request that you release him with time served."

Lucifer chuckles. "I agree, especially not that bastard. Aamon's right. He was bad. Even for a demon." His smile drops.

"My concern is Aamon. The power to kill a prince isn't something I take lightly. What if someone hurts you?"

Aamon growls, and Madoc places a hand on his arm. "What if he were to live with creatures stronger than him? Would that ease your fears?"

Intrigued, I tilt my head, wondering where that could possibly be.

Lucifer looks at Callyx and Evren, who both nod their approval. "Since he wears our brand, I'll need to know his location at all times."

Madoc takes a deep breath. "I believe The Wild Hunt will allow him to live with them. They'll take care of him and teach him about the world in a way he'll understand. I'll be able to regularly visit and check up on him."

It's Lucifer's turn to look intrigued. "That's a pretty big assumption. How can you be sure The Wild Hunt will even listen to your request?"

"Right now, they won't," Madoc returns with a scowl. "But they will once I get back the power Leandra stole. I need time to set things straight. For now, Aamon can live in the outskirts of the Wilds, and nobody will bother him." Back ramrod straight and jaw locked, he waits for Lucifer to decide Aamon's fate.

Tension rises as Lucifer studies Madoc. Aamon moves restlessly, but Madoc only meets Lucifer's probing look with one of his own, each taking the measure of the other. Suddenly, Lucifer's demeanor changes to one of supreme satisfaction. He raises an eyebrow at me, but unsure of what he's asking, I can't answer his silent query. That surprises him.

"Remember this moment," Lucifer tells Madoc with a chuckle. "I'll consider Aamon's term served, but I want regular updates."

Madoc dips his chin in acknowledgement. "Understood. Thank you."

I step forward. "One more thing… We need permission for Aamon to help us hunt Leandra."

Lucifer narrows his eyes. "Fine. But, Cormal, he'll be under your supervision during those times. Fuck up, and you'll find yourself in one of my dungeons."

Smiling broadly, I bow. "Thank you, oh so generous and benevolent leader."

"Get out." He waves a hand, and we find ourselves standing outside the forbidding, dark palace.

I slap Madoc on the back. "Well, that went well. Now we don't have to worry about Callyx hunting down Aamon and taking our heads. Let's return to my office, then we'll drop Aamon off in the Wilds."

It feels good to accomplish so many things in one day.

The news I get at the office brightens my day even more. Lot, the demon of greed, sent me an update. His contact, the shadow demon, is dead and all leads are going cold. He asks if I want him to return, but I've been at this game too long. If demons are dying, it means we're close. I tap the desk, thinking of how to proceed.

Sending one of my shadow demons to you. Set him up as the contact. See who bites.

CHAPTER SIXTEEN

MERI

Cormal slides into me from behind. "Mm, you're very, very wet. Dreaming of me?" His hand cups my breast and squeezes. "Or maybe Rivan?" Kneading the fullness, he licks the side of my throat and finds my ear. "Dark and brooding Madoc, perhaps?"

Phantom hands move all over my body as if they were all here, touching the places that turn me on most. An image of the three of them, thrusting into my mouth and body, each one filling me up brings me to a fever pitch. Panting at the thought, I press into Cormal.

"All three of us," he concludes. "Fuck, you're beyond drenched at the thought." With a twist of our bodies, he pulls me to my knees and thrusts in hard from behind. Dark magic swirls around us, and I lose all sense of time. Only the pull of Cormal's seduction and the plunging of his body into mine registers.

Coming in a sea of darkness, I cry out, my body pulsing and clenching his. He continues to slide in and out, faster and faster, until he slams his body deep into mine and stops, coming a second later.

Tiny kisses pepper my shoulder, until he releases me to lie on the bed.

Twisting from my knees to my side, I stare at the scruff covering his face. "That's one hell of a wake-up call." I reach out and sweep the hair back from his face. "Is everything okay?"

"Long day," he murmurs. He continues, telling me about taking Madoc and Aamon to Lucifer.

Startled, I stare at him with a troubled look on my face. "Why did you do that? Because you thought they were ready? It could have gone horribly wrong. What would you have done then?"

He sighs and gets out of bed. With a wave, he clothes himself, then paces across the room. "Everything worked out."

Exasperated, I jump up and stand in front of him. "Cormal, it wasn't your call to make. Why not offer it to Madoc and let him decide? You always have to manipulate things to your satisfaction, but that doesn't make it the right way to handle things."

"Thank you," Madoc says from the door. "Someone understands…" His voice trails off into silence.

Curious, I peer around Cormal to find Madoc staring at something on the far wall. Swiveling around, I find a full-length mirror, reflecting my entirely naked body. With a strangled curse, I clean and dress myself. My eyes meet his slate-grey ones, widening at the heat in their depths. His nostrils flare, and a small carnal smile appears.

Fresh air swirls around the room, and Madoc's gaze swings from me to Cormal. "Now I know why you were in such a hurry to return."

"Hard to resist when her dreams are filled with such passionate images," Cormal reflects with a satisfied smile.

"Although I wasn't the only one in them. She seems to have a thing for dark and broody men."

Madoc turns to me and crooks his finger. "Come. Tell me what I was doing in these dreams of yours." His voice is gravelly, as if the thought of me dreaming about him is turning him on even more.

Tossing a glare at Cormal for revealing my secrets, I ignore the ache Madoc's words are igniting. "We need to get going, but I want to check on Rivan first."

Cormal smirks and heads out the door. "Let's go."

Madoc moves to the door but stops at the threshold. I wait for him to continue, but he mockingly motions for me to go first. Walking toward him, with his eyes watching my every move, my heart races in anticipation. Two feet away. One. There's plenty of room for me to get through the door without touching him, but it's like my body has a mind of its own, and I deliberately brush against his. Hard muscles slide across every aching part of me, and I gasp at the sensation.

It's his turn to suck in a breath. His head dips down, and he huskily murmurs, "One day soon, I'm going to take you up on that offer. The things I ache to do to you. It's all I think about when I smell you or see you. You wrapped around me. Me buried inside you. And that's only the beginning."

Dragging air into my lungs, I stumble past him, reeling from his words, barely resisting the overwhelming urge to throw myself at him.

"I'll meet you in the lobby," I stammer as I walk into the elevator, leaving him standing in the hallway with a sinful smile on his face.

I manage to gain some semblance of calm on my way to the training room. When I enter, Rivan's standing by the door, taking a break. He slowly lowers his water, but thankfully, doesn't look away.

"Hi," I say softly, walking over to him. "I've come by a few times, but you always seem to be training." Flicking a glance over his body, I notice the sheen of sweat coating his lean muscles and burnished skin. I swallow hard. "You look good."

His mouth twists, but he remains silent.

"I'm sorry," I assure him. "I should have told you I was giving up the crown, but some part of me didn't want that to be the reason you came back. It didn't have anything to do with you being weak. You'd been through so much and had so many changes forced on you, I didn't want to add to them."

"Instead, you took away my choices," Rivan says bitterly. "The reason doesn't matter."

I look around the training room. "Doesn't it? You haven't left this room, have you? All you do is train. Why? Because Brixton thinks you're weak? Who gives a shit what that deranged psycho thinks?" My voice rises with every question until I'm practically shouting at him. Horrified, I close my mouth.

He gives me a pitying look. "You can't even yell at me because you're worried about how it will make me feel." His hand comes up as soon as I open my mouth. "I doubt you even think twice when you're yelling at Cormal. Go away, Meri."

I watch him stalk over to his sword and pick it up. The second his hand touches the hilt, the room comes alive with enemies trying to kill him. Rivan instantly becomes a blur, striking them down with a ferocity I haven't seen in him. Because of me. It's obvious my visit only made things worse between us. I sigh and let myself out.

The portal is open when I get to the lobby. Madoc takes one look at me and shares a silent look with Cormal, but I ignore their unspoken conversation.

"Where are we going?" I ask Cormal. There isn't a place I've lived that he doesn't know. I always knew he had someone watching me, but he would never admit it.

"We've got three places to visit today," he says, taking my hand in his. "The Cauldron, Dead Rock, and the Slag."

I inhale sharply. "My day might have started out great, but it's going to hell fast." With a mirthless laugh, I walk into the portal, holding tightly to him.

When witches began arriving in hell, demons feasted on them. Weak witches were killed on sight. Strong ones were forced to create potions and spells to survive. Over three hundred witches died before they banded together on this very ground to fight their common foe. They won and claimed this land for themselves, calling it The Cauldron.

Designed after a small town in the human world, witches bustle here and there, shopping and visiting with each other, while their children play on sidewalks or in the street. Postcard perfect, or so they want you to believe, but witches aren't sent to hell for practicing good magic.

Hundreds of years ago, I stepped into this town and fell in love. Clean streets. Lots of food. Nice places to live and clothes to wear. It was a dream come true until I blinked, and it became a nightmare. It took them less than a week to run Leandra and me out of town.

Madoc swivels around in surprise. "It's nice."

I snort. "It's a façade. Deception at its finest. Stay alert."

He tilts his head. "What happened?"

I wave a hand. "Jealous of Leandra's power, they wanted her to share it with the entire coven. When she refused, they tried to force her by holding me hostage. It didn't end well."

That's an understatement. Leandra almost destroyed the entire town.

A beautiful witch with dark hair appears in front of Cormal. Her lips twist into a sneer when she sees me. "I'm Carmela. Per your rather forceful request, we've agreed to escort you to the lodgings Leandra and her abomination used while they were here." Her eyes dart to Madoc, and she holds up a hand. "We did not agree to let a Fae into our town."

Cormal waves a hand, changing Madoc's appearance to that of a human male. "All I see is a witch."

She huffs but motions sharply for the three of us to follow her. It only takes us a minute to get to the studio apartment I shared with Leandra.

"It looks the same as the day we left," I say in surprise.

One room with a tiny kitchen. A small bed sits in one corner. A couch along one wall. Leandra slept in one and I in the other. It was comfortable. The room is one of the nicest ones we ever stayed in. "There's not even a speck of dust in here."

"That's because nobody has lived here since you left," Carmela reveals from the hallway outside the apartment. "They're afraid Leandra might have left a few nasty surprises behind."

I laugh, noting her position. "That would be something she would do." Even now, they are scared of Leandra.

Madoc tilts his head and looks at me. "Sometimes you sound like you admire her."

I look at the witch standing outside the door and shake my head not wanting her to hear my reply. Walking over to the fireplace, I use my magic to light a fire. Once the flames are high enough, I reach through them to the back wall and open the hidden safe. Empty. I run my hand along the inside to make sure. "Nothing. We can go."

Carmela escorts us to the edge of town where Cormal's portal stands. "We will not honor any additional requests. Don't come back." She disappears.

"Leandra had more power than all of them put together," I tell Madoc with a sneer on my face and a hint of pride in my voice. "To someone with no power, I thought her magnificent, larger than life and bigger than her enemies. For a long time, I was grateful she gave a dud like me a home."

When he looks confused, I explain. "No powers. A dud. I thought myself a Fae orphan she picked up along the way, but then I learned the truth of my existence, and I hated her with every fiber of my being. Flip a coin and that's how I felt any given day."

125

CHAPTER SEVENTEEN

<u>MADOC</u>

Dead Rock is exactly what I thought it would be—a dirt road town in the middle of The Underworld. A pile of rubble sits where Meri's home used to be. I study the pitiful stack of wood planks and guesstimate this hellhole was roughly eight by eight. How the hell did it fit two people?

She raises her hands and sifts through the boards, but there's nothing of Leandra's here. "Damn it. This is useless. She's a paranoid bitch on her best day."

I reach over to pat her shoulder, but she's already turning toward Cormal and his outstretched arms. Hot wind blows across my face, and I pivot to block it. "Let's go."

My gut tightens when I step out of the portal this time and find Callyx standing in front of it. "What are you doing here?"

He dismisses me with one look and turns to Meri. After

giving her a hug, he blasts Cormal. "What the hell are you thinking bringing Meri to The Slag?"

"We're searching for anything Leandra might have left behind. We need a scent for Aamon to follow," Cormal admits in a low tone. "This is our last stop today. How the hell did you find us?"

Kavi, along with several other large demons, step away from the side of the building. "Sorry. Forgot he hides in the shadows. Bastard followed us."

Cormal shrugs. "We can use the back-up while we're here." Dark blue eyes dart suspiciously from one end of the alley to the other. "We need to get in and out."

"What the hell is this place?" I ask as I look from one tense face to another.

"Lesser Demons trade unscrupulous services to Higher Demons in exchange for power," Cormal states tersely. "It's a brutal, lawless place."

Dirt and grime cover every surface, but you can barely see it in the near dark. "Is that why there aren't any lights?"

"Lights attract attention," Meri inserts quietly. "One of the first rules you learn here. Never bring a light to The Slag."

She lived in this forsaken place. Ripples of anger build inside me. No wonder her first instinct was to duck the knife coming at her. I throw Cormal a murderous look, and he nods in agreement.

Moving closer to me, he murmurs, "It took me a week to find out Meri was here. I almost killed Leandra over it. Instead, I gave her money to get them out of here." All these years haven't dimmed his fury.

"Why didn't you?" I ask, furious at him for not doing something permanent to save her.

He raises a finger to his lips. "We're here."

I store the anger away for later.

Cormal opens the door to the stairs and points up. Silently, we follow him in single file all the way to the roof. Once we're at the top, he points to a metal shed nestled into one of the corners.

Made of flimsy corrugated metal, this structure is tiny. Five feet long, eight feet wide. The screech of metal makes me wince, and I see Kavi motion for his men to fan out over the roof.

Cormal steps in first, then motions for Meri to join him. I move in closer but hesitate at the doorway. There's an underlying current here. Like a predator, it waits.

"Be careful," I whisper harshly. "There's something wrong with this place."

Meri snorts. "There's a lot wrong with this place."

For the first time, I hear a hint of fear in her voice. This place frightens her. My anger at Leandra increases for making her live in this hellhole.

Cormal sends his magic out. It streams across the walls of the shed without interruption. "I don't feel anything."

Frustrated, I step farther into the room and send my magic to probe the same walls. Alarm bells ring violently in my head, and I instinctively clamp my hands across my ears to stop the sound. Excruciating pain drives me to my knees, but I silently tell Cormal to get her the hell out of here.

For a second, he tilts his head in confusion.

Does he not hear it? I look from him to Meri. Neither of them are holding their heads. I push the word out through clenched teeth. "Attack."

Cormal immediately moves in front of Meri and orders her to make her way to the door. "Out. Now."

The words are barely out of his mouth when the room shifts and a gigantic monster peels itself from the walls. Cormal's the closest. It grabs him and flings him back and forth like a rag doll. Meri jumps forward to help him. Hairless beasts erupt from the monster and begin stalking her.

Dark magic leaves Cormal's hands and wraps around the

grotesque beast, but it dissipates the second it lands on its target.

Cormal curses and shouts something unintelligible to Kavi.

Meri cuts off a large piece of the shed with her magic, lights it on fire, then swings at the smaller beasts, but it doesn't deter them.

Callyx crams his body into the small space and starts swearing. "Fucking hell, it's a shade." Pulling his sword, he raises it high and slashes down and across the creature, but the sword passes straight through its now transparent body. He rears back. "This sword is infused with Lucifer's magic and should easily kill a shade."

Meri screams and slashes at the clawed hand on her arm. "Not if Leandra created it." Faery fire erupts from her hand and turns the creature to ash. She stares at her arm in wonder. "I did it."

Callyx steps in to take care of the other two. Apparently, the sword works on these beasts, easily cutting them down.

"Watch out!" I yell, lurching to my feet.

I shove Meri back, then step into her spot. Brutal strength wraps around my body and squeezes. Dark Fae power flows out of me and into the creature, but instead of killing it, the damn thing grows bigger.

"Fuck!" I roar when it cracks a couple of my ribs.

I release the faery fire inside me and it singes the fur on its arms but doesn't turn it to ash. Astonished, I stare up at the creature. "Shade. Phantom. Whatever the hell it is, the usual rules don't apply." Jerking my arms out from under his, I grab him around the waist and throw him against the shed.

It doesn't faze him.

Cormal jumps on its back and plunges his fingers into its eye sockets. Magic as dark as sludge slides into the empty spaces, filling them up.

With a roar, it stumbles backward, blindly swiping at

Cormal. One of its claws happens to catch on his neck, almost decapitating him. He falls to the floor in a heap.

Meri screams and screams. Before either Callyx or I can stop her, she throws herself at the monster and begins slashing at him with all her strength. Deep gashes appear across its chest as it roars and shakes in agony. Relentless in her attack, she continues to shred the outer layer until a cavity opens.

The monster stumbles again, and she shoves forward, plunging her hand into the dark hole and removing a black, withered heart. I still. Phantoms don't have hearts, and I'm willing to bet shades don't either.

She drops it to the ground and turns it to ash. The monster falls and begins fading into the shadows, but not before it sends a pulse of magic out into the night. A warning to its maker.

I move forward to help Cormal, but Meri turns her head and snarls at me. Freezing, I stare in horror at the sight before me. Her eyes are gone. Replaced with white sockets and the faint image of a skull. She points a bony finger at me, stripped of its flesh and muscles, and opens her mouth. Dread pours into me, filling me from head to toe. This is why Denir and Leandra are after Meri.

"Stop. If you say the wrong words, it could kill everyone here. Permanently," I interject. Hands up, I show her I'm not a threat. "Callyx, get out."

He starts to protest until he gets a good look at her face. Backing away slowly, he takes up a stance in front of the entrance but continues to watch the scene in the shed unfold.

Meri tilts her head side to side, the power inside her studying me.

I point to the floor where Cormal is laying. "I need to help him, but I can't do that with you standing between us."

Her eyes narrow, but then she follows my finger to Cormal.

Some part of her is hearing me. "Take a deep breath. Move a little to the right. That's it."

I slide past her and pull out a healing potion. It will speed up his recovery. *Wake up, you bastard.* We desperately need to show her he's alive.

Meri sways and crashes to her knees, but her eyes never leave Cormal.

Finally, he stirs, blue eyes blinking rapidly. He frantically looks around until he spots her, then yanks her into his arms.

I throw up a shield around them. A second later, she sags against him and loses consciousness. Thank the goddess.

Cormal shakes her, but I stop him. "She'll be out for days. I'll explain after we get to The Abbey. There are too many ears around here."

He tries to stand with her in his arms, but he's weaker than he realizes and almost drops her. I take her from him and cradle her tightly in my arms. She feels good. Tiny, but full of curves. I look down at her beautiful face. It all makes sense now. I was first drawn to the darkness inside her. How did I not realize it was my power?

"Where's the monster?" Cormal asks, his eyes darting around the shed.

"Dead," I say flatly.

Callyx comes striding in the door, his brows lowered in a thunderous scowl. "I assume it's safe now that she's out?"

Cormal tenses. "What the fuck does that mean?"

With a hiss, I zap the two of them. "Not here. We need to return to The Abbey."

Callyx swings an arm around Cormal to help him walk, but the snarl he receives has him backing off. "Fine. Fall on your damn face. Let's go." Within minutes, he has everyone mobilized and moving toward the portal with Cormal's team protecting us from the rear.

The derelict citizens of The Slag slither out of the shadows to watch us pass, whispering about the monster's death and Leandra's anger.

"Where's Kavi?" I ask Cormal.

"He went to get Lux," Cormal replies with a hard laugh. "He's the last resort when things go sideways." He picks up the phone and calls his second in command. "Stand down. It's dead." He narrows his eyes and looks at me. "I'm not sure. Will touch base later."

"Before it died, it sent out a warning to its maker," I murmur to Cormal. "Leandra knows we're actively hunting her."

CHAPTER EIGHTEEN

<u>CORMAL</u>

Madoc places Meri on the bed and carefully sweeps her platinum hair back from her lips and face. For a brief second, he leans down as if he's going to kiss her but stops himself before their lips touch. I conjure a chair by the bed and sit down, lacing my fingers with hers. His lip curls, but he says nothing. He better fucking stay silent. Not once did he let me hold her on the way back. Snarling like a damn beast every time I tried to kiss or touch her.

Callyx arrives, bringing everyone else with him, including Rivan.

Rivan, Solandis, and Arden step toward the bed, but Madoc holds up his hand. "She'll be out of it for a few days. Her body is recovering from the power she inadvertently invoked."

Solandis' delicate brows rise. "What power? Is this something new she picked up?"

Madoc runs a tired hand down his face. "To explain the

power, I need to first take a step back and explain the Dark Fae Kingdom and how the crown chooses its ruler. As you may or may not know, the light Fae crown uses wisdom and foresight to choose its ruler. Unlike its counterpart, the dark Fae crown searches for blood and power, specifically the blood of Konnyr and the power of The Wild Hunt."

Knowledge sparks in the depths of Theron's violet eyes. As the only other dark Fae in the room, he quickly jumps ahead. "You're the son of Madox." There is an awe to his tone I've never heard before and based on the expressions of Arden and the rest of the cadre, neither have they. "You went missing a little over three thousand years ago." He frowns.

"I am," Madoc admits in an arrogant tone. "I was to inherit the crown after my father passed, but the night before the coronation, Leandra stole the power from me and gifted it to Denir."

Fear rises inside me. "Are you telling us Meri somehow picked up this power from Denir? Is she mimicking it?"

Madoc's jaw clenches. "It can't be replicated in any way. Only those with Konnyr's blood can wield it. My guess is Leandra accidentally or hell, purposely, took that power from Denir when she created Meri. It's why they're both after her."

Theron whistles. "And time is running out," he continues to explain for the rest of us. "To keep the crown, the dark Fae ruler must show his continued ability to wield this power every thousand years on the anniversary of his coronation, which for Denir is in less than two months."

"Meri's nine hundred and ninety-three years old. Leandra must have stolen the power right after the last anniversary and created Meri," I tell them, rubbing my thumb across the delicate bones in her hand.

My mind latches on the explanation Madoc gave to Lucifer. "Why didn't she kill you instead of dumping you in The Below?"

"She couldn't take the chance my death would cause the power—and subsequently, the crown—to search for a ruler with the strongest bloodline. It would not have been Denir. He only has a drop of Konnyr in him." Madoc sneers. "Enough to wield the power for the coronation ceremony, but like Meri, he doesn't have enough of the bloodline to wield it in times of war—the purpose for which it was created."

It hits me. "Lucifer knew, didn't he? Or at least, he figured out some of it out." The smug bastard is going to hold this over me forever.

Madoc's lips twitch when he sees the irritated look on my face. "It felt good to be recognized by another ruler."

Rivan raises his head and looks at me in utter horror. "Meri has to die to release the power, doesn't she?"

Everyone starts talking at once. I place my fingers under my tongue and whistle like my sister taught me to do long ago. They instantly stop. "Madoc?"

He shrugs. "Leandra took the power from me, and I'm still here. I'm guessing she can do the same for Meri, but will she? She constantly threatens to unmake Meri, yet she kept her alive all those years. I think she intends to use her as a tool of revenge against Denir. How? I don't know. Placing Meri on the throne will never work."

He's silent for a minute as he thinks it through. "She made her with both Nyssa's and Denir's essence. There must be a tie between them."

Solandis slips past Madoc to go to Meri's side. Her graceful features twisted in anger. "I refuse to let that happen. We need to kill Leandra before she unmakes Meri." Her turquoise eyes assess me closely. "Tell me what you've done to find her."

"Very little," I return with a frustrated sigh. "The amulet prevents her enemies from finding her. We were visiting past places they lived in hopes of finding an item of Leandra's to use in a hunt."

"What's the origin of the amulet? How did Leandra get it?"

Arden asks with a frown. "We might be able to use blood magic to trace it."

I shake my head. "My guess is blood was used to create the spell to hide its wearer from their enemies." When everyone looks hopeful, I scan the crowd, landing on Daire. "Evren made it."

Daire, Arden, Vargas, and Callyx exchange hopeless glances. "I see."

Rivan, who met Evren and helped her defeat the brùid, locks eyes with me. "I'm sure you've exhausted every other avenue. We don't have a choice. We need to ask Evren."

"Right now, we need to wait for Meri to wake," I tell him, unwilling to leave her side. I watch Solandis press her hand to Meri's forehead.

Madoc comes to stand beside me. "Meri will be out of it for at least three days. We know Leandra was warned last night. We don't have much time." He presses a hand to my shoulder. "We won't leave her alone for one second. I swear."

Rivan comes up to us both. "If you want, I'll go with you."

I tear my eyes from her to look at Rivan. "I'd rather you stay here. Keep training. We're going to need you at full strength." It's the truth, but it's not the sole reason I said it. He needs to snap out of this destructive phase and focus on the bigger picture. "If Leandra manages to unmake Meri, you're going to have to step in and bring her back to us. So, train. Do whatever you have to do to prepare, but you might be the only reason she survives."

Rivan's at his finest under pressure. I plan to keep reminding him of his role.

Daire glides over to us. "You're going to need back-up. I'll go with you." His bright blue eyes hold a hint of worry in them. "We should bring Vargas, too."

Vargas walks over to us. "His favorite son and favorite commander." He motions to Daire and himself. "And the biggest pain in his ass." He dips his head toward me and laughs. "At least we know who he'll kill first."

Daire chuckles. "Hopefully that means I'll make it out of there alive."

We joke, but asking Lucifer and Evren for her blood is the scariest fucking thing I've done in a long time.

"Swear to me you will have someone by her side at all times," I order Madoc.

Dark, angry brows draw together in irritation. "I already swore to you. Take my fucking word for it and get into the damn portal. We've got this."

Arden turns from giving Daire a kiss goodbye and adds her promise to Madoc's. "We've already put together a schedule. We won't leave her alone."

Rivan points to the portal. "Go."

Vargas shoves me into the portal and immediately follows. Underworld guards look confused when they see their commander, but they quickly snap to attention and salute him.

"Prince Daire is arriving. Look sharp," he orders them in a hard voice.

Straightening, the two soldiers thrust their shoulders back and chins up.

Daire steps through, looking every inch the prince in his navy windowpane suit and light blue tie. "At ease." The guards spread their feet but stay alert.

As we walk away, I hear him lean down and whisper to Vargas, "Guess you've still got it. But you're confusing the hell out of them with this face."

Vargas waves a hand. "By now, they all know I've died and

come back. It doesn't hurt to wear this face once in a while to remind them who they fucking report to."

"Me?" Callyx says jokingly. When Vargas moves toward him, he holds up a hand. "Easy, old man. You're still the big chief. All I do is spy on people and kill Lucifer's enemies."

The Duke of Greed happens to be walking by and overhears Callyx and almost walks into a marble pillar. I chuckle. His shoulders stiffen when he hears me, and he turns, mouth open to say something, but when he sees the four of us staring back at him, he gulps and rushes off.

"Shall we?" Daire suggests softly, his hand raised toward the hall.

I straighten the black silk tie I'm wearing. "How do I look? Respectful?"

Callyx laughs. "Arrogant, as always."

"That's the look I was going for," I say smugly. "Let's go."

When I requested the meeting with Lucifer, I made sure to let him know it was a request involving Evren. Surprises suck. It's better that he's on guard from the start.

Walking into his office, we find Evren sitting behind Lucifer's desk with him standing tensely by her side.

"Daire!" Evren says, jumping up to come over and give him a hug. "It's been too long. You really need to come to dinner. Bring Arden and the cadre. We'll play old records and dance the night away."

Lucifer snorts. "She's been watching way too many movies."

Daire ignores his father. "We'd love to. Let me know when." To my surprise, he walks over and gives Lucifer a hug. "Keep your temper in check and hear us out."

Lucifer shakes his head. "I make no promises, but it must be important for all four of you to have banded together on this request. What is it?"

Instead of returning to the desk, Evren folds her legs underneath her and drops into an upholstered chair. When Lucifer clears his throat and motions to his desk, she wrinkles her nose. "It's uncomfortable. I don't know how you sit in it for an hour, much less all day. This is much better." She props her chin on her hand and looks at me.

"I'm sure Callyx told you about Meri's new power," I begin, glancing at Callyx for confirmation. When he nods, I continue. "We need to find Leandra and get her to remove the power from Meri and, hopefully, restore it in Madoc. Denir needs the power for his coronation anniversary. He'll become more desperate the closer it gets."

Lucifer drops into his desk chair. With a frown, he shifts from side to side. Finally, he looks up. "You want Evren's blood to trace the amulet. First, let me be clear, I would never give her blood to you or anyone else." Power rises in the room, nearly suffocating in its intent.

A cool breeze of power sweeps through the room and, relieved, we all take a deep breath.

"There. Much better." Lucifer flashes Evren a murderous look, and she winks back at him. "I didn't use my blood to make the amulet. So that means…" She looks at me expectantly.

"You used a spell," I reply with a shake of my head at the power she must wield. Something of that magnitude usually requires blood to activate. "Would you share the spell with me?" Maybe I can trace the words.

She frowns. "I gave the amulet to Leandra in exchange for the information she brought me. I can't, in good conscience, give you the spell." Slipping her bangle off her wrist, she offers it to me. "Meri is going to need a way to control the power within her while you search for Leandra. Make sure she wears this at all times."

Disappointed, I take the piece of jewelry from her. "Thank you. This will help." The intricate bracelet has no clasp, but it does have a deep red ruby on the top. "It's beautiful."

She lifts a shoulder. "I find metal to be a great conductor of spells, and I like to wear pretty things. Jewelry allows me to combine the two."

My eyebrow rises at her words, and I hold the bracelet up to the light. Engraved inside is a spell written in Viridian, which is Evren's natural language. At the end of the spell is a symbol of a diamond overlapping a triangle. Almost like a signature. This is how we'll find Leandra.

"This means more than I can ever repay," I tell her. "Meri is everything to me."

Lucifer clears his throat. "Glad to see you finally know Madoc is the true heir to the Dark Fae Kingdom." There's a hint of superiority in his expression.

I roll my eyes. "I was waiting for you to bring that up."

He leans forward. "Denir is weak. If the Dark Fae Kingdom falls, the imbalance will break the Fae. Tell Madoc The Underworld will stand with him and the crown."

Inhaling sharply at the message, I bow my head. "I'll tell him." Madoc must have the crown to call upon his allies, but when he does, they will come to his aid. "Thank you."

With the bangle clenched in my fist, I leave them all to visit with each other, unable to stay away another second. There's the tiniest sliver of hope inside me, and all I want to do is share it with her.

CHAPTER NINETEEN

<u>MERI</u>

Opening heavy eyes, I find Madoc sleeping in a nearby chair, feet propped up on the bed. The squinched shoulders and pained expression on his face tell me he isn't the least bit comfortable. Frowning, I scan the room. Clothes and weapons are strewn everywhere, but it's just the two of us.

Based on the low level of light coming into the room, it's early, barely past sunrise. My brain is pounding. Why is he sleeping in here? And where is Cormal?

Memories filter into the dark recesses of my brain. An image of Cormal lying on the floor with his head barely attached. Slashing through skin and bone. A blackened and withered heart. Panicking, I sit up and look around for the shadowy beast. A large, scarred hand reaches out and coaxes my hand in his.

"Cormal is fine. He went to see Lucifer," Madoc says, his voice rough from sleep. "How are you feeling?"

Like I can't catch my breath. My heart races from fear and something I can't quite grasp. I lift up my hands. The bones ache as if the skin is too tight. I put a hand to my head. Images continue to bombard me, showing me the truth. There I am... slashing at the monster with my bare skeletal hands, slicing through the shade as if it has flesh. Using an unnatural strength to pierce its chest and pull out a heart that shouldn't even exist. My entire body begins to shake.

"Did I really do that?" I ask hoarsely, barely able to get the words out.

Madoc picks me up and enfolds me in his arms. "I've got you. Just breathe. Don't think. Let your mind go." He turns and sits back on the bed with me across his lap, surrounding me with his strength as his words work to ease the panic inside.

Cormal is fine. I'm a monster. Cormal is fine.

He runs a hand down my hair over and over. Safe and protected, I let my eyes drift close, unable to deal with it all, smothering reality under the blanket of sleep.

Light fills the room when I wake again. Still cradled in Madoc's arms, I open my eyes and tilt my head back to find him watching me, his grey eyes full of concern.

"Thank you," I murmur softly, visually tracing his full lips. "The panic was dragging me under."

He reaches out a finger and runs it down my cheek. "We need to talk. Do you feel up to it?"

A shiver cascade downs my spine. Madoc's usually surly demeanor is noticeably absent. "This is bad, isn't it?" I trust him to give the truth without sugarcoating it.

"You killed the monster by invoking the power of The Wild Hunt," he begins. His voice is even and soothing, but his words are nothing but alarming as he explains what the power is, how it's essential to be king of the dark Fae, and how it came to me.

"Why didn't it show up before?" I ask with a hysterical note in my voice.

He runs a hand down my back to calm me. "We're not sure. Based on what we've pieced together with Solandis and Cormal, the power to mimic was the only power you had before you physically met your mother. Once you met her, you started picking up light Fae powers. This is a dark Fae power. Maybe Denir's presence activated it." He pauses for a second, as if he's debating something.

"What?"

"After I left The Below with Aamon, I was drawn to the light Fae court and specifically to you. I believe the power has always been inside of you and the severity of Cormal's injury triggered it," he divulges. "I'm not a hundred percent sure, though."

"You were drawn to me? Or to the power?" I ask with a frown, although I'm not sure I want to hear his answer.

"Likely the power drew me," he reluctantly admits.

"I see," I mumble.

A harsh laugh. "You see nothing."

"I sort of thought… never mind," I stammer, unsure of what I even want to say. *I thought you liked me?* Juvenile, but sort of how I feel. Honestly, it took him forever to even accept my friendship. Although, things have been changing between us. Little moments that felt like more.

"It might have been the reason I came, but it's not the reason I stayed," he croaks, as if he's forcing the words out.

"Right," I drawl, one eyebrow raised high.

Cursing under his breath, he confesses, "I followed you when you left the palace. Using the shadows." He peers down at me to see my reaction to his words.

I stare at him, not entirely sure what he's telling me. "When?"

"Never mind."

"Fine."

Apparently, he doesn't like my answer. "Do you think I

would hold you like this if all I wanted was the power inside you?" His voice is gruff, but his gaze is intense.

Wow. Man of few words. But I still can't help the smile spreading over my face. "Mmm, do you think I'd let just anyone hold me like this?" I inch forward, my eyes on his full lips, but the rest of his words stop me. "Wait. You want the power inside me?"

His arms tighten around me. "Leandra stole it from me." He places my hand on his chest. "This scar is from her."

Reeling, I connect the dots, and a lot of things start to make sense. His arrogance, ability to fight, the level of power he wields, his stint in The Below, and so much more. "King of the Dark Fae?"

"I was supposed to be, but I can't be crowned unless I have the power," he informs me. "The Wild Hunt gave it to Konnyr in case they needed to call upon him in times of war. Only dark Fae can wield it. The power passes from the strongest in our bloodline to the next. Denir was never meant to possess it. He can't control it."

"How do you propose to get it out of me?" I ask, but then the answer hits me. "Leandra. You're hoping she'll transfer it back to you." I look him straight in the eye. "She won't. I'm her revenge against Denir. If he can't use the power, he'll lose the crown."

"If she gives it to me, she can still get her revenge," he insists, almost desperately.

Another thought occurs. "If I can't control it, what will happen?" I'm afraid to hear his answer, but I have to ask.

He tightens his arms around me. "I'm not going to let that happen." His finger lifts my chin higher. "I promise you."

"Tell me," I implore him. "Knowing the worst-case scenario is how I deal with bad things. Please. Tell me."

He hesitates but seeing my set jaw and narrowed eyes, he

finally relents. "It would consume you, making you a permanent rider in The Wild Hunt."

"Bloody hell," I curse. "Why does everything have to be so damn difficult? I mean. Where is the karma here? Leandra should be writhing in the pits of hell. With Denir at her..."

The smallest of smiles appears on his scruffy face and stops my ranting in its tracks. It's the first one he's ever given to me. It looks so good, I want to see more of them. Although I don't mind his gruff and surly nature, either. Or his blunt approach to everything.

It makes sense with every little bit I learn about him. If he was groomed to be king, was he even allowed to be carefree? I try to picture him laughing and joking with others, but the image eludes me.

Closing the gap between us, I place my lips on his, peppering them with small kisses and nibbles. His smile disappears, and I wait, breath held, to see if he'll push me away. Full lips open under my tender onslaught and return my affection with the sweetest, deepest kiss I could never have imagined.

I thought he would want to dominate, not seduce, demand, not give. This is sensual and enticing. My body melts into his, humming with need, but in no rush to move beyond this moment. Sliding my hands around him, I shift my body until I'm fully wrapped around his torso. Who ever thought he would let me hold him like this? I bring one hand up and slide my fingers into his thick hair. Luxurious and soft, I play with it while we kiss.

He pulls back a little to suck on my bottom lip, then swipes his tongue across it. His tongue plays with mine, then delves deep again, taking ownership of the kiss.

I scrape my fingernails lightly against his neck, and his lips harden a little. Of course, I do it again. He shifts my lower body until it's flush with his. Fingers tighten on my waist, but his kiss remains languorous and sensual.

My body settles on his and I pull my lips from his to groan. "Goddess, you feel good."

"Mm, I want to touch you all over," he says in a low, husky tone.

My shirt disappears, and his hands slide up and down my bare back as if he's mapping all the ridges and valleys.

Desire courses through my veins, and I brush my breasts against his chest. "Touch me." My voice is surprisingly guttural and almost harsh.

Madoc jerks away from me. "Stop."

Confused, I slide my hands from his body, and when I do, I see the faintest impression of skeletal bones superimposed over the skin. Fear tries to take hold, but with us joined so closely together, I know I can't let it. Sucking in a huge amount of air, I hold it in until my heartbeat slows.

Large hands glide gently across my back and over my shoulders. "That's it. Just breathe." He picks me up and turns me around until I'm sitting across his lap and puts my shirt back on.

If I wasn't extremely scared, I'd be pissed off. I finally get him to smile and give me a kiss, and we have to stop.

The door opens, and I turn my head to watch Cormal stride into the room. He pauses when he sees us on the bed, but not for very long. In his usual arrogant fashion, he strides over and sits right down beside us.

"You look like you've been thoroughly kissed."

I blush and glare at him, hoping he doesn't make Madoc uneasy.

Cormal shrugs, then leans over to give me a hard kiss. "About time you woke up." His words are simple, but his tone is heavy with relief.

My hand stretches out and slides around his throat so I can feel its strength for myself. "You scared the hell out of me."

He picks up my hand and nibbles on my fingers. "You can't

get rid of me that easily. I've waited too long to be denied forever."

My mind embraces his words. The events from our past are no longer hidden by an impenetrable curtain. The episode I had must have wiped away the barriers. Or the power inside me did. Either way, I know. All of it. This man has sacrificed a lot to claim me as his without Leandra standing between us.

"I remember," I tell him.

His eyes flick to mine, and he freezes. "What do you remember?"

"All of it. Our past. The love we shared. The night I attacked Leandra with her own powers. You… accepting my punishment." My voice breaks when I think of the caning he got and the scars it left on his back. "Leandra threatening to unmake me. Going to Rivan to get the rune."

The last thought makes my blood boil, but when the power inside me stirs, I have to shut off the sharp emotion.

Madoc stands and passes me into Cormal's arms with a warning. "Go through the memories later. She needs to stay calm. The power is near the surface."

Cormal holds up a beautiful gold bracelet with a large ruby on it. "Evren sent this. She said it will help you to control the power." He slides it on my arm.

Cold metal dangles from my wrist. "It's gorgeous, but I don't feel any different."

"Did you get Evren's blood?" Madoc interjects impatiently.

"No," Cormal replies with a grin. "She only gave me the bracelet." His hand grasps my chin. "Let's test it out, shall we?" Pulling the two of us up until we're standing in front of Madoc, he bends his head and captures my lips in a devastating kiss.

The past blends with the present, and my passion rises hard and fast.

Cormal pulls my head back. "Let me see your face." He darts a glance at Madoc. "I don't see anything, do you?"

Madoc peers down at me, his steel-grey eyes growing dark. "No."

Cormal moves in closer and presses my body against Madoc until I can feel every inch of their hard bodies against mine. "She dreams of all three of us."

Madoc's hands settle on my hips. "Rivan, too?"

"Yes. Tell him," Cormal demands.

Unable to say the words, I stare mutely at Cormal.

"Or should I show him?" His wicked smile is the only warning I get before my shirt disappears.

Madoc growls behind me, then his hands slide up my sides and stop.

Taking a deep breath, I twist my head to look up at Madoc. "Touch me."

Calloused hands slide forward and cup my breasts, weighing them, learning their curves. His breathing becomes harsh, but his hands lightly skim over the mounds, pausing only to pinch or play with my nipples.

Arching my back, I revel in the feel of his hands on me. "More."

Hearing my demand, Cormal removes all of our clothes.

Madoc freezes, then his hands fall away from my body.

I immediately turn to face him, taking his hand in mine. "Talk to me. I thought you wanted this, but if you don't, that's fine. Or if it's something else, tell me."

Madoc's expression is unreadable.

I lay my hands on his bare chest and lean forward to kiss the place where Leandra stole his power. "Please, tell me." Unable to help myself, I map the contours of his muscular body as I wait for him to answer me.

He lifts his chin. "This... doesn't bother you?"

Puzzled, I look up at him, then back to his body. My gaze dips down and finds his cock. Thick with hard ridges. I lick my lips. "Define bother."

Cormal leans in close to my ear and chuckles. "She doesn't see them the way you do. To her, they're a testament to your strength and ability to survive."

I give Madoc an incredulous look. "This is about your scars?"

Madoc searches my face, and whatever he sees must convince him. He cups my face in his hands and destroys me with a kiss full of broken dreams and hope. "Thank you."

I lick my puffy lips and give a dazed nod. "Are we good to continue?"

"Yes," he says gruffly.

Relieved, I sigh and glance back at Cormal with a silent request.

Cormal's hand slides down my body and parts my folds. "She's drenched with need." His fingers slide into me, and his thumb makes small circular movements on the most sensitive part of me.

Madoc watches Cormal pleasure me with a look of satisfaction on his face. His hand grabs his cock, and he strokes it a few times. "You want both of us?"

"At the same time," I say breathlessly. Heat scores my cheeks as my body trembles on the edge of an orgasm. "Cormal!" My cry has him picking up the pace until I thrust forward, surrendering to the overwhelming need to come.

I lean against him, chest heaving, and let the waves crash over me until they're nothing but a ripple. Tilting my head back, I bring Cormal's lips to mine for a deep, wet kiss. "More."

Madoc picks me up and places me on the bed.

Looking up at them both, I spread my legs and wait for them to join me.

Cormal slides up beside me to continue our kiss.

Madoc crashes to his knees and jerks my body to his mouth, where he literally devours me. Firm lips cover my core as his tongue dips and swirls. He flicks a glance at me, his eyes dark with desire and intent.

The kiss with Cormal gets wilder and more carnal as we both enjoy the sight of Madoc's mouth dripping with my juices. Dark shadows spill from Cormal, wrapping around my wrists and pulling them to the sides.

With his wicked tongue, he leaves my lips to carve his own path of destruction on all the most sensitive parts of my body.

Abandoning all control to the two of them, my body trembles and shakes beneath their sensual attack. Lost in a haze, I'm only cognizant of them and the pleasure they're wringing out of me.

"I want you. Inside me," I whimper, looking first at Madoc, then Cormal.

Madoc immediately stands, his hands pushing against my thighs to widen them, then he thrusts into me. "Goddess, you feel so fucking good. Your wet heat wrapped around my cock." His hands raise my hips higher, then he plunges slow and deep inside me. "Better. Lean up. Take what Cormal's offering you."

Automatically following his command, I turn toward Cormal, who's kneeling beside me and open my mouth.

Cormal's hand tangles itself in my hair in a firm grip.

Relaxing my throat, I take all of him into my mouth. He curses. Humming, I move up and down, wanting to torture him as much as possible before he comes. I peek up at Cormal and see the utter bliss on his face. I wink at him and begin sliding up and down on his shaft, sucking and swirling, faster and faster. His cock swells in my mouth, and a bolt of pleasure shoots through me. My body begins to tremble.

"Now," Cormal orders Madoc and me, his own body releasing itself into my mouth.

My body contracts, and I clamp down on Madoc's cock, milking him with my own orgasm. I hear him curse as he comes, too, his body twitching and thrusting a couple more times. Calloused and scarred hands run over my legs and body lightly until the waves slowly subside.

They both ease from my body, and I can't help but stare at them as we all try to catch our breath. Dark hair plastered to their heads, chests heaving, and cocks semi-hard. Fierce expressions on both of their faces.

"Remind me to thank Evren." My tone is full of innuendo, but damn if I don't mean it. "That was incredible."

Staring at Madoc, I could wonder if this means anything, but I know he rarely lets his guard down for anyone. For now, that's enough.

CHAPTER TWENTY

<u>MERI</u>

Bright light wakes me the next morning, and the first thing I see is Cormal's blue eyes. Propped on his elbow, he's staring down at me with a pensive look on his face. He sweeps my hair back before kissing me good morning. I rise and see Madoc's gone. As usual, he didn't even say goodbye. I sigh.

"So, you remember?" Cormal asks. His tone is flat and unsure, as if he still can't believe it's true.

"Everything," I confirm with a sad smile. "I didn't intend to go up against Leandra with my magic that night. All I wanted to do was leave and be with you. Everything kind of snowballed when she flipped out on me." It's important he knows I didn't intentionally ruin things.

After we left Hiemal, Cormal and I continued to see each other behind Leandra's back. He was right. It had been sweet and innocent and full of those stolen moments you think will last forever.

After he shared his power to mimic, I worked to accumulate as many powers as I could, but not to fight her. I thought if I showed her I could protect myself, she'd let me go. But when I showed her my magic, she laughed and told me I was never going anywhere. She made me for revenge, not love.

"When she told me I was a thing she created, I lost it," I admit, even knowing Cormal lived the story with me. "She threatened me. Told me she'd unmake me." His serious blue eyes flinch as if she's standing here screaming the words at us. "She can, can't she? That's your biggest fear."

He meets my gaze. "I refuse to let it happen, and we're not alone this time. We've got Madoc and Rivan fighting with us, too. Solandis, and all the rest of your family. Leandra's time is coming to an end."

"Goddess, I hope so," I pray. "What do we do now?"

"We're going to hit this from two sides," he informs me. "Arden and Astor are using a tracing spell to find all the objects with the Viridian language or Evren's symbol on them. By searching for something innocuous, we think it will allow us to bypass the enemies rule."

"Do we know how long that will take?" I ask, aware of how fast time is slipping through our fingers.

"A few days," he assures me. "In the meantime, Madoc's left to speak to The Wild Hunt and inform them that the current king doesn't have the power. He hopes that by being transparent, they will favor him over Denir if they both end up fighting for the crown."

"That's an utterly terrifying statement," I croak. "Seriously. Who drops by for a chat with The Wild Hunt?"

Madoc's in a league of his own.

Cormal chuckles. "Actually, I'm quite jealous." He stands and pulls me up for a hug. "I'd love to lie here all day with you, but I need to go check on one of my men. Don't leave The Abbey."

For a second, I cling to his hand. "I love you, Cormal. Then. Now. Forever."

"Never-ending?" he drawls with a smile.

"Never-ending." That's my hope.

After one last kiss, he strides out, leaving me standing there, fiddling with the bracelet on my wrist.

Is Rivan with us? Cormal and Madoc both told me he watched over me while I was out, but since I've been awake, he hasn't come by. Not once.

Needing to get out of this room, I change into workout clothes and head to the gym. I miss my sessions with Madoc. Maybe Rivan will teach me how to wield a sword. He's pretty damn good at it.

The clashing of swords rings throughout the gym. I round the corner and see Rivan, drenched in sweat, fighting Theron.

"Meri," Arden loudly whispers, motioning for me to join her against the wall. Blond hair high in a ponytail with a few damp tendrils plastered against her neck, she must also have been training this morning.

I find a seat beside her and lean back against the concrete wall. "How long have they been at it?"

"Only about thirty minutes," she whispers. "But that's the longest a single warrior outside of the cadre has held out against Theron and his two swords. It's quite remarkable how much progress Rivan's made over the last couple of weeks."

"He spends enough time in here," I remark with a wry smile. "Solandis told me he was once the greatest warrior of the Fae. Until Nyssa made him a prisoner."

She swings her gaze to me. "You need to stop feeling guilty. It's not helping you or him. You set him free. It's up to him to make his life what he wants it to be. That's how it is for all of us."

She waves a hand at me. "Look at you. Once you had your freedom from Leandra, you blossomed. The crown chose you for a reason and look at all you accomplished in such a short time. Here you are at a crossroads again, and I have every faith you'll forge your own path forward."

My eyes water, and I reach over and hug her tightly. "Thank you. I needed to hear that today." I follow her gaze to the men. Maybe it's time I ask Rivan what he wants.

Ten minutes later, Theron calls a halt to the match. "You're flagging. Take a break."

Rivan doesn't even question the cool order. Sheathing his sword, he picks up a bottle and gulps half the water down. As he lowers it, he spots me sitting by Arden and hesitantly makes his way over.

"You're looking better," he states, scanning me from head to toe. "How are you feeling?"

I hold up my wrist and show him the bangle. "Evren sent it to me. It stops me from turning into a monster." Well, this is awkward. Hurting from the distance between us, I stand and look up at him. "Can we talk?"

He walks over to the corner, and I follow.

"According to Arden, only the cadre can hold out against Theron in a sword fight. She's impressed with your skills, and that's a lot coming from her. She lives and breathes warrior," I say with a grin.

He blows out a relieved breath. "I thought... Never mind." His smile is rueful. "Frankly, I was glad he called a halt. My arms were killing me. Damn Fae is a machine."

"All this training," I begin. "What do you want to do after this? Kill Brixton? Fight with the Water Fae? Lead the Fire Fae?"

He shakes his head as if he can't believe I'm asking him these questions. "I won't know until I'm done."

"How will you know you're done if you don't have a goal?" I ask, genuinely wanting to hear his answer. Is this going to take days, months, or years? Does he want me to wait, or is he even thinking about us?

He gives me an obstinate look. "Why does it matter?"

A tear slips down my cheek, and I angrily brush it away. "I care about you more than I ever thought possible. More than anything, I want you in my life. Warrior or not. It doesn't matter to me. I'll support whichever path you take. As your friend, I want the best for you."

Amber eyes glow brightly when he stares down at me.

"But I won't wait for you. I don't want my life to be in limbo. For almost a thousand years, I allowed Leandra to dictate my every move. Never again. Being queen showed me how to take risks and trust in myself," I explain, trying to get him to understand why I won't wait.

Pushing through the pain, I make myself finish. "I'm moving forward. Either step up and be in my life or tell me it's over."

Angry and hurt, he snarls, "You don't understand. I need to get stronger. You keep saving me, but it should be me saving you. I need to be the warrior who can stand proudly by your side. Until I am, I can't make any promises."

"Out of all the people here, I understand you the most. You're a survivor, which makes you a warrior in my book," I remind him, trying to tamp down my anger, knowing it won't do any good. "Look, I'm not asking you to stop training. I'm asking you to make *us* a priority in your life."

He laces his fingers together and places them on the back of his head. Staring up at the ceiling, he says nothing. I don't know whether he's thinking or avoiding. I wait for him to say something, but several minutes pass in silence.

Men can be such idiots.

"We should know Leandra's location in the next few days. Once we do, we're going after her," I tell him. "The window for you to decide is closing. Barring death, I'm getting my life back."

The tic in his jaw jumps, and his stares down at me, his eyes full of thoughts and emotions, but he remains silent.

I let him get one good look at my face. I'm serious. This is our last chance.

Madoc's standing behind me when I turn around. There's a proud gleam in his eyes that would normally make me smile with pride, but I'm irritated with him, too.

I walk right up to him. "You need to tell me when you're leaving and how long you'll be gone. If not, I worry, and worrying gives me wrinkles. Got it?"

He raises an arrogant eyebrow, but to my surprise, he gives me a quick nod. "Got it."

I crook my finger, asking him to bend down. "And I want a kiss goodbye. And hello. This is non-negotiable." I'm tired of them doing whatever the hell they want. All I'm asking for is a little consideration.

His lips twitch, but he grips my chin and lifts it higher to meet the kiss he lays on me. Long and deep, it goes way beyond hello. "I hope this will count as two—one for the goodbye I missed earlier and one for hello."

"That works," I breathe out. "Thank you."

I go to walk away, but he stops me and points to Rivan. "Hyne called Cormal. Brixton is dead. His body was found hanging from the mast of one of his ships. The head in ashes at his feet. Eternal death. He won't be regenerating."

Shit. "Did Hyne kill him?" I hope not. The last thing we need to contend with right now is a war between the Water and Fire Fae.

"No, he insists he didn't kill him, and he has an ironclad alibi," Madoc remarks. "Brixton had a lot of enemies. It could have been any number of people. Maybe Denir got tired of him." His tone is indifferent, as if who killed him doesn't matter, but it will to Rivan.

With Madoc by my side, I walk over to Rivan.

He looks at each of us but stops on me. "What happened?"

"Brixton is dead," I blurt, then wince. I relay the information Madoc told me.

Rivan stumbles back against the wall. "My sister, Aeris. She must be devastated. I need to leave.

"Do you want us to go with you?" I ask him.

"You're not fucking going anywhere," Madoc decrees with his arms crossed over his chest. "It's too dangerous."

"I did say 'us,'" I huff out. "You, me, Cormal. And don't remind me about Leandra. Or Denir. I'm aware of the risks." I turn toward Rivan. "Well?"

He shakes his head sadly. "The Phoenix won't want me there. I only want to see Aeris. Tell her I'm sorry. Ask her if she needs anything."

Knowing it will be too dangerous for Rivan to go alone, I narrow my eyes at Madoc, silently telling him to do something.

"Let me talk to Cormal. See what we can arrange," he growls in gruff voice, then stalks off.

Feeling the teensy bit triumphant, I turn to Rivan. "He'll return soon. You should grab a shower." Still angry and hurt, I leave him standing there alone.

CHAPTER TWENTY-ONE

RIVAN

Cormal comes storming into the room, shadows spilling out around him, barking orders into the phone. "Find out what the hell happened. It looks like Lot escaped, but I wasn't able to follow the trail. Send me updates on the hour. I need to take care of something here, but I'll join you as soon as possible. Kavi, be careful. Whoever is at the other end of this is damn powerful." He slides the phone into his pocket.

Cormal has entirely too much on his shoulders. Feeling guilty, I offer him a way out. "You don't need to go." I glance at Meri and Madoc. "I'm meeting Aeris, not the Phoenix army."

Cormal stops pacing and stares at me. "Have you even spoken to your sister since you saved her from the light Fae all those years ago?"

My sister was one of the children held hostage and released when my elite squad and I surrendered. Stiffening, I shoot him

159

an incredulous look. "You can't believe she would kill me." She looked happy and content walking with her daughter the last time I saw her.

Cormal's lips flatten. "She's lived under your father's thumb for thousands of years. I can't predict what she'll do, which means we'll take every precaution. Got it?"

I give him a curt nod. "What's the plan?"

Madoc produces a map and places it on the table. "We need to meet on neutral ground but in a place where your sister will feel comfortable. Not Avalon." He cuts a sideways glance at Meri.

I stare down at the map. "Anywhere close to the water is out." My eyes scan inland. "Here. On the border of the Winter and Autumn courts. The Phoenix have well-established relationships with the Autumn Court. And we have one with Theron. I'm sure he'll give us permission to enter his land."

Squinting, I examine the border, looking for an ideal vantage point. "Here, where the land is flat." Southland Meadows. "We'll be able to see each other coming for miles."

Cormal and Madoc both nod in agreement. "It's perfect."

Meri picks up her phone to send a message. It pings a moment later. "Theron and Arden are on their way. A map doesn't always tell us everything we need to know."

"True," I admit with a small smile, which she doesn't return. I'm not going to lie, it hurts. All I've been focused on the last couple of weeks is getting stronger for her. I don't understand why she doesn't see it.

Theron strolls in dressed in his usual suit, although his tie is a tiny bit skewed. Arden, lips swollen, rushes in a second later, her hands smoothing down her shirt.

Ignoring the obvious, I motion to the table. "My father, Brixton, died. Aeris, my sister, is the only family I have left. Well, besides her daughter, I guess. I want to meet with her, but given my current status with the Phoenix, I'm not welcome there. So, we need somewhere neutral." I turn and tap the map. "This area on the border of your land and the Autumn Court would be ideal."

Theron and Arden step forward to peer at the map.

"From what we can tell, Southland Meadows runs right up to the border, and it looks fairly flat. What do you think?" I pause and wait for him to answer.

Theron thinks about it, but then nods. "It will work. Miles of sight line in every direction." He turns his head toward me. "How many do you think she'll bring with her?"

"I'm going to limit us both," I tell him but look around at the others. "Meri, Madoc, Cormal, and I make four. Is there anyone else we should consider?"

Theron gives me a wry look. "My land. I'll be there."

Arden flicks a glance at Theron, then adds, "Me too."

He stiffens the tiniest bit, but he doesn't argue with her. She's better in battle than most men, even if he doesn't like her going. "Fallon, too."

I take a deep breath, a little worried by the size of our group. "Okay, that's seven of us. Still reasonable."

Madoc shakes his head. "The Phoenix are damn hard to fight. I'm fine with limiting the number to seven, but I think we need another advantage. One they won't see." He looks at Arden. "Do you have any curare? Or another toxin that causes temporary paralysis?"

She opens her mouth to answer him, but I slam my fist on the table. "Absolutely not. This is supposed to be a peaceful meeting."

Cormal holds up his hand. "The Fire Fae are at war with the world. Do you really think they won't be taking the same precautions? Tell me, Rivan, are you planning to leave your sword behind?"

"Of course not," I reply stiffly, understanding his point, but a weapon isn't extreme. Poison is.

Frustrated, I stare down at the map. Maybe they're right. I'm not sure. I used to instinctively know what to do, but that was when there was no doubt as to which side I was on.

Madoc leans forward. "I'd rather not kill them, but if you refuse to let us take the toxin, we may not have a choice." His grey eyes are completely serious.

Maybe I should have gone alone. "Fine."

Arden picks up her phone. "Let me text Astor. It's his lab."

Meri frowns. "How do you propose to get a message to Aeris? We don't know where the Phoenix are hiding."

"Actually, I do," I inform her. "They moved from the old mines to the Gora Mountain. That's where Brixton and I fought before he took my body to Avalon." My mouth twists at the memory of all the Phoenix sneering at me as I walked through the tunnel into the mountain. "But location doesn't matter because we use the fire network. I'll send word, asking her to meet tomorrow. The less time we give them to prepare, the better."

Everyone nods in agreement.

"Is there a fireplace here?" I ask Arden.

She looks up from her phone. "Yes, there's one in the library. Also, Astor says we only have a small stash of curare here. Not enough for what we're planning."

Madoc pivots and heads toward the door. When he gets there, he stops, then returns to Meri. "I'm going to see Aamon. Be back shortly." Bending down, he places a firm kiss on her lips. "Better?"

Meri's turquoise eyes brighten with happiness. "Thank you."

I peer at Cormal to see what he thinks of them kissing, but the faint smile on his lips assures me he's fine with it.

Meri walks over to Cormal. "Are you okay? What happened earlier?"

He murmurs, "Later."

She leans into him. "Okay."

Her easy acceptance of his request to wait irritates me. "I'm going to the library to send the message."

Fire Fae use the fire network to send coded messages. The Phoenix keep a fire lit at all times for this very purpose. It's an old method of communication, but one of the most secure. Very few races can intercept them.

Comfortable furniture and shelves filled with old books gives the small library a cozy feeling. The fireplace stands in the center, surrounded by white marble, and it takes a mere thought to light it. Once the fire is roaring, I write a message to Aeris, asking her to meet tomorrow and include all the details.

Once the message arrives, a sentinel will have to find Aeris. I prowl around the library while I wait. There's a curious number of artifacts in here. Weapons stored in glass cases. Oddities from the supernatural world. A MacAllister grimoire.

I make my way toward the military section. Once upon a time, I enjoyed reading books on the histories of wars, armies of old, and battle strategies and tactics. I run my finger down the spine of a familiar friend. *Aerial Combat Strategies*. One of my favorite books. It was written by a dragon, but many of the tactics served us well during the Fire Fae Rebellion. The elite squad I led was one of the best. Pride surfaces from somewhere deep inside me. For the longest time, I've made myself forget that part of me. Not anymore.

Whoosh! Her reply. I reach into the fire and grab the message.

She agrees to the meeting, and my terms, but refuses to stay long. The only reason she wants to meet is to say the formal rites of passage for Brixton, a traditional Phoenix ritual to send the soul on its way to the afterlife.

Looks like Cormal was right. Her allegiance to Brixton supersedes her past affection for me. Abandoned by the very race and family I sacrificed everything for is a betrayal so deep I can't breathe. All this time, I thought it was my father's need for blood and war that made him reject me. Tiernan was right. Very few remember what I did for my people.

My palm itches, and I stride out of the library heading directly to the training room. I need to burn off the emotions and thoughts swirling around inside before tomorrow. Sentiment will only cloud my judgement. I swing the sword, and Arden's training spell activates. For the next two hours, I battle imaginary foes and nameless faces as I try to forget those I left behind.

When my mind is clear and my muscles are on fire, I sheath my sword and head toward my room. Passing Meri's door, I hear the quiet murmurs of conversation between her and Cormal. I stop and raise my hand but drop it when I hear her laughter. Now isn't the time to talk, but she was right earlier. I've been too wrapped up in my own torment to see a way forward, but that ends with this meeting. It's time to let go of the past and embrace my future. With her.

CHAPTER TWENTY-TWO

<u>RIVAN</u>

Dawn in the land of Winter is bright with the light bouncing off the ice and snow. Theron brings us in several miles from the meeting point to make sure they haven't infiltrated his land in an attempt to surround us. High in the mountains, he surveys the area below. Once assured it's empty, we head down.

Brutal winds slam into us as we begin the journey to meet the Phoenix. From the valley to Southland Meadows is only a few miles. Thankful for the parka's thick protection, I burrow into its warmth. Except for Arden and Theron, who are wearing Fae armor, the rest of us are bundled from head to toe, trying to conserve our magic in case the meeting doesn't go well. I eye the thin, almost impenetrable fabric covering their bodies. It must also regulate temperature, as neither of them seems to be the least bit cold. There is one big disadvantage to the armor…

it doesn't protect against faery fire. Let's hope nobody regenerates today.

Both the light and dark Fae armies thought themselves superior with their lightning fast skills, high-level magic, and armor, but the Fire Fae proved them wrong during the rebellion. Defeating the Phoenix means finding a way to bring about eternal death. If not, they end up fighting the same soldiers over and over.

Coming out of the mountains, Madoc signals for us to stop, then pulls a jar of clear, thick liquid out of his pocket. "Dip the tips of your weapons into the toxin. Be careful not to get any of it on you."

Taking a deep breath, I unsheathe my sword and step forward. "What is it?" I want to be sure it isn't something that will permanently damage my kind. They may not want me in their ranks, but I still consider myself a Phoenix.

He wrinkles his nose. "Aamon's saliva. It's a mild toxin that will incapacitate our enemies for ten minutes tops, giving us only enough time to disarm them. So, if we end up in a fight, we need to finish before they're able to move again."

"Ewww," Meri drawls, as she dips a pair of gold daggers into the mixture. She pulls out the tips and watches the thick glob separate and slowly slide down into the jar. "Gross."

Theron's eyebrow twitches as he eyes the mixture. "Does it wash off?"

"Yes, but I'd sterilize your weapons with an astringent like alcohol, too," Madoc suggests.

Once everyone has added the mixture to their weapons, which includes a wide assortment of swords, daggers, throwing stars, and arrows, he dips a wicked-looking black curved blade into the mixture. As well as several other sharp, pointy things. But my eye keeps returning to the blade. It looks familiar, but I can't place it right now.

As the valley meets the meadows, the ice disappears, leaving only a few inches of snow to cover the land. I stop the group when I see my sister and her men. They're almost at the meeting point. I scan the skies, looking for wings of flame, but spot only a few. Uneasy, I count the soldiers with her on the ground and add the ones flying above. Ten. More than we agreed.

Aware it's not just me, I turn toward the group. "They have more than the seven we dictated in our terms. What do you want to do?"

Theron shrugs. "Three more makes little difference to me. Fallon? Arden?"

Fallon squints at the sky. "Something seems off to me, but I can't figure it out."

We all stare at the blue-grey sky above us, but it's not until I turn my head to the side that I catch something with my peripheral vision. I turn back, but there's nothing but sky.

Meri shades her eyes with her hands. "The sky is moving."

"What do you mean?" I ask her, moving to view the sky from behind her so I can see what she's seeing.

"I don't want to point, but if you look at my six o'clock, you'll see the slightest movement," she murmurs, aware of the way sound carries across the land.

"I'll be damned," Madoc says with a hint of admiration in his voice. "They're using mirrors to reflect the sky and hide more soldiers. If you look closely, you can see a cloud drifting the wrong way or the same piece of sky replicated several feet apart."

I raise an eyebrow at Fallon. "Good instincts." Now that we know what we're searching for, I'm able to get a better idea of the count. "Maybe fifteen to twenty soldiers."

Theron's violet eyes harden, and he picks up his phone. "We were right. Wait until we give the signal."

"Valerian, Astor, Daire, and a half dozen of my best men," he explains to Cormal, Madoc, and Meri. "Rivan's suggestion."

When all three turn to look at me, I shrug. "Last night, I realized you were right, and thought we should have back-up ready in case we needed it. Theron and the cadre agreed."

Madoc's scowl eases into something like approval, and Cormal slaps me on the back. "Good thinking."

"Let's go," I say, urging everyone forward. I'm furious, but I manage to shove the emotions down deep until my face is completely blank.

Twenty feet to go. Aeris drops down in front of us and folds in her wings.

Startled, I look at the dark-haired woman leading the Fire Fae to the meeting point, and she smirks as if I'm a fool for believing she was my sister.

Aeris strides forward, her features so strikingly similar to our mother, I can't breathe. She raises her fist and Phoenix, including those who are shielding their presence with the mirrors, reveal themselves. Gold triumphant eyes lock with mine, victory shining in their depths, and I see our father in the lines of determination on her face.

"We agreed to seven," I remind her, instinctively tracking the movement of the Phoenix in the sky. "Were you scared to meet with me?" Deliberately taunting her to see if she can stay cool.

She lifts her chin. "Never trust a traitor. That's what Dad always said."

Surprised, I stare at her, then bark with laughter. "Ironic coming from him. I'm not a traitor. In fact, I'm pretty sure I've sacrificed more for the Phoenix than anyone else still alive." I watch several of the older Fire Fae shift from one foot to the other. Some people remember me.

She presses her lips together.

"You look like her," I blurt, unable to stop myself. The last time I saw my mother was a week before we surrendered. Both the elite squad and I had needed a break, so I ordered everyone home for a couple of days.

She sweeps me with a furious gaze. "Don't you dare bring her into this."

"How did she die?" I ask, desperate to know.

Her brows draw together. "Father didn't tell you?"

When I shake my head, her shoulders drop. "She died trying to protect me and the rest of the Fire Fae children from the light Fae." She spears me a look of speculation. "It happened the night before you and the elite squad surrendered. Dad… told me you knew. Said it changed nothing."

Shocked, I shake my head, unable to say anything. The entire time I spent in the light Fae court, nobody had ever mentioned her death to me.

She scrubs her face. "It doesn't matter. She died. Life moved on."

I step forward. "I'm sorry. She was the best of us." Taking a deep breath, I offer my hands to her. "Do you want to say the rites?" Which is it going to be, Sister? Peace or war? I wait for her to decide.

For a few seconds, she stares at my hands with a wistful expression on her face. One of the men next to her says something, and I watch her wipe the expression from her face. The moment is gone.

"Do you really think I'd say the rites with his killer?" She sneers, looking away for a second. She scans our side and points to Meri. "I'm only here for her head."

She never could lie worth a damn. "For the record, I didn't kill Brixton, but I can guess who did."

She shuffles back and forth.

"You know what? It doesn't matter. He was the wrong leader for the Phoenix. Maybe now you can find a leader who puts the needs of the people first," I state firmly, staring directly at her.

She lifts a defiant chin. "The Fire Fae want our freedom. Our next leader will accept nothing less." The ones with her yell in agreement and raise their fists.

Inspired by their actions, she raises hers again.

Damn it.

She opens her mouth, but I interject before she can say a word. "This is Theron, Lord of Winter. Do you think the dark Fae won't avenge this attack?"

Her eyes dart from me to him, and for a second, she wavers, but the man next to her murmurs something to her that solidifies her resolve, and she brings her fist down.

"Now!" I shout to Theron, pulling my sword to fight the Phoenix landing in front of me. In a flash, I nick several of them with the tip of my sword, and they slide to the ground, immobile from Aamon's toxic saliva.

A portal opens to our right, bringing our back-up into the fight. Valerian immediately takes to the sky in dragon form, flying toward the approaching Phoenix. Several scatter, panicking at the sight of one of the few creatures who can render them an eternal death. Dragon fire is lethal to our kind.

Aeris spins around in astonishment, yelling orders at the soldiers around her in an almost chaotic manner. It's clear she isn't versed in battle, nor did she expect us to bring our own reinforcements.

It's been two minutes since I took down the first few Phoenix. Cormal shouts at us and points to the portal he's opened to Gora Mountain. Arden immediately sends their weapons through the opening.

I spare a moment to view the battle. Cormal's magic whips through the men, blinding them, before he nicks them with his xiphos. Madoc's a blur by his side, the black blade making a brief appearance against his enemies, dropping them one after another. The rest of the cadre and Theron's soldiers are working just as quickly to take them all down.

Turning back to Aeris, I leap forward and attack the soldiers nearest to her. Under a time crunch, I slice through them quickly, but when I stop and face the last soldier, I realize the gold eyes and black hair are familiar. Tiernan.

In a fast maneuver, he steps to the side and brings up his sword, only to find Meri's dagger meeting it.

"Kill her!" Aeris shouts at Tiernan.

I tense, but he immediately takes a step backward. "I can't. I swore an oath."

Meri smiles at him, then slices his arm with her dagger. He drops to the ground.

Furious, Aeris screams and comes running toward Meri with her sword drawn. I stop her advance with my own. The two swords collide in a loud clang that rings across the near silent land, but she doesn't stop. Going on the attack, she parries and thrusts, her intent clear.

I flash a taunting smile at her. "You're good."

It's clear she learned everything she knows about sword fighting from our father. With a flick of my wrist, I use a move Theron taught me a few days ago. Her sword goes flying out of her hand and into the portal.

"But I'm better."

Chest heaving, I lay the point of my sword on her neck and look around at the clearing. Phoenix and other Fire Fae litter the ground.

Her eyes widen as she stares at her fallen comrades. "You'll pay for their deaths. The Fire Fae will hunt you for the rest of your life."

I laugh. "I doubt it. Not once they find out you killed Brixton." My aim hits its target, and she glances around in panic. "Why?"

Her chin lifts. "He's been working with Denir and the dark Fae. All he wanted was more power. We want our freedom from both the light and dark Fae. It's all we've ever wanted."

I sigh, understanding her reasoning. "They're not dead, only temporarily paralyzed," I assure her. "Despite what you think of me, I don't wish to harm the Fire Fae, especially not the Phoenix."

She snorts in disbelief. "Right. That's why you're with her." Her head tilts toward Meri. "Are you going to stand with the light Fae this time?"

Meri laughs. "I willingly gave up my light Fae crown. We represent the dark Fae, but we do count the Water Fae as our friends and allies." Her point is clear, and my sister stares at her in confusion.

Cormal, Madoc, and the rest of them start tossing the immobile Fire Fae through the portal, and I wince as their bodies thud against each other.

"Go home to your daughter," I urge Aeris. "Think about her future. We've been caught up in the past, never stopping to think about what we truly want. Personally, I'm tired of letting what others think define my path."

I turn to stare at the beautiful soul who led me out of the dark and into the light. "The path I choose going forward will include Meri. She's my future, not the Phoenix."

Meri's breath catches in her throat.

My eyes return to my sister, and I kiss her cheek. "Goodbye." Digging the point of my sword into her neck, I send her to sleep, then sheath my sword and carry her into the portal. When I return, Cormal immediately closes it.

I return to Meri and wrap my arms tightly around her. "I choose us." Holding her, I turn to the side to include Cormal and Madoc. "And whatever future we carve for ourselves." Madoc sheaths his dagger, and they both silently move closer, enclosing Meri and me between them.

It suddenly hits me where I've seen Madoc's curved blade. In a painting in the dark Fae palace. In the hand of the first Fae king, Konnyr.

CHAPTER TWENTY-THREE

CORMAL

"I've got to go. Kavi says the trail is leading into Aerie Wells. As a chaos demon, he isn't familiar with the area, and I don't want him to end up a prisoner of some damn Red Cap or worse," I inform them, sliding more weapons into the black fatigues I'm wearing.

Meri waves a hand, dressing herself in a fitted black outfit complete with knit cap, and lifts her backpack. "Let's go."

This isn't a trip. "You're not going," I snap. "It isn't safe. Just because it's in the land of the Fae and not The Underworld doesn't mean Leandra can't find you there."

She folds her arms across her chest. "I'm not asking your permission."

Madoc heaves a sigh and stands. "Hell, Aerie Wells is in the Dark Fae Kingdom. I'm the most familiar with it. It makes sense for me to go with you." He scowls at Meri. "I agree with Cormal.

It's too dangerous. Besides Leandra, the creatures in Aerie Wells are walking nightmares."

She lifts a shoulder. "And?"

"And we can't protect you and search for my man," I shout, throwing up my hands. "What if something attacks you and your bracelet comes off? Think for a second."

Rivan strides into the room. "What the hell is going on? I could hear you from the elevator."

"Cormal's sister went missing a long time ago. One of his men found a lead, but when they tried to follow it, Cormal's other man, a very tough chaos demon named Fluk, died. They've been trying to catch up with the first man, but someone keeps interfering with their search," Meri explains to Rivan.

"Lot was last seen in Aerie Wells twenty minutes ago," I toss out. "My second in command, Kavi, isn't familiar with the area."

Rivan whistles. "I've been there quite a few times with my father. Kavi will be a target the second he enters. Let's go."

"Why did Brixton go to Aerie Wells?" Madoc questions him with a puzzled expression on his face.

"To talk to the other leaders of the Fire Fae Rebellion," Rivan reveals with a shrug. "They were too easily recognizable everywhere else."

Madoc turns back to me. "We have more knowledge than you. We're going with you."

Meri steps forward and spears me with a narrow-eyed look. "Me too. I'm not changing my mind. You need to trust us to be there for you." Her fingernail taps her wrist. "We need to go."

Exasperated, I point to Rivan and Madoc. "She's your priority. If anything happens, get her out of there. I can take care of myself and my men."

Both Madoc and Rivan snort but agree.

My phone pings. "It's Kavi. It says JI #3." I raise an eyebrow and look at Madoc and Rivan. "Well?"

"Juba Inn, room three," Rivan murmurs. "We should go in the rear entrance to avoid anyone seeing us."

Damn it. I was hoping he was bluffing about his knowledge. Without another word, I storm out the door with the three of them. As we pass Astor in the lobby, I tell him where we're going in case anything happens.

His eyebrows shoot up. "Good luck."

When we arrive in Aerie Wells, it's pitch black.

We head to the Juba Inn and around the back. Old wooden stairs lead up to the second floor, and Rivan nods when I point to them. Once inside, we tread softly down the hallway until we reach room three. After knocking twice, then once, I push the door open and find Kavi and Lot arguing.

Relieved, I wave a hand to get them both to shut up. "Shut up. This isn't the kind of place where you want what's in the shadows noticing you. Not if you don't want to be eaten or worse."

Kavi throws a murderous glance at Lot but folds his arms and closes his mouth.

I point to Lot. "We've been searching for you. Why haven't you answered my texts or sent us updates?"

"Too dangerous," he spits out, running a hand through his red hair. "We made contact with the Fae and informed him that we had the info he needed. We set the time and location, then we fucked up."

He lifts a shoulder. "Apparently, nobody uses a phone around here. Not in the open. The second Fluk picked up his phone to text you, the locals killed him for being a spy or some crazy shit."

Unbelievable. "We lost our contact?"

"No, I made it to the rendezvous, but without Fluk, I knew he would get suspicious. Better to pretend we didn't show and follow him. So, that's what I did," he excitedly corrects me. "He's here."

"In Aerie Wells?" I ask, afraid to hope.

"In the inn," Lot replies. "He's downstairs. I was going to try to follow him from here, but Kavi found me first."

"When was this?" I whip around toward the door. "Madoc, Rivan, and Meri. Head outside. If he gets past us, I'll text you. Kavi and Lot with me." I get to the hallway and stop. "Which way?"

Lot hurries past me, taking the lead. "Stairs to the bar around the corner."

We head left, and I look back to make sure Madoc turns right to lead Meri and Rivan to the rear exit. Before we reach the common room, I grab Lot's elbow. "I'm going to slide into the shadows with Kavi. We're too recognizable. All I want you to do is go in and sit down near the contact. Order an ale and blend in."

Lot dips his chin, then hunches his shoulders and opens the door.

Slipping into the shadows, we watch him shuffle into the bar. A few of the patrons look up when he enters, but they quickly dismiss him and return to whatever they're doing. Except for one.

That's him. His height alone gives him away. I stare at the tall, dark hair man with bright green eyes, sitting there, nursing a tankard of ale. Not once does his eyes drift to anyone else, not even when Lot walks over and sits two seats down from him. It's puzzling. Lot said he was paranoid. Those aren't the actions of a paranoid man.

I text Madoc, asking if he can take the shadows to meet us in the common room. Near the interior entrance. Seconds later, he slides up beside us, and I add a sound barrier between us and the room.

"Lot says that's him, but all he's done is sit there. Do you recognize him?" I murmur, pointing to Fae.

"Aristocratic Fae. At least a lord or lady based on the reading

I'm getting from their magic. Hard to tell with his glamour," Madoc replies softly.

Glamour, of course. "Can you remove the glamour?"

"For a brief second, but they will instantly know it's gone and bolt," Madoc cautions me.

Modern technology working with old magic. Got to love it. I pull out my phone and aim the camera toward the Fae. "Do it. Now."

Magic pulses out of the shadows, and the Fae turns toward it. The glamour lifts and I snap several pics of the now blond-haired, brown-eyed lord.

Flipping up the table, the lord takes off toward the door. I step from the shadows, with Madoc and Kavi, and wave to Lot. The four of us leap after him, intent on following him as far as we can.

Rivan: Small incident. We're leaving. Might want to send Kavi to bury the bodies in the back. 3 Red Caps. One pile of ash.

Cormal: ...

I show Madoc the text. "Will you go with Kavi and check it out? I'm going to keep following these two. Catch up when you can."

Madoc pulls Kavi into the shadows, and they disappear.

Winding through the town, I spot Lot standing in the corner of a dark alley. Deliberately letting him see me, I walk past his hiding spot. He flicks a finger at the stables nearby, and I slide into the shadows.

Light streams through the slats from the lights outside. The cool interior is dark and mostly silent except for the occasional whinny from a horse. For the next hour, I stand in the shadows, waiting for him to make a move.

The front door slides open, and light spills through the

entrance. Several Red Caps, muttering angrily amongst themselves, make their way to the wagon in the corner. Hitching up the jackass next to it, they lead it out of the barn and close the doors. The sound of clucking and the wagon pulling away echoes in the darkened room.

A huge beast of a horse rears up in the corner of the stables and changes from animal to Fae in a blink of an eye. Glamour gone, he leaps up on the nearest horse and sends a biting cold wind into the doors to open them wide. In a flash, they're gone.

I rush outside and see Lot and Madoc standing in the alley. "Where's Kavi?"

"I helped him drag the bodies out of town and burn them. He's scattering the ashes throughout the woods," Madoc replies with a shake of his head. "Based on the evidence, Rivan killed the three Red Caps, and Meri used faery fire to kill a hag. We need to leave. They'll be searching for royalty."

"I have an idea where to go next," I tell them. "Lot, find Kavi and head back to The Underworld. Collect your bonus. You've earned it. Well done."

He reaches out and shakes my hand. "Thank you. That money means a lot to me and my family."

I make a mental note to find out more about his circumstances. "No, thank you. I've never gotten this close to finding my sister, and I wouldn't have now if it wasn't for your perseverance. I'll let you know how it turns out."

When he's gone, Madoc turns to me with an eyebrow raised. "Where to next?"

His easy acceptance of my need to follow this through is unexpected. "You're turning out to be better than I hoped."

He scowls and stalks off.

Catching up, I flash him a broad grin. "We're returning to The Abbey to check on Rivan and Meri. Then we're going to find Theron and ask him about a man on a horse."

Meri and Rivan are waiting for us in the room. She immediately rushes over and gives me a hug. "Sorry we had to leave."

I smooth a hand down her platinum hair as I scan her from head to toe for any injuries. Thankfully, there are none.

Madoc inserts himself between the two of us. "Hello." He dips his head and captures her lips in a deep kiss.

She grabs onto his shoulders and leans into him. "You don't have to kiss me like that every time."

He draws back. "You prefer a peck on the cheek like Cormal gives you?"

I growl in response to his asshole comment.

"I'll take every kind of kiss from you three," she breathes in a sultry voice.

Clearing my throat, I tilt my head and focus on Rivan. "What happened?"

"Some Red Caps were a little pissed because they lost family in the rebellion," Rivan says nonchalantly. "I would have walked away, but they tried to take Meri as recompense."

Meri's turquoise eyes are brimming with laughter. "While he was ferociously fighting the Red Caps, a gnarled hand reached out from the shadows and touched my hair. Told me it was pretty, then tried to snatch it off my head. I might have gotten a little pissed and lit it on fire."

I chuckle. "You've always been a little overprotective about your hair." This little skirmish seems to have helped her and Rivan find their rhythm, too. "We followed the Fae to the stables. I think he's a Winter Fae lord. I'm going to show Theron his picture."

She frowns. "Theron's brother is the only other lord in the Winter Court. His name is Oryn, and he lives in the palace with Denir. He's the one who gave me the information about the Phoenix."

"Full circle," I murmur.

How the hell does Oryn know my sister?

CHAPTER TWENTY-FOUR

<u>MERI</u>

Cormal thrusts his phone into Theron's hand, then proceeds to explain everything from his sister's initial kidnapping to this Fae's search for her background. "Tell me you know him."

Theron's gaze slips to the phone and back to Cormal. "It's Oryn, my brother. How did you know to come to me?" He passes the photo to Fallon, who's standing beside him.

"In Aerie Wells, the rider used a wintery wind to open the doors of the stables," I recount with a shrug. "Dark Fae territory. It was bound to either be Autumn or Winter."

"I'm surprised he even used a disguise," Theron notes with a shake of his head. "Oryn's never faced hardship in his life. And to go out of his way for someone else isn't like him. I'll order him to Winter Court, where we can meet with him in private." With his phone in hand, he walks away.

Minutes later, he returns. "He was waiting for my call.

Told me he would meet me in Winter in an hour, then hung up. Fallon, will you go? I might need a voice of reason if it's bad."

Fallon brushes his long hair back from his face and tucks it behind his ear. "Of course. Don't want you to kill your favorite brother."

Cormal eyes Madoc, Rivan, and me. "I'll fill you in when I return."

"Take Madoc," I urge him. "Oryn lives at court with Denir. He might know something that could help us."

Cormal swoops down and gives me a deep kiss. "Good call. I'll see you later." He throws his elbow into Madoc's ribs when he passes him.

Madoc's grey eyes are full of laughter, although his surly countenance never changes. "Someone is jealous." He bends down and whispers into my ear. "Think about me when I'm gone."

An image of me sitting in his lap naked, me naked and laughing as he feeds me, him chasing a naked me through a forest, flickers through my mind.

My face flames, but I don't tell him to stop. Nope. I wink and send him an image of his head between my thighs, worshipping my body.

He groans, and his goodbye kiss is a little deeper and rougher than usual. "Remember, keep your shield up."

I flip him off as he leaves.

Rivan slides up beside me. "Up for a surprise?" His voice is deeper and huskier than it usually is, and I look up to see the desire in his eyes.

"Does it turn you on to see them kiss me?" I ask him, running my hands down his torso. "What kind of surprise?"

"Yes," he admits gruffly. "It wouldn't be a surprise if I told you." He pulls out a blindfold from his back pocket. "Close your eyes."

Intrigued, I let my eyes drift close. A second later, the cloth slips over them, snuffing out the light.

Taking my hand, he leads me down the hall to the elevator. When we get off, the air is different. Damp and heavy. His hands grasp my shoulders as he walks me where he wants me and stops.

Whipping off the blindfold, I see the hot springs he took me to when I was queen. "We didn't leave The Abbey, did we?"

He chuckles. "No, I like my head attached, thank you very much." He stretches out his arm. "The Abbey creates what you need. I wanted to take us back to the moment when I first started falling for you."

I take a deep breath and turn to face him. So many moments full of longing between us, but we never crossed the line when I was queen. The kiss I gave him when we pulled him off that mountain was our first kiss, but it was to bring him back to me.

Raising my chin, I slide my hands up his defined chest to his shoulders, then clasp them behind his neck. "All those times you stopped. Show me what was in your heart."

Bending his head, his lips draw closer and closer until they finally meet mine in a kiss so beautiful it was worth the long wait. Emotion pours from him to me. Like our friendship, it starts off slow and sweet, then gradually moves into something deeper and more intense. His lips break away, hovering closely next to mine, but never touching, reflective of the break between us. They suddenly capture mine, and there is joy and desire and love all wrapped into one. It's the story of us in a kiss.

A tear rolls down my cheek, and he breaks away to capture it with his lips.

"Don't cry," he murmurs. "We know each other in ways nobody else ever will. The part of us that is strong enough to survive the terrors in the night and still see the light in ourselves the next day."

"I didn't think we would ever get to this point," I admit to him with a tremulous smile. "Not just because of the crown on my head but because the wounds of the past were incredibly deep and prevented me from asking you to stay with me in the Light Fae Kingdom."

He squeezes me tightly. "I know. If our roles were reversed, I wouldn't want you to return to a place of torment, either." His hands smooth down my shoulders to the buttons on my shirt. He slips one through the hole, then another. "I've dreamed of this moment so many times."

It takes him several minutes to get my clothes off. By the time he finishes, I'm already wet with need. Impatient, I wave a hand and make his disappear instantly.

He throws his head back and laughs, and the sound echoes throughout the chamber. His hand grabs mine and I lift it to the light to see the hard callouses on his palm. "From the sword." The pride in his voice is all I needed to hear, and I link our pinkies together.

He helps me into the warm pool, and I groan as the heated water eases my tight muscles. "Lean your head back and I'll wash your hair."

Remembering how good his fingers felt, I tip my head back, but this time, I don't hide myself from him. "Like this?"

"Perfect," he replies huskily.

I hear his hands rubbing briskly together. Then he gathers up my hair and begins to coat each strand with the shampoo, until every single one is well lathered. Strong fingers slide behind my neck and up the back of my head, massaging every single inch along the way. I moan at the amazing feeling.

Minutes later, he tips my head back farther and carefully rinses away the suds.

Unable to resist, I wrap my arm around his neck and pull his lips down to mine for a sweet thank you. At least it starts out that way, but the longer I kiss him, the more my body aches for his.

As if to answer my silent plea, his hand skims the top of the water to my breasts. "I wanted to touch you so badly that day. Cup your breasts in both hands and play with the teasing peaks."

He pulls me backward until my shoulders are resting against his chest. "Better." Cupping my breasts fully, he plays with them while his mouth finds my neck. "I love the sexy slope where your neck joins your shoulder." His tongue laves the area, then slides up to kiss my ear.

His hands glide down my body, mapping the dips and mounds, until it reaches the heart of me. Fingers part my folds and slide up and down as if his goal is to know my body using only touch. He dips a finger inside, then circles it around the nub at the top. Over and over, until the slickness covers me.

A muscular arm wraps around my middle, and he holds me closer. Two fingers dip inside while his thumb presses firmly on the most sensitive part, swirling around and around. I arch into his hands, then retreat.

He stops, and I gasp. Flipping my body around to face him, he pushes against my shoulder. "Lie back. I've got you. That's it."

When I'm floating on my back, he places my legs over his shoulders and pulls me closer, his hands under me for support.

He bends his head and makes love to me with his mouth. Incredibly intense, I'm truly lost at sea, awash in sensations, with only him to anchor me. The water laps over my breasts, reinforcing the feeling, and when my release hits, it's continuous, rolling over me in short bursts like the waves breaking on the shore.

He eases my legs off his shoulders and guides my body down to his. "Still with me?" His chuckle is low and sensuous, but I hear the underlying need in his voice.

I rise and wrap my arms around him while I let gravity pull me down until his body is at my entrance. "All the way. I'm yours." I sink onto him slowly, watching his face the entire time.

Little flames appear in his amber eyes, and I move up and down until he's fully inside me. His fingers grip my hips, and he lays his forehead against mine. "It's better than I dreamed." Biceps bulge as he pulls me down and thrusts up at the same time.

Steam rises around us, but the heat building between us is like an inferno. It rages and flares, making our cheeks red and our breaths short. Pleasure tightens my body, but I don't want to let go yet.

His mouth firms, and I feel him swell inside me. He reaches down and swirls his thumb against me, bringing me with him as he falls. Strong arms wrap around my body, and he hugs me tightly.

"I don't want to ever let you go."

"You don't have to," I reassure him, content to stay in his arms. "Although Cormal and Madoc may come to find us if we don't surface."

He draws back and mockingly frowns. "I guess I have to share you with them, don't I?" His eyes twinkle with mischief, and it makes me happy to see him so lighthearted.

I lick my lips. "How do you feel about foursomes?"

He hardens inside me.

"I'll take that as a yes," I groan.

With a wave of my hand, a bar of soap appears. "It's my turn to wash you."

CHAPTER TWENTY-FIVE

<u>MERI</u>

Madoc strides in and pecks me on the lips, then turns me toward Cormal. "Go to him. He needs you." There's a disturbing glint in his eye that tells me their visit with Oryn didn't go well.

Worried, I swivel to the door and see conflicting joy and devastation in Cormal's eyes. The second I get close, he jerks me in his arms and eases down to the floor. Silent tears roll down his face until he buries it in my shoulder. I wrap my arms and legs around him the best I can and hold him tightly.

"My sister's alive," he begins, his voice haggard with conflicting emotions. "She's queen of the dark Fae and has been for the last nine hundred years. Almost the entire time she's been gone. That's why the trail went dark and cold."

His tone changes to something bitter and unrecognizable. "That's the good news. She's trapped. Denir is controlling her with a torque, and he's the only one who can remove it. In the meantime, he taps into her power as if it's a well."

Dropping his head back against the wall, he takes a deep breath. "Oryn says most of the time her eyes are blank, displaying little emotion. But he noticed that there are days when he sees a flicker of light in her eyes. A glimpse of anger or a spark of humor. It's why he's tried to check into her background without Denir finding out."

He sighs. "He's an ally and will do anything to help us get her away from Denir. I didn't tell him our plans, but he'll be ready, regardless."

"Oh, Cormal. I'm sorry." My voice breaks, and I pause to gather my thoughts. "She's alive, right?" When he nods, I brush his silky dark hair from his face. "Which means you can save her, and lucky for her, you're damn good at saving people."

The torment in his expression eases.

"We have to kill Denir, anyway," I reflect with a casualness I don't feel. It hurts me to see him so broken when he's done everything he can to find her. "But maybe we can find some way to torture him first. Crush him until he begs for mercy."

The smallest smile appears.

"We all want a piece. Me, you, Madoc, Leandra, and your sister, of course," I drawl. "But I say, whoever gets to him first wins. A competition. We both know how competitive you are, and Madoc... the man is a machine. Doesn't know when to stop."

A loud snort sounds from across the room.

Cormal's hands wrap around both sides of my head. "Thank you."

His hoarse voice is still tight with emotion, but the lines of his face are beginning to set in the expression I love most on him. Determination. The implacable will of someone who rules his world.

I nod at the sight. "Good. Are you ready to get up and start kicking some ass?"

He chuckles and produces his trusty notebook.

I roll my eyes. "After we plan, of course. I mean, it's not like we can spontaneously jump into the abyss. Or ride off and kill someone."

A knife clatters to the ground beside me, and I turn and glare at Madoc. "Good try. My shield is up."

The surly Fae winks at me, and my jaw drops. "Cormal, you better call Kavi and make sure hell didn't freeze over."

Cormal waves his hand and sends the knife straight toward Madoc, who catches it with his bare hands.

Show off.

"Did you check with Arden while we were gone to see if the tracing spell is working?" Cormal says, standing with me in his arms. He lets my feet drop.

I peek at Rivan and silently urge him to say something.

"We were busy," he replies with a huge grin that makes it obvious what we were doing.

Madoc spears him with a look that borders on murderous. "I checked with them." Surprising all of us. "They are close. Should have a location for us within the next hour or two."

"While you get the coordinates and plan the attack, I'm going to see Solandis," I inform them.

In the light Fae world, I saw her almost every day. I miss her. And I need to see her before we go after Leandra to remind myself what real love is and how it feels.

Vargas opens the door, clothes wrinkled, and a surly expression on his face.

"What's going on?" I murmur, stepping into their suite of rooms.

He merely extends his hand toward the couch.

Solandis is sitting on the couch, feet propped up on the coffee table, eating ice cream. Showing considerably more than she did a week ago. Her eyes are puffy, as if she's been crying.

"What's going on? Is it the baby?" I ask, starting to panic.

Solandis licks the spoon and gestures down to her growing stomach. "The doctor says everything is fine. I mean, Fae are born relatively quickly, although not usually this quick." Tears begin to flow down her face, and Vargas curses.

"It's okay," I assure her. "You've got this. And us. We'll help you through everything."

She sniffs and points to the ice cream. "I can't stop eating."

I look at her bowl, then dart a glance at Vargas, who's throwing his hands up in the air. "He or she must really love ice cream, and right now, they're growing so fast, they need more of everything."

She stops for a second to think about it. "Maybe. It was never like this with Callyx."

Tilting my head, I stare at her in disbelief. "Really? I mean, he was pretty unique too, right? Son of a chaos demon and the Princess of the Light Fae. And he turned out great."

She puts down her spoon and hands me the bowl. "You're right. Maybe I wasn't like this. All these years later, it feels different."

Vargas comes over and sits down beside her. "All better?"

Solandis grips his hand tightly. "Definitely better, but my emotions are all over the place." She raises an eyebrow and turns to me. "Tell me what's been going on."

It takes the better part of an hour, but I bring her up to date on everything.

She studies me for a long minute. "Don't let Leandra get to you. You're not the same person anymore." She sighs. "I wish I could go with you. Give her a taste of my power."

It's my turn to sniff. "That would be fun to see." It would too. Solandis is not the sugary sweet princess she portrays. "Thank you."

She lets go of Vargas to pull me in close, and I hug her tightly, breathing in the scent of her. "Give Cormal a hug from me, too. Tell him to focus on the things he can fix, not the past." She places a kiss on my cheek. "I love you."

"I love you too," I murmur.

Arden walks into the room with a bag full of food. "I've got a little of everything in here for all of your cravings." She hands the bag to Vargas. "We narrowed it down to two possible locations, which I handed to Madoc a few minutes ago. Leandra could be at either one. We offered to go with you, but all three said they had plenty of back-up."

I shrug. "I haven't heard the plan yet, but if I need you, I'll call. Thank you for finding her." I give her a hug. "Does this place have secure dungeons?"

"Very," she replies in a smug tone. "Plus, she won't be able to harm any of us who live here. The Abbey won't let her."

"Thanks," I say with a grim smile. "See you soon."

Everything is packed and ready to go when I return. Madoc's pacing from one end of the room to the other. Cormal's meticulously ticking off his list. Rivan's studying the strategy.

"So, where are we going?"

"They have two possible locations for Leandra. One is in the Underworld and one in the human world," Madoc grumbles with a wave of his hand.

Cormal instantly says Underworld at the same time I say human.

"Leandra hates humans," Cormal reminds me.

"Precisely," I stress. "Not once did we think to search for her here." Not in a million, gazillion, quadrillion… whatever, years did I think of checking for her in the human world. I wouldn't even know where to start. Near a coven? Far from civilization? In the heart of one of the cities? She could stand in the middle of a busy sidewalk, and we wouldn't see her.

"All right. We check here first," he agrees, clapping his hands together. "My magic is pushing at the seams, itching to burst free and kill someone."

"We can't kill her," Madoc barks. "Maim her. Take off a couple of limbs. But don't remove her tongue or hands. Everything else is fair game."

I look at Rivan, but he's storing weapons in every conceivable area on his body.

I glance out the window and see it's near sunset. Running a hand down my body, I change into form-fitting grey clothes. Picking a color between night and day will help me blend into both.

"Let's go."

The portal takes us to a house in the countryside. The little brick cottage sits alone on the dirt road. Ruffled curtains blow in the breeze. Window boxes overflowing with flowers sit on the sills. The lawn is freshly mowed.

Full of doubt, I ask Madoc, "Are you sure you have the right coordinates?"

He gives me a droll look, then points down the dirt road to another house. "There. Aamon is joining us here. Leandra's magic won't work on him."

Hmm, good to know.

Rustling in the bush has us all grabbing our weapons, but Aamon laughs when he steps out of them. "Just me."

"Hi, Aamon," I greet him with a smile, which he returns. My eyes widen in alarm, and I look at Cormal. His silent laughter brings an even bigger smile to my face.

"Make sure you smile at Leandra, Aamon," I urge him. "She'll love it."

He tilts his head to the side, then shrugs.

Madoc shakes his head at my comment, but I don't care. Aamon's smile is utterly terrifying, with multiple rows of very, very sharp teeth. One bite and you'd be gone. He might be a sweetie, but Leandra doesn't know that.

Madoc and Cormal take to the shadows. I walk up the road to the other house with Rivan on one side and Aamon on the other. When we get close, Rivan kisses me on the cheek and shoots into the sky. I continue along until I'm standing in front of the house.

This is definitely more her style. Completely rundown. Derelict. Rotting siding, peeling paint, overgrown yard, you name it. The dirty, half torn curtain in the front window twitches open, then closed. I tense. Magic buzzes around my fists, and Aamon lets out a soft growl.

Leandra walks out of the house and down the front steps, looking every bit as regal as the last time I saw her. Lush, dark brown hair cascades in waves to the middle of her back, framing her perfect body. Square jaw meets high cheekbones in a stunning visage. Everything about her is designed for seduction, except for her eyes.

Windows to her soul, they terrify everyone who meets her gaze. Cold and calculating, with wild sparks of madness and magic, they return my stare. "Took you long enough to find me."

Those aren't the words I imagined her saying.

"You were the one hiding. If you wanted me to visit, all you had to do was send me an invitation."

She holds the amulet out to me. "Timing wasn't right. I knew exactly when you would find me, and poof, here you are," she asserts. "Everything is falling into place. Denir's coronation is close. I'm sure he's panicking, and I plan to be there to see him fall."

I chuckle. "From where? The dungeons? Do you think we're going to leave you alive?"

She lifts her chin. "I've seen my death, and it's not by your hand. Nor Cormal's." She peers at the walls of her house. "You can come out from the shadows. I know you're on the porch."

But it isn't Cormal on the porch, it's Madoc. With his usual arrogant stride, he walks up to her wearing an expression so dark and full of hatred, she should count her blessings that her death isn't on his agenda, then snatches the amulet from her hand.

She blanches. "How did you get out?"

"An angel gave me his wings," he says sardonically. "With my freedom and power, I'll take my crown and kingdom."

Leandra throws her beautiful head back and laughs and laughs. "Wouldn't that be the greatest twist? To return the power I stole and make you king in his stead. The deliciousness of that moment is worth considering." She holds her hands out to me. "Put on the golden cuffs. Go ahead. I won't bite."

Aamon steps forward with the cuffs and grins at her.

She falters for a second, but then moves to meet him. "I meant what I said. I've been waiting for you." She cackles loudly. "Guess you finally met the monster inside you, Meri, my pet. Good thing I'm going to remove it."

"Can you remove it without killing her?" Madoc asks, his voice harsh.

"Good question. Can I?" Leandra asks, tapping her finger against her thigh. "For the right price, maybe."

CHAPTER TWENTY-SIX

<u>MERI</u>

"One of the most powerful witches in the world who gave it all up for love. Excuse me, scorned love," Cormal taunts her. "You could have ruled the world, but you chose to focus everything on your revenge. Why?"

She presses her lips together.

"For his mate, right? At least that is the story I heard." I throw it out there to see if she'll bite. "You were his mistress. He met his true mate and kicked you out."

I pause. That doesn't make sense. Cormal's sister is the queen, albeit a forced one, but she didn't come along until a hundred years after Leandra and Denir parted ways.

"It's a lie, isn't it?" I ask her. "One you made up or him?"

She scoffs and fluffs her hair. "What do you think?" Settling on the cot behind her, she crosses her long legs and waves her hand in an imperious manner that sets my teeth on edge. "Go on."

There's a lot to unpack here, and it's not as if the queen of secrets herself is going to tell me anything. So, what do I know? I hold up a finger.

"Denir and Nyssa became rulers of their respective kingdoms around the same time. Neither was supposed to inherit, but because of the power you stole from Madoc, Denir was crowned king. Talks between Nyssa's father, the King of the Light Fae, and the Fire Fae began not long after. He supported their independence. Unfortunately, dark Fae killed Nyssa's father, the king, and her mother, leaving the crown available for Nyssa to grab. Of course, she was behind the assassination of her parents, and since the perpetrators were dark Fae, I assume Denir assisted her. Maybe he thought she would be a less formidable adversary than her father. I'm not sure the reason matters, but it's the first time the two of them collaborated. With your help, I'm guessing. After the Fire Fae Rebellion, the land was divided, and life resumed for them both."

For the first time in my entire life, Leandra spares me a look of approval. Guess that means I'm on the right track.

"You spent two thousand years by Denir's side. That's a hell of a long time. It would have taken something drastic for you to leave him. Something that also involved Nyssa, who had become the incredibly powerful Prime during that time," I speculate. "Because you used the essence of them both to create me a few years after you left him."

Leandra claps her hands. "You learned something while you were queen, didn't you? Very good. But why? That's the burning question, isn't it? Denir knows. Ask him."

She could tell me, but because she's a narcissistic bitch, she won't.

"I learned a lot of things while I was queen. After I gave up my crown, too." I pull the chair across the floor to sit in front of her cell.

"I learned how strong I am. Stronger than you, certainly," I coolly inform her. When she scoffs, I smile. "You could never endure the things I did. You were a tyrant, pulling and tugging on my leash when the whim took you. Constantly trying to crush my spirit. I used to think you did it out of sheer joy, but I realize you did it to escape the misery inside you. And no matter how hard you tried, my spirit remained intact. Hell of a feat in itself and a clear victory for me."

I scan her from head to foot. "Something crushed your spirit, and instead of fighting, you went into hiding. Pathetic." I sneer at her. "Every day, I got up and faced you. Over and over and over. Hiding wasn't an option. Neither was running. For someone who had little power, that's pretty damn amazing. The only thing I regret is not believing in myself enough to find a way to leave you sooner."

She jumps to her feet. "There would have been nowhere to hide. I created you. Like the shoes on my feet, you were mine."

Madoc comes striding in, darkness swirling around him. "Shut up. If you speak to her like that again, I'll let Cormal dump you in The Pit or Below for five minutes. That's how long it would take to have you weeping and begging."

He grits his teeth. "Tell us. What's your price? Denir's life? Happy to oblige." At my request, he'd left us alone to chat, but having her within reach is driving both him and Cormal crazy.

Her eyes are distant as she stares at something only she can see. "Soon, I'll tell you."

Infuriated, his power builds, but I place a hand on his arm. Torturing her will only piss her off. We need to show her we have options, too.

"You told The Wild Hunt Denir doesn't have the power. What will they do when he can't display it at the anniversary of his coronation?"

"End him," Madoc says with a gleam in his eye. "Too bad you won't get to rub your revenge in his face."

Leandra stands and makes her way to the bars. "Clever." She looks from Madoc to Cormal, who's been sitting in the corner listening to everything. "Unfortunately for you, Cormal, they will end your sister, too."

She laughs at his furious roar. "Yes, I've known for a long time she was Riona. It played nicely into my long-term plans." A mocking tone to her voice, she adds another dig. "You're not very good at keeping the women you love safe, are you?"

Furious, Cormal holds out his hand and aims at the floor beneath her feet. Electricity sparks and rises. With a twirl of his finger, it flows from the floor into her. Leandra's body jerks as it moves through her body. She raises her hand to stop it, but her magic is gone, stripped by the cuffs on her wrist and the bars surrounding her. Falling to her knees, she spits at him.

Her shoulders slump for a brief second, but something inside her rallies. "I will never surrender. Revenge is the only thing left to me. It is my right."

The way she says it tells me this isn't about jilted love. Needing to think, I leave them in the dungeons, torturing Leandra, and go find Rivan in the training room. He takes one look at my face and opens his arms wide.

"Any progress?" he asks, cupping the back of my head and holding me to him. His thumb rubs softly across my neck in a soothing manner.

"I may have to wear this bracelet forever." My pitiful statement is muffled by his chest, but I can't bring myself to raise my head from the haven of his arms.

He scoops me up. "Let's take a break." He carries me into the elevator, and when the doors open, the sweet smell of roses and honeysuckle fill the air around us. Theron's garden on the roof. He and Fallon spend quite a bit of time up here close to nature. Their own kind of rejuvenation.

Rivan sits in one of the chairs and stares up at the night sky. "Wherever we decide to call home, I want a place on the roof to escape from everything."

I smile, thinking of the secret place he showed me on top of the light Fae palace. "Yes, but with comfy chairs. And blankets. And snacks."

He bends his head and kisses me. Butterflies dance in my stomach as the warmth of him spreads through me. "And lots of kisses."

"Mmm, yes, lots of kisses," I agree. My hands skim his biceps, enjoying the feeling of the muscles he's developed in such a short time. "Why haven't you added the runes back to your body?"

He's silent for a few minutes. "I don't need them around you."

The words make my heart ache and sing at the same time. He purposely left his skin blank to show me he doesn't need their protection, because I won't hurt him like she did.

"I love mine," I remark, showing him my palm. "And I think I want more of them. They're beautiful."

"Dangerous, too," he murmurs, but a smile lurks in the corners of his mouth.

"The island protected me," I confide. "When the Phoenix soldier was regenerating on top of me, it shielded me from his faery fire."

His head tilts. "Really? I knew the runes on your body woke up the old magic, but I didn't know it protected you, too. Interesting." He settles back in the chair. "You know. There is a rune that will reinforce your shield. We could start with that one."

I roll my eyes. "Madoc."

"Madoc worries about your safety. He talks about it all the time," he confides, probably hoping it will win Madoc points.

"Maybe he should talk to me about it instead of barking at me all the time," I say, snuggling further into his arms. Staying up all night, trying to get Leandra to agree to transfer the power from me to Madoc, has worn me out. "Let me close my eyes for a few minutes, then I'll go back down there."

It's much later when I wake, and the warmth of Rivan has been replaced by a darker, earthier scent. I open my eyes and find Madoc staring down at me. His steel-grey eyes are full of worry, and his usual snarl is absent.

I run a finger over his lips. "Hello, friend."

The corner of his mouth twitches, but he bends down and nibbles on my lips in a sweet kiss. "Hello, friend." Deep grooves line his face. He appears worn out.

"She has waited almost a thousand years for this revenge," I remind him. "Why? Not for love scorned. Or power. What did Nyssa have to do with it? She was the Prime. I doubt she even cared about Denir."

He tilts his head to consider my words. "But she owed him a huge favor, right? For helping her get the crown. Maybe he came to collect. But for what? We continue to circle back to that one point." He drops his head back with a sigh.

"Do you want to be king?" I ask.

He's done all this to get his crown back, but is it because his kingdom was stolen from him, or because this is what he really wants?

He stares across the rooftop at the city lights around us. "All my life, I was groomed to be king. Forced to sacrifice friends, spend hours of my day learning diplomacy, military strategy, combat, cultures, and traditions. Riding with my father to meet the people. Hearing disputes in the court. I didn't really question whether I wanted it or not. It was my duty and privilege."

"What about now?"

His eyes fall to me. "Yes, I want it. Not because it's mine by birthright or because it was stolen, but because I'll be a good king. My people deserve to have someone with their best interests on the throne. With the Lesser Fae rising and the light Fae in turmoil, we cannot let the Dark Fae Kingdom fall to the revolution. There's more at stake than their rights."

"There is one way to get this out of me," I begin, but his mouth cuts off the rest of the words.

Usually, his kisses are sweet and demanding, but this one is hard and tinged with anger. At me or the situation, I'm not sure, but there is a lot of emotion simmering under his surly surface.

He moves us from the chair to the ground, where he's conjured a fluffy quilt for us to lie on.

"I don't want to hear you say it, much less think it," he retorts with a fierce expression. His hands are busy, stripping the clothes off me. "All I want to hear are sweet moans when I sink into your body. Or the word yes, falling from your lips." He stares down at me. "Take my clothes off."

I wave a hand and remove every stitch. "Mmm, I like this side of you." My hands tiptoe up his shoulders and across the many scars on his body. "Are all these from the monsters below?"

He stills. "No. Training to be king isn't for the weak. Or so my father used to say." He eyes me closely. "Are you sure they don't bother you?"

"The abuse bothers me," I return angrily. "Not the scars." I rise and kiss the ones nearest his heart, paying extra attention to the ones with the smooth edges.

"Say my name," he demands, his voice hoarse with emotion.

"Madoc," I murmur, then gasp as his mouth and hands descend on my body.

"Again," he demands, plunging his fingers inside me.

"Madoc," I cry out, scoring my nails across his broad shoulders before reaching down to grip him in my hand. Soft, velvety skin with a steel core. Using a little magic, I make my hand slick to glide up and down his shaft.

Inhaling sharply, he pulls it away from his body and laces his fingers with mine. "Not that way. I want to feel you wrapped around me. Say yes."

"Yes," I moan, wrapping my legs tightly around his body.

Instead of thrusting, he slowly sinks into me. "I want you to know every inch of me." His hand pushes against my inner thigh to spread my legs farther apart. "Mmm. So deep." He flexes inside, making me gasp.

His eyes meet mine. "I never expected you," he tells me with a serious expression. "You've irritated me from the moment we met. Fae. Human. You act like both. Making friends with every dangerous stray you meet. Me. Lux. Aamon. You show fierce loyalty to those in your circle. Tolerance to those outside it. You live life without absolutes like good and evil. You hate being unique, but you defy the norms. You ask for little, but demand everything."

Lips suckle as his tongue dips into every crevice.

Arching, I offer myself up to him. "You're no better. Surly. Content to be in the shadows, yet you yearn to wear the crown. Loyalty to Aamon and the few you deem important. Fae. Monster. You act like both. Unyielding integrity packaged in an uncivilized beast with fierce emotions. You ask for little, but demand everything."

He pulls out and slowly pushes in again, and I moan at the feeling of us joined together.

"Oh, and you're an incredible lover."

"Mm, I especially like that last one," he drawls with satisfaction. "I can't get enough of you and your delectable body. You might say I'm obsessed."

My eyes flick to his. "Don't say things you don't mean. I can do casual, but I can't fall for you and have you walk away."

His eyes narrow, and he spits out, "There will be no casual between us. Intense. Consuming. Obsessed. Those are your only options. Do you understand?"

I raise an eyebrow at his tone. "Respect. Consideration. Love. Do you understand?"

"So, we're in agreement?" His body moves in and out as he waits for my answer.

My body quivers underneath his. This certainly feels intense and consuming. He stops, and I loop my arms around his neck and pull him down for my kiss of surrender.

"Yes, yes, yes."

He continues his slow torture, driving us both to the edge of madness before he lets us fall.

Lying together, the cool night air dries the sweat on our skin, and I reach up to push the dark silky strands back from his scruffy face.

"My turn."

CHAPTER TWENTY-SEVEN

<u>MERI</u>

Dawn is cresting the horizon when I leave Madoc and head to the dungeon to check on Leandra. The air is saturated with dark, disturbing magic, but Cormal is nowhere to be found. Leandra is lying limply on the bed.

Immense satisfaction fills me. "I've always admired Cormal's ruthlessness."

"Definitely a brutal bastard," she agrees in a hoarse voice, likely from screaming most of the night. "He'll do anything for you. Even make a pact with me." Her chuckle is strained. "I had someone like that once."

"No, you didn't," I correct her. "Denir is weak and pathetic. Nothing like Cormal." I squat down to peer into her eyes. "Tell me what you want most in this world?"

A tear slips down her cheek. "You can't give me what I want most in this world, but you can give me my revenge." She slides a hand to the bed and raises herself halfway up to stare at me with swirling eyes. "I want to see his face when he realizes this is his end."

"You want to go to the anniversary celebration," I deduce. "Show him to be a fraud in front of everyone. Watch him lose the crown you gave to him."

"Yes. And I want the world to know why I did it," she admits with a strange expression on her face. "That is my price for removing the power from you. I want him to see the power and know it will never be his again. I want him to watch as I return it to Madoc, knowing he will wear the crown."

"Will it kill her?" Cormal and Madoc ask in unison.

Startled, I turn to see them standing at the door.

She lifts a shoulder. "If the host is strong enough, it shouldn't."

They both start yelling at her, but I raise my hand to stop them. "The celebration is a month away. We have time to figure it out."

She cackles and moves her head from side to side in an exaggerated way. "The public celebration is in a month. Denir's real anniversary is in two days. He didn't want to take a chance the crown wouldn't accept him, so he had me place it on his head early. Only his court will be in attendance."

Her words echo in the silent chamber. I glance at Cormal. He trembles with fury.

"Stop. It won't do any good."

He says nothing, only continues to shoot murderous looks at Leandra.

She eases down to the cot and turns away from us. Done with all conversation.

Madoc grabs his arm. "Come on. We need to pull together a plan."

The three of us head upstairs to grab the others, including Rivan, and make our way to the war room. Ironically, I believe it's the same room the cadre and their allies gathered in to plot Nyssa's downfall.

Solandis waddles in and kisses me on the cheek. Her stomach is growing by leaps and bounds. Soon, the baby will be here. I hope I get to meet her. Or him.

Arden and her men arrive, crowding into the room. Fallon and Theron take point with Cormal, Madoc, and Rivan.

Once everyone is assembled, Cormal brings them up to date. "In two days, we have to get in the dark Fae palace without Denir knowing, let Leandra confront him, then shield her while she transfers the power from Meri to Madoc." He pauses. "This is her price."

"Will it kill Meri?" Solandis asks with a frown.

"We don't know. At this point, I think we have to assume it will and plan accordingly," Cormal states gruffly, his worried gaze locking onto me.

Everyone begins to talk over one another, and he lets out a piercing whistle. "Our hope is that Rivan will be able to revive her."

Rivan flicks me a determined look. "I'm ready."

At his confirmation, I take a deep breath in and slowly exhale. "We can access the palace through a secret tunnel into the library." Leandra used to send me on errands there all the time.

"That's where you got the book on the history of witches, isn't it?" Arden remembers with a smile.

"Yes, and I know almost every inch of that place," I inform them.

Callyx comes strolling into the room. "Heard you were having a party without me."

I walk over and give him a hug. "Given where we're headed, you might have to sit this one out." When he folds his arms and tilts his head, I shrug. "Going to see dear old Dad."

He flicks me a glance. "Please. I'm Lucifer's spy. Been in

everyone's palace at least once. But this one is tougher than most. Denir's alarm senses anyone walking in the shadows."

"Good thing to know," Cormal says, marking it down in his notebook.

"Besides, Lucifer already knows," Callyx drawls, glancing at Cormal. "Evren sent you a note." He hands him a sheet of paper.

Cormal opens the note and stares down at it for a minute. With a satisfied smile, he folds and slips it into his pocket.

"Since Leandra is aware of it, too, it makes sense for us to split up," Madoc warns. "Cormal and Callyx will take Meri and Leandra through the secret passageway with them. Rivan and I will enter a different way."

Cormal flicks a glance at Theron. "Can Oryn get them inside?"

Theron picks up his phone and calls Oryn. "Is it possible for you to let my friends into the house?" He listens, then hangs up. "He wasn't able to speak freely but mentioned being in the garden later. I assume he means the garden is the best way for him to get you inside. He'll call me back in about twenty minutes."

Madoc produces a map of the dark Fae palace. Yellowed with age and wrinkled, it's obviously been handled a lot over the years. "Show me where the tunnel is into the library. It didn't exist when this map was produced."

I lean over and study the lines. "There. In the kitchen pantry. She built a tunnel from the back wall to the library. Once there, a bookcase opens with a spell." Tracing the invisible path with my finger, I show him how to get from one place to the other.

"Why the kitchen?" Arden asks. "Wouldn't that be one of the busiest areas in the palace?"

"Leandra used to say... nobody notices a servant," I reply with a snide tone in my voice. "It's true, they don't."

Arden winks at me. "Guess she won't mind dressing down for the occasion."

"The good news is that this will be a smaller ceremony. According to Leandra, only his court will be in attendance, which includes lords and ladies, servants, and guards. Similar to your ceremony, Meri," Cormal explains.

"That's a lot of people," I remark with a frown. "How are we going to get in there without anyone else noticing?"

He flashes a wicked smile. "The best way to hide is out in the open. We'll walk in with the rest of the crowd. That's what I did for your coronation. I slipped in with the servants. We might need to mix things up for this one." He looks at the crowd in the room.

The memory of him standing on the balcony bowing after my coronation will stay with me forever. At the time, I was incensed to see him there, but now I'm glad he witnessed it.

Theron holds up a hand. "Arden and I, along with Oryn, will be in attendance as part of the court. Usually, I delegate these things to my brother, but I think our presence can help sway the aristocratic masses into standing down as it plays out. The rest of the cadre will stay behind but close to the portal in case they're needed."

He inclines his head toward Madoc. "Maybe we can also remind people that Madoc is the son of King Madox."

Madoc inhales sharply at this statement. "Thank you. The last thing I want is an insurrection because they aren't aware of my lineage."

Theron scans his attire. "Maybe we should find you something more royal to wear." He shakes his head when everyone groans. "Court dress is elaborate. I'm not suggesting he don peacock feathers or jewels or whatever the latest is in fashion, but formal attire is a must."

I laugh. "True." With a mischievous smile, I wink at Arden. "The women were extravagant with their luxurious gowns, but the best part is how they used magic to showcase their power."

Arden's lips quirk upward. "This might be fun, after all."

Solandis chuckles. "It's quite absurd, but I love it. Of course, as a princess, I can choose to wield my power or not."

Vargas lifts her hand to kiss it. "You looked magnificent at Meri's coronation." He tucks it into his arm, then his mouth turns down. "I'm sorry I won't be there to fight this time."

I walk over and hug them both. "I'd rather you stay here and protect her and the baby."

Then I move to the front of the room to stand with my men. "Honestly, I've been a bit bored lately. This should liven things up, don't you think?"

THE DARK FAE palace is nothing like the gilded golden palace of the light Fae. Deep weathered grey stone stands resolute against the land with its straight lines and symmetrical exterior. From the front, two separate wings extend back for at least a mile, creating a u-shape in the rear. There's nothing particularly pretty or fancy about it, but that's always been part of its appeal, at least for me. I like the strong, solid feeling it gives. As if it's stood unchanged against the ravages of time and strife.

Cormal, Leandra, Callyx, and I head to the rear of one of the wings and stroll confidently into the kitchen. Wearing simple clothes, Callyx lifts the box he's carrying and mumbles something about the pantry. Everyone shuffles out of the way to let us through.

"Idiots," Leandra cackles, and I dig my dagger into her ribs to shut her up. She glares down at me, but with the glamour rendering her eyes a dull brown, it doesn't have the same effect, and she knows it.

In the pantry, I close the door and Cormal steps into my spot next to Leandra. Squatting down below the bottom shelf, I flip a lever and watch the back wall swing open. "Let's go."

Callyx, still holding the box, goes in first. Then, me, followed by Leandra. Cormal enters last, protecting our rear and shutting the door behind us. For a second, it's dark, but I murmur a spell and faery lights turn on one by one, illuminating the path to the library. When I had no magic, I often walked this path in the dark.

"It's nice to have magic, isn't it?" Leandra taunts. "I'm surprised to see you have all this power, considering you had to give up your crown."

"Well, I did regain full use of the magic Cormal gave me." I smirk at the ugly expression on her face. "It nets me quite a few interesting powers." The ability to walk in the shadows is one of my favorites, but I don't share that tidbit with her.

Callyx comes to a halt. "Meri?"

I squeeze past him and hold up my hand, murmuring the spell Leandra taught me long ago. Previously, I had to carry an orb with her magic in it to open the door, but that's not necessary today. A huge smile spreads across my face as I watch the door silently swing open.

Callyx enters and sets the box down on a nearby table, then immediately moves to secure the area. "Clear."

Stepping into the vast library, I breathe in deeply. I love this smell. Of all the places Leandra used to send me, this was one of my favorites. Surprisingly, Denir is a collector, and he's made it his mission to get a copy of every known book in existence. Cormal said Lucifer often asked him for rare editions.

There's a sad expression on Leandra's face when she enters. "We spent many hours in here together." She walks over to the seat by the window and runs a hand over the cushion.

We who? But I say nothing. This isn't going to be an easy day for her. As usual, my feelings are a mixed bag of everything. Sometimes I wish I could hate her.

She motions to her worn clothes. "Where's my dress?"

Cormal opens the large box and pulls out a smaller box with

a silk bow on it, which he hands to me. He hands a similar sized one to Leandra, then takes out two smaller boxes for him and Callyx.

The only elaborate thing I had in my closet was my coronation dress. Stunningly beautiful, I thought it would be nice to wear it again, but instead, I have to turn away before anyone sees the tear roll down my cheek. Maybe I can go as a servant.

Cormal takes my hand in his and pulls me back to the box. "Open it."

With a heavy sigh, I tug on the ribbon and let it drop to the side, then lift the lid. Instead of champagne-gold silk, acres of dark red silk embellished with sequins and feathers fill the box to the brim.

Lifting the dress out, I stammer, "Where did you find the time?"

He runs the back of his finger across my cheek. "For you, I'll always find the time. Plus, it helps to have two more sets of hands to do things. The dress is from all three of us." With a wave of his hand, a familiar mirror appears.

I hold the dress up in front of me. Against my pale skin and platinum hair, the dress practically glows. The fitted bodice plunges to a deep vee in the front with sheer panels on the sides and a sheer back. Sexy. The bottom half of the dress is a very short peplum skirt, hand embroidered with the sequins and ostrich feathers I noticed first. Laughing, I run a finger across their downy softness. Sheer panels flow from beneath the bell-shaped skirt to my feet, with slits on both sides.

"It's stunning," I breathe out. With a wave of my hand, I put the dress on and style my hair into a simple updo.

I move into Cormal's arms, my gaze silently asking if he's going to be okay. This will be the first time he's seen his sister in centuries, and I know he's wondering how to save us both. Reaching up, I capture his lips with mine, needing a kiss to carry with me into the court.

His hand cups my cheek as I draw away, and his intense blue eyes burn with unspoken words for me.

"Someone cleans up nice." Leandra's smoky voice is mocking. She peers down at her own dress and gives Cormal a stiff nod. "Thank you for getting the purple." Her draped dress is equally beautiful in an ombré silk dyed in different shades of purple. Hugging her body, it showcases all her best assets.

Leandra never wore purple. Ever. I didn't realize it until now. I watch her fingers gently smooth the fabric. The way she's fingering the dress makes me think her choice of color is sentimental.

Her brown hair is also in an updo, although much more intricate than mine, and her swirling eyes are on full display. She takes a deep breath and flashes me a satisfied smile.

Cormal's suit is black, of course, and in the same style as the one he wore to my coronation, but this one has accents of deep red to match my dress. Callyx suit is all black as well, but with zero embellishments.

I flick my hand and silver threads appear, making it seem like a fancier version of a pin-striped suit. "Better."

He gives me a dry look. "Are we ready to go?"

Cormal holds a hand to his ear. "Rivan says they're at the side door. Let's move."

The plan was for Oryn to meet Madoc and Rivan at the back door of a secret garden in the rear of the palace. They will then make their way through the lush flowers and bushes to a side door very few use. We'll meet them in the ballroom.

"Ready," I murmur.

My nervous stomach feels the same as it did during my coronation, except the stakes are much higher. Tonight could be the beginning or end of Leandra and me.

CHAPTER TWENTY-EIGHT

MADOC

Over three thousand years ago, I stood in this very spot, staring at the same obsidian throne. My father was ailing and the time for my coronation was near. Nerves were getting the better of me, so I came to assure myself I was ready.

Gleaming black spears, made from the same obsidian material, extend from the back like a spiked halo, a reminder to all dark Fae that their ruler wields the power of The Wild Hunt and all the duties it entails, including the command of the creatures in the Wilds.

Surrounding the dais, brilliant diamonds adorn dark velvety walls and the ceiling, in a pattern reflecting the feeling of a cold starry night. Platinum chandeliers flicker tiny lights across the room and over the lords and ladies standing with me in the starkly beautiful great hall.

Double doors open wide, heralding Denir's entrance. Striking his most debonair pose, the one I found him practicing often in the mirror when we were children, he waits for the court to pay him homage. After, he arrogantly waves a hand, motioning for them to rise, he strides through the crowd. Tall and lean like most Fae, the ladies used to consider him handsome and suave. It doesn't seem like he's changed much. Slightly fuller in the face, and if you look closely, a cruel twist around his mouth.

His eyes swing toward the area I'm standing in, and I slide behind Lady Karee from the Autumn Court, who's wearing an outrageously orange gown with a matching headpiece.

When he passes, I slowly make my way to the servant's entrance on the side and open the door. Callyx moves into the room, like a shadow, dark and swift. Leandra is light and quick like a bird, picking a spot behind a tall pillar. Meri is a burst of fire in the cold dark of night. I almost choke at the sight of our dress on her; suddenly wishing we had picked something more substantial.

"Mmm, court attire suits you well," she says in a low, husky tone when she passes by me and takes her place near Leandra.

Cormal's low chuckle tells me I've been staring at her for several precious seconds.

"More material next time," I growl to him, but he lifts a lazy shoulder in response.

"Wait until Rivan sees her," he returns, his eyes anxiously scanning the room.

Not for Rivan, who's positioned on the other side of the room, but for his sister, the current Queen of the Dark Fae.

"She's not here yet," I tell him.

The crowd parts, and I spot Lord Theron and Lady Arden. Regal in his navy court attire, he's the perfect foil for her form-fitting ice blue dress. Usually stoic, he's clearly irritated by the looks the males in the court are giving the woman on his arm.

Ice spreads from beneath his feet, pushing back those crowding around them.

She laughs and whispers something into his ear. The ice melts around them.

Cormal reaches out and grabs my arm. I turn toward him. He's staring at the dais.

My eyes shift to the front of the room and find Oryn escorting the queen to her throne. The careful ways he handles her tells me a lot about his feelings for the stunning royal. Dark hair, same as Cormal's, but instead of a vibrant blue, her eyes are ice-blue and blank. Like the most exquisite porcelain doll, there's not an ounce of emotion in her eyes or face. Once seated, she folds her elegant hands in her lap and pastes a serene smile on her lips. Dressed in black with a gleaming gold torque around her long neck, she sits there staring at nothing.

"She may not recognize you," I warn him. Again. "Remember Rivan's visit with his sister. It didn't go well." I've had this conversation with him several times over the last two days, but he's brushed me off.

Until now. His jaw clenches along with his fist, but I hear his soft exhale, as if he'd been holding his breath until he saw her. Alive and within reach.

Denir holds up his hand, and I tap Cormal's shoulder. He tears his eyes from Riona and gives me a firm nod. Leaving him, I make my way to the pillar closest to the dais.

Denir holds out his arms. "For three thousand years, I've served as your king. To mark this momentous occasion, the coronation anniversary ceremony will be held during the public celebration. With the current winds of revolution flaring high in the Light Fae Kingdom, my people need to see the power that protects them now more than ever."

The crowd shifts silently on its feet, but then the whispering begins. Growing louder by the second, they talk about this latest change.

Incensed at their lack of applause, Denir motions to his queen. She steps forward. He bends down and whispers something to her. Pale lips move, and the crowd becomes silent.

I open my mouth, but nothing comes out. Puzzled, I turn to look at Cormal and see him murmuring and weaving his hand to counteract the spell she must have placed on the crowd. A minute goes by. He dips his chin, telling me to proceed.

This time when I open my mouth, the words flow out. "The power must be displayed tonight, on your anniversary." My voice is loud in the silenced room. "Or you will forfeit the crown."

Angry, he swivels to face the crowd nearest to me. "Who dares to speak that way to their king? Show yourself."

I step from behind the pillar onto the dais. "You're not my king. Never will be."

He stares at me, eyes widening in recognition.

"What? Not happy to see me, cousin? Well, it has been a few thousand years." I hold out my scarred arms and hands. "As you can see, I've been a bit busy fighting monsters. Literally."

With the exception of Theron and Arden, the crowd shuffles back a few steps. Scars aren't the norm in Fae society.

Denir motions to the guards nearest to him. "Remove this imposter."

Callyx claps a hand on their shoulders, and they pale when they see who's holding them. "This is between family. Let them hash this out."

"How dare you enter my court!" he shouts at Callyx. "Wait until I inform Lucifer."

Callyx flashes him a taunting smile. "Lucifer knows you've lost the right to rule. Do you think he cares? He backs the true heir to the Dark Fae Kingdom."

Red-faced, Denir motions to the lords nearest him, and they move to intercept on his behalf, but a shield of ice forms around them.

Theron pulls his two swords. "Madoc, the son of Madox, deserves our respect and allegiance. Hear him out."

"Madoc is dead," Denir shouts at Theron. "How dare you interfere in my orders! Once I've taken care of him, I'll strip you of your lands and title."

"Only the king has those rights. Either display the power to rule or give up the crown," Theron states cooly.

Denir murmurs to his queen, and a wave of power penetrates my shield and wraps around me, squeezing so tight my bones crack. Her black magic creeps up to cover my face.

"Riona, it's me. Your brother," Cormal says, moving to my side. His hands silently weave in and out, setting his magic against hers. "Our father, Brennus, was the first Druid. Remember?"

The binds around me break, and she stumbles back. "I know you?" For the briefest moment, her eyes flash a darker blue, but Denir whips his hand up to touch the torque around her neck.

Infuriated, I jerk him away from her and punch him in the face hard. "Fight someone your own size."

He stumbles and raises his hands, pushing magic toward me. Typical Fae response. Curling his hand, he looks to his lords and ladies, but the power that is usually on tap is gone. Only the king can pull from his subjects.

Throwing my hand out, I shove him against the wall with magic, then follow with another right cross. And another. Bones crunch beneath my fists, and it's so satisfying it makes me want to beat him to a bloody pulp. Magic collars me, jerking me away from him.

"Fuck!"

Riona comes to stand next to Denir.

He spits out blood and drags his sleeve over his mouth. "Her number one priority is to protect me." With a flick of his finger, he taps her cheek, then the torque. "Isn't that right, Riona?"

"Get your fucking hands off my sister," Cormal snarls at

Denir. "You're a weak, pathetic piss-ant with little magic to call your own. Everything you wield is hers. You struck gold when you bought her from that last demon, didn't you? She goes free tonight."

Denir strokes a light finger over the collar around Riona's neck. "She's my queen. Of course, she shares her power with me. Who the hell are you?"

Cormal raises a dark brow high. "Cormal, king of a dark empire full of the worst of the worst. You don't want to fuck with me."

"That explains it. This is all an attempt to take my queen from me. It's a ruse," Denir states jovially. "Who else have you brought with you?"

Denir gestures behind Cormal, and Riona parts the sea of people surrounding Meri. "Well, well, well. The replacement. Your timing couldn't be more perfect."

Meri's mouth goes slack, and she turns to look at Leandra behind her. "Replacement. The first time I met him, he called me your *replacement daughter*. Is that what I am?"

"She stole the power from me," he says, raising his voice to the crowd who crane their necks to see Meri.

Several lords shout and magic begins to fly toward Meri.

Arden raises her hands and traps the magic with a golden net. "Riona isn't the only powerful magic wielder here."

A tall Fae pulls his sword and swings it at Arden, only to be interrupted by Theron's sharp blade across his neck. "Hurt one hair on her head, and I'll take yours."

With the two of them holding back the crowd, I turn toward Denir.

Leandra strolls forward, her purple dress swishing elegantly around her. "Meri isn't my daughter, she's my revenge. I took the power from you and hid it within her. Almost a thousand years I've waited for this moment."

He gestures to the people. "This isn't funny, Leandra. The

power is mine. Give it back and we'll talk. I promise. It's been too long. I've missed you, and I regret how things ended between us, but taking my power is the action of a woman scorned. It's been a thousand years. Surely, you're over my rejection."

She stares at him as if he's lost his mind. "This isn't about you. You and Nyssa killed my daughter!" she screams, the heart-wrenching pain in her voice ringing in the air. "She was my world, and you took her from me!"

He stares at her in disbelief. "You did all of this for the girl?! We had everything together. Power, a kingdom. I wanted us. You. Not her!" he shouts back, as if he's repeating an old argu-ment. "She would have ruined everything."

Leandra's fury rises, and she shoves Riona away from Denir with a flick of her hand. "Alia was beautiful and brilliant, and you loved her until you found out she was more powerful than the two of us combined. Her love was pure and good. She worshipped you. But all you could see was her taking your crown." Her hand reaches toward him, but Riona steps to his side and blocks her magic.

"Tonight, you will lose it all, including your life. This is my declaration of love to the daughter I loved more than anything in this world. My sole reason for existing the last thousand years is this moment. When I visit our daughter in Elysium, she will know the depth of my love by the breadth of my revenge," she says, holding her arms out wide and whipping the wind around the room.

"Give me the damn power, Leandra, or I'll have Riona end your life," he roars at her.

Riona sends a wave of magic against Leandra, but she merely flicks a finger to hold it off. "Did you forget how powerful I am?" She scoffs. "When you called in your favor from Nyssa and killed our daughter, I vowed to take the crowns you both loved more than life. Nyssa is gone. Her kingdom in ruins. I'm only sad I couldn't be there to watch her die."

She drags him closer to her. "Tonight's revenge will be even sweeter. I originally intended to let the power go back to The Wild Hunt. But it's only fitting that the power returns to its original owner, don't you think?"

Denir darts a glance at Madoc. "He never wore the crown. It will return to me."

"Shall we see?" Leandra asks in a husky voice. Her power rises, and she wraps an arm around Meri and places her hand over her heart. Magic arcs from her into Meri's body.

Tears roll down Meri's scrunched face and the tendons in her neck pull tight as she fights to keep from screaming. Leandra's hand moves away from Meri's heart and a pulsing ball of swirling black follows.

Meri lets out a blood-curdling scream and instantly falls to the ground.

Leandra pushes the magic toward me, but I refuse to take my eyes off of Meri. I wait for some sign of life. Her chest is still. I slide over and put my ear near her mouth. Not a single breath escapes.

"Cormal! She's not moving!"

CHAPTER TWENTY-NINE

MADOC

When he doesn't answer, I swivel around and find him engaged in a silent battle with his sister to keep her from getting the power. Waves of magic batter against each other, with neither gaining the upper hand.

"Rivan!" I yell. "Meri's down!"

The Phoenix's wings snap open, and he begins to fly toward us, but several lords and ladies fling magic toward him, stopping him in mid-air. He drops to the ground and pulls his sword.

My gaze swings from Meri to the power to Leandra and, finally, to Denir. His eyes are locked on the power. He frantically whispers to Cormal's sister, whose look of fierce determination nearly matches the expression on her brother's face.

Denir moves to intercept the power, and Leandra moves in front of him.

I glance back at Rivan and see him surrounded by the court. Theron and Arden are battling their way toward him.

Calling to the shadows, I shove the power up to the rafters and pull the dark sword at my back. Sliding into the darkness, I surf the shadows to Rivan and come up beside him. "How much time?"

"A minute, if we're lucky," he grits out, slamming the pommel of his sword into the chin of a nearby guard. "I need to get to her."

Every time I try to grab on to Rivan and slip into the shadows, someone else grabs him and shoves him farther away from me. *Damn it.* To resurrect Meri, he has to get to her within the next thirty seconds.

A loud roar sounds from across the room. Unable to see what's happening, I keep fighting to get to Rivan. Meri is more important than anything else. Even the crown. I slam the heel of my foot onto the toes of the lord behind me, bone crunches under my boot, then I slam a left hook into the next one who gets too close.

Callyx steps from the shadows like the angel of death and grabs Rivan, flinging him into me. "Go! I've got this." Sword swinging, dark magic pours from him, and suddenly, there are six of him standing there ready to fight.

Damn. I think he glamoured the shadows.

I drop into the darkness with Rivan and come up beside Meri, well aware we're past the window of time he gave us. "Don't say it. Just try. Please."

Rivan gathers her in his arms. Cradling her to him, he nods at me, and I send a wave of magic directly into his heart. Killing him. He erupts in faery fire, taking her with him into the afterlife, leaving their ashes behind on the floor.

My heart races as I stare at the pile on the ground, waiting for a sign. A minute ticks by. Then two. Three. Cormal looks at me, and I shake my head. Even Leandra darts a glance at the empty floor. Five minutes have passed.

Rivan promised not to return without her. Are they both gone?

Ashes swirl in the wind, creating an intricate pattern. Slowly, two bodies reform in a storm of fire.

Rivan stares down at Meri, his eyes burning with emotion. "Open your eyes, my love." His voice is firm as he calls to her. "Open your eyes."

I drop to my knees beside him. "Meri, open your fucking eyes."

Rivan shoots me a murderous look. "Come on, my love. I know you're in there. That's it. Bat those gorgeous blues at me."

Her dark lashes flutter and her turquoise eyes open, and it's the most beautiful sight I've ever seen. My hand moves up to wipe the wetness from the corner of my eye.

"I love you, Rivan."

His lips find hers in a crushing kiss. "I love you so damn much. You were almost lost to me forever." There's a break in his voice that tells me how close she was to never returning.

I take her from him. "You scared the fuck out of me." Unable to stop shaking, I wrap both of my long arms around her.

Rivan stands and taps me on the shoulder, but I hold on to her a minute longer, needing to feel her heart beating against mine. Finally, I help Meri stand between Rivan and me.

Leandra calls out, "Madoc! The power." Her finger points toward the ceiling where the black swirling ball is zipping from one side to the other.

With a pop, it disappears.

"NO! Where did it go? Bring it back, you bitch!" Denir roars, his eyes darting around the hall, desperately searching for the power.

Leandra's face is white when I give her a deathly glare. "I swear. I don't know where it went."

There's something dark behind my right shoulder. It's still

here. I feel it. Closing my eyes, I try to pinpoint it, but it's moving rapidly from one place to another.

Denir yells, and I open my eyes.

"The power is still here. Can't you feel it?" Taunting him. I know he can't feel it because it was never supposed to be his. It belongs to me.

He looks at me blankly, then shrugs off my question.

Desperate, he turns to Riona and orders her to give him all her power. She struggles, but his hand on the torque forces her to pour her magic into him.

Cormal sways, and I realize the toll it's taken to pit his magic against his sister's. They must be pretty evenly matched.

"Now, Rivan!" Cormal shouts.

Rivan's a blur as he bullets toward Denir and Riona, his hands outstretched. His body slams into theirs, knocking them to the ground.

Denir stands and peers down at his chest, his brow furrowed. Blood seeps from the outer edges of the golden scarab attached to his chest, its onyx eyes unblinking as it stares back at him.

He stumbles over to Riona and pulls her to her feet. When he sees a similar one on her chest with golden unblinking eyes, he begins to roar.

"No, no, no," he rages. His fingers claw at the edge of the scarab, trying to peel it off, but it refuses to budge.

Cormal's harsh chuckle makes Denir swing around. "I found these little beauties in the light Fae palace. In a storage room, of all places. Tossed in there like an old sword. They called to me, so I took them. It wasn't until I received Evren's note that I realized what they do. They break all binding chains, turning the master into the victim."

Denir glances from him to Riona, and he knows what will happen when she gains the upper hand. In one last burst of fury, he raises his hand, but not toward Riona. His head swivels to where Leandra stands on the sidelines, and faery fire erupts from his finger. She ducks behind the nearest pillar.

Enraged, he turns toward us, and I raise the shield I was taught from birth. The only one capable of withstanding the faery fire he flings toward us.

Cormal steps up and recites the spell on the piece of paper sent to him by Evren.

> Khepri, hear my plea
> Let the scarab sun undo
> And the scarab night release
> Undone is done

The faery fire ceases, and I lower the shield around us. Hands trembling, I fist them against my thighs. It takes a tremendous amount of power to create that particular shield.

Leandra moves out from behind the pillar to watch the scene unfold, pure satisfaction in the depths of swirling, mad-filled eyes. This is the moment she's been waiting a thousand years to see.

Dark blue eyes light up, a fierce flame in their depths. Riona cracks open the torque around her neck and destroys it. Gold dust rains to the floor. She jerks Denir to her.

"Your reign has ended. Death is your reward."

His body turns to dust in her hands.

Leandra laughs, and we all turn toward her. Dust is flaking off her skin as her body begins to decay right in front of us. "I tied my life to his long ago, but the years meant nothing without her. My revenge is complete. I go to be with my daughter." Seconds later, she, too, is gone.

The crowd looks from one to the other, then starts shouting. Callyx, Theron, and Arden move to stand with us, and we close ranks. The court pushes forward, but suddenly stops, pointing to the dais.

I follow their gaze and find the power zipping in circles around the throne. Holding out my hand, I call it. Slowly, it stops moving and turns in my direction.

A massive hand reaches out and palms the power. "I'll take that."

The crowd scrambles back a step. Massively tall, with a long beard, the fierce old man on the throne squints at me with his one eye. Hard to believe he leads The Wild Hunt.

Furious, but unable to do anything against him, I bend a knee and bow.

"Odin," I hiss at Cormal and the others. "The Wild Hunt. Kneel or die."

Cormal must decide the power Odin wields is more than he can fight because he slowly kneels beside me.

There's a collective movement as the rest of the room follows our actions.

Odin heaves a huge sigh. "Whatever. Get up. I know your respect is real." He holds out his hand and shows me the swirling orb of power. "I listened to everything and waited for the dust to settle. Unfortunately, you didn't get Leandra to transfer the power from Meri to you. According to our laws, you failed to get it back."

He stares at me with blue starry eyes. "This predicament pisses me off because I do think the power should be yours, but rules are rules. You have to earn it. To get it back, you'll have to run the gauntlet." Standing to his full six feet nine inches, he lowers his brows and jerks me to him. "The clearing in the Wilds. You know the place. Midnight. Tomorrow. Bring them with you."

In a flash, he disappears.

Lifting my chin, I pivot to face the dark Fae court with my usual scowl. "This might take another night to resolve, but make no mistake, the crown will be mine."

Oryn walks up to the dais where Riona stands and takes her hand in his.

Standing beside the throne, I watch the crowd digest what just happened. Denir is gone. I'm likely going to be their next king. One they tried to kill. Without a single acknowledgement, they shuffle out the door, murmuring amongst themselves.

Cormal jumps up on the dais and strides over to his sister. He reaches over to hug her, but she backs away. She rips the scarab off her chest and studies it closely. He points to the eyes, then steps over and grabs the one from the pile of dust on the floor and shows it to her as well. Hand outstretched, he waits for her to give it back to him, which she does.

"The kingdom will be in an uproar until Madoc gains his power. If you want to stay at my place in The Underworld, it will be safe for you," he offers in a gruff voice. Unable to take his eyes off her, he scans her from head to toe. "I never forgot you. All these years, I searched and searched. Became immortal so I could continue to look for you. I followed up on every lead. That's how I found you. Oryn asked about your background, and one of my spies reported it back to me."

Riona's blue eyes flicker to Oryn, then down to their linked hands. "Thank you."

Oryn sweeps a piece of hair behind her shoulder. "I could see you in there. Once I realized he was controlling you, I tried to find more information on your background so I could figure out what to do."

Meri goes up to them and holds out her hand toward Riona. Her wide smile must convince Cormal's sister that she's not a threat because she grasps her hand. "I'm Meri. Cormal's better half. If you want to know anything about him, ask me. Him and I have known each other for a long time."

Riona's smile is weak, but it's the first one she's given. "Nice to meet you." For a second, she pauses, then continues, "I'm sorry. I don't remember him."

Meri pats her hand. "It's okay. It will come back to you. Give it time." She flicks a glance at Cormal. "The first thing we need to do is get you away from here."

Oryn steps forward. "I've got a small place by the lake in Winter. She'll be protected on Theron's land. It's peaceful too."

Meri raises an eyebrow. "What do you think? Does that sound good?"

Riona slips her hand from Meri's and gives a firm nod. "For now."

Cormal steps forward and holds out his hand. "Please. For a second. I need to know you're real."

When she places her hand in his, his emotions break and his eyes water with unshed tears. "It feels so good to see you, but touching you reassures me this isn't a dream. Thank you."

She pulls her hand from his. "Can we go now?"

Oryn hesitates, his eyes sliding toward Cormal. "Let her decompress for a couple of days. I'll call you every day and give you an update on her progress."

Cormal reluctantly agrees, and Meri takes his hand in hers. They stand there while Riona and Oryn walk away.

Meri throws her arms around him and squeezes him tightly. "She'll come around. Give her time."

He takes a deep breath. "I know." He lifts her chin and kisses her deeply, devouring her lips for several minutes. "That's the last fucking time I want to see you dead. Do you hear me?" His blue eyes glance at me. "Can we get the fuck out of here now?"

Rivan turns toward me. "What the hell is the gauntlet?"

"It's a brutal test of strength and endurance. Pain delivered at the hands of the elite soldiers and monsters of The Wild Hunt. The last, and only person, to come out of it alive was Konnyr," I explain. A laugh bubbles up and escapes my infamous control. Everyone stops to stare at me. "I'm literally fucked."

"First, we need to take care of them," Meri reminds me, pointing to the two piles of dust.

I'm tempted to have the servants sweep Denir out with the trash, but he did rule for three thousand years. Beckoning one of the brownies over to me, I motion to Denir's remains. "Please see to it that he's buried in the royal crypt."

She nods, and with a twirl of her finger, scoops him into a royal-looking vase and seals it, then heads out the side door.

Meri walks over to the pile on the floor. With a wave of her hand, she conjures a water pitcher and magically scoops up Leandra's ashes. "Remind me to replace the one at The Abbey."

Cormal steps forward and places a hand on her back. "Where do you want to take her?"

"To the Flames of Hell," Meri replies thoughtfully. "Her soul is gone to be with her daughter, but I want there to be zero chance she'll be resurrected by anyone."

I turn to Arden, Theron, and Callyx. "I can't thank you enough for all of your help. I'm not used to having friends. But I know we couldn't have done this without you. We'll return to The Abbey once we take care of Leandra's ashes."

MERI STANDS at the edge of the black, jagged cliffs. The Flames of Hell burn below us, a field of eternal death. She taps the glass with her nail as she chews on her bottom lip. "I don't know what to say. All these years, I never thought I was enough. Not enough power, not smart enough or mean enough or pretty enough. The list goes on and on."

She shakes her head, then smiles. "Now I know she never even saw me as a person. I was a tool for revenge. Nothing more or less. Honestly, I don't know if she could care for anything. Her heart died with her daughter. She chose her path a long time ago."

Tipping over the pitcher, she pours the ashes into the fire

below. "Today, I take with me the lessons of the past but not the bitterness of it. Strength. Courage. Freedom. Love. Those are the pillars of the path I choose to follow going forward. Our destiny is ours to define." She tosses the empty pitcher into the fire, turns her back, and throws her arms around the three of us. "Right?"

My heart swells with her words. "Fuck yeah it is. Let's get out of here."

CHAPTER THIRTY

MERI

Leandra and Denir vanquished. Cormal's sister saved. Power removed. We're alive. All wins. Yet Madoc faces another trial, and according to him, only one other Fae has ever survived it. Biting my lip, I try to squelch the fear rising in me. At least we get to come with him.

Alia. Leandra's revenge for her daughter's death may end up costing thousands of Fae their lives. Tensions are high among the light Fae. Many are picking to fight with the Fire Fae instead of holding out hope for the rights the treaty promises. Dark Fae, especially the Lesser Fae, were already leaving to join the revolution, and the death of King Denir will only increase their numbers by the thousands.

The light Elven land is still in chaos, according to Fallon. His mad father the king rules a small portion of the kingdom, but the rest are trying to understand the benefits of freedom. He's helping them establish a coalition to continue their commerce with other realms and lands. It's slow going. Most Elven are used to the land and king providing for their needs, but he says they're finally starting to understand that establishing a strong economy is necessary for their future.

The dark Elves are flourishing under Arden's father's rule. All the years he spent as one of the people helped him gain valuable insights into the challenges they face in their daily lives. He's been working to establish rights for all his people. Arden said he's using the treaty we drew up with Fisk as a guideline.

If Madoc doesn't get the crown, what will become of the Fae? If he does get the crown, he'll have to go to war.

The Water Fae were content with the treaty to establish their rights. They dreamed of owning land in the Light Fae Kingdom and passing down those rights of equality to their children.

The Fire Fae sneer at the same rights, demanding their freedom. But I see the feverish light burning in their eyes. The repression they've endured for years. They want war.

The three of them find me on the roof, staring out at the massive city surrounding The Abbey. A mix of supernaturals and humans, it accepts everyone. Is this the future? Will the individual lands and realms eventually wither or implode until all that's left is this one?

"Mm, we thought we'd find you here," Rivan remarks, jumping up on the ledge to peer at the people on the streets. "It's hard to think of living in a place like this with no space to breathe. Everyone scurries from one place to another. Pockets of community but no tribes."

Cormal lifts a shoulder. "I quite like the teeming masses of sin and corruption. Maybe I should open up a casino here. The profit margins would be astronomical and the seedy underbelly a bottomless source for The Underworld's eclectic tastes."

I raise an eyebrow. "You mean the demons who would pay you to point out a greedy customer or one willing to sell their soul."

Cormal's grin is sin itself. "Exactly."

Madoc stares up at the sky. "I want to go home. Where the constellations differ, and the land is as familiar as the lines on my hand. You can't even wear a damn sword here."

Sensing his turmoil, I wrap my arms around him. "What you have survived, no other Fae can claim. Not even your precious Konnyr. Monsters so dark and depraved they can only live in The Below." He drops his head to look at me. "How long were you there again? Ten years? A hundred? Nope. You're badass. Spending three thousand years in the blackest of holes. The gauntlet should be a piece of cake."

He snorts, but I can see his mind restructuring itself.

I trace a few of his worst scars. "Maybe you'll even get some new souvenirs."

Shockingly, he winks. "Only for you."

Rivan jumps down and picks up his backpack. "I've picked out a few runes I think will work for what you've described. Still within the rules. None of them will dull the pain as they strike you, but once you're through, the numbness and healing will kick in."

Madoc stares at him in surprise.

Rivan tilts his head. "We're in this together. The four of us. Forever, right? I'm sure as hell not leaving Meri, even if I have to put up with the two of you. I know Cormal's never going away. What about you?"

Madoc walks over to the nearby table and chairs. "I'm in. For all of it." His steel-grey eyes soften when they turn toward me. "Where should I put this new ink?"

My gaze drops to his cock, but his fierce expression makes me burst out laughing. "I'm kidding. A piercing, maybe, but not a rune."

"Why don't we create a design on your bicep? An intricate link of the runes interlaced with geometric shapes. Very few will be able to see the difference," Rivan suggests, sketching a quick design to show Madoc.

Madoc grumbles but agrees.

Cormal keeps staring at his phone.

"She may not even understand the whole phone thing," I remind him. "Once we get back, call Oryn. See if you can have coffee or tea with her. And him, of course. I doubt she's ready to do things on her own."

He puts his phone in his pocket and wraps his arms around me. "I still can't believe we found her. Alive. I'm incredibly grateful."

"But you wanted your sister Ri´ back, not Riona, who has lived under Denir's thumb for such a long time," I remark. "It's too early to know what she'll remember. Stop being impatient."

He chuckles and places his chin on my head. "Mm, bossy. Maybe I should put you in charge of my new casino."

I wrinkle my nose. "Not on your life. Although once this is over, I want to find something to do. Maybe help the Fae get their rights."

All three of them nod. "Maybe there's something we can all do."

Rivan finishes tattooing the design onto Madoc's arm. "Done." He glances around. "Anyone else want one?"

I prop my arm on the table. "I do. Something pretty and useful. You pick."

Rivan takes my hand and turns it over until the underside of my arm is facing up. "It's something I drew up the other day. Three images in a line." He pulls out the paper from his box of inks, and I smile when I see it.

"Perfect," I tell him. "And I want my clarity tattoo back, please."

For the next hour, we all ignore the ticking of the clock as we spend the time relaxing in the afternoon sun, basking in its warmth, and joking with each other. Madoc slips up and smiles twice, which thrills me but earns him harsh taunts from the other two.

Rivan puts away his tools and peers down at my inner arm in satisfaction. "I'll have to finish your palm another day."

"I love them. Thank you." I raise my face to his for a sweet kiss, but Madoc pushes him away and claims it for himself.

The sun sets, and we all stand.

Madoc isn't sure why they want us to come too, and it makes him uneasy. Aamon is already in their camp, but he feels we should bring Lux, too. Cormal thinks it will be a disaster, but he wants someone who will protect me, and Lux is the best option. The Wild Hunt won't let anyone in, but Lux, like Aamon, is unique.

"It will take us a few hours to get to the clearing," Madoc informs us. "We need to gather supplies and be ready to leave within the hour." He shakes his head when Cormal opens his mouth. "We can only portal to the edge of the Wilds. We have to hike to get to the clearing."

It doesn't take long to pull together the necessities. Blankets, water, food, weapons, a massive first aid kit, and several lighters. When I question the number, Madoc gruffly informs me that cauterizing bleeding wounds works the best. Okay. Good to know.

Everyone is at the portal when we get there. Their faces are carefully blank, which is worse than sad or grim.

I shake my head. "When we return, we're celebrating, got it? Callyx, Lucifer, Evren, Kavi, Oryn, Ri', and everyone else in this big family of ours. Got it?"

Refusing to give anyone a hug, I enter the portal, after Madoc, and find Lux waiting for us on the other side.

"Meri!" he squeals in delight.

"Lux!" I squeal right back, making him dance around in happiness.

The other two men step through and join us.

Madoc takes the lead, Cormal the rear. Rivan, Lux, and me in the middle.

Wide-eyed, I step into the Wilds and find myself completely enchanted with the world around me.

Madoc gets in my face. "Don't touch one fucking thing along the way. I mean it. The Wilds are a mixture of wonder and death. Pretty things are deceitful. Plants have a mind of their own. Everything will take a bite out of you. Some will devour you. Got it?"

I put my hands behind my back. "Got it."

Lux nods his head. "Dangerous. Don't touch."

Well, damn, if Lux thinks it's dangerous, that's bad. "Thanks, friend."

He grins up at me. "You can hold my hand."

Probably for the best. Ignoring temptation was never my strong suit. "Thanks, I will." Grasping his strong, leathery hand in mine, we swing our arms between us.

Cormal mutters curse words behind us.

Lux darts a glance at me, and I whisper, "He's just upset he doesn't have a friend to hold his hand."

"Fucking hell, Meri," Cormal bites out. "I'm fine, Lux…. Maybe a little bit grumpy." His blue eyes flash a warning look at me.

It takes us three hours to get to the clearing, and I could have sworn we were going in circles, passing the same trees and flowers several times, but Madoc assures me that's not the case.

Madoc walks up to the widest and tallest tree I've ever seen and knocks on it. He listens intently, then pricks his finger and smears it on the bark. A door opens in the trunk, and we walk through the tree into a small city.

"In the old days, it was a clearing with huts and campfires," Rivan murmurs to me. "Over the years, they've picked up small modern conveniences."

I swivel to look at him. "You didn't tell me you'd been here before. Does Madoc know?"

He shakes his head. "As a daughter of Avalon, my mother was often called to obscure places. She came here to tattoo runes when requested. I usually went with her."

"Every day, you surprise me," I whisper back. "What an incredible story."

As we near the main area, Odin appears with several large men and women. Muscular, fit, wearing a plethora of weapons. Warriors. Part of The Wild Hunt?

"Welcome," he greets us. "Feel free to mingle, grab some food, or catch a nap. The gauntlet begins in an hour at the stroke of midnight."

A gorgeous red-haired woman eyes me with curiosity.

"Hello, I'm Meri," I say, introducing myself.

She tilts her head, studying me intently. "Brynhildr. You're the queen who gave up her crown."

"Good news travels fast," I quip. "Can you point me to the restroom?"

She lifts a leather clad arm and points to a small building nearby. "Why?"

I pause and turn back toward her. "Family is everything. Blood or not, I'll do whatever it takes to keep mine."

Hmph. Maybe Leandra taught me something after all. By not seeing me as anything but a tool of revenge, she lost out on the daughter she could have had all those years. Smiling, I turn on my heel and head toward the building.

Expecting an outhouse situation, I'm pleasantly surprised to find real bathrooms. After finishing, I step outside and find Lux standing near Aamon.

"Aamon," I say, smiling up at him. "We've missed you. Tell me how you like living here? It seems nice. Have you made any friends?"

He motions for us both to follow him. I glance around and

find Madoc staring at us with a bemused expression on his face. Cormal, on the other hand, is scowling. I swear. It's like they've switched places today. I motion walking with Aamon, and Madoc nods.

Aamon takes us to the training gym. The mess hall. And last, his house, which he shares with a few other equally terrifying creatures. He introduces each one, and I shake their hands.

One snarls at me, but Lux turns on him. "She's my friend. Be nice."

The beast's dark eyes shift from Lux to Aamon to me, then slinks away.

"Friend?" another asks.

Lux explains to them what friend means with Aamon nodding in agreement, and I couldn't be prouder of them.

My phone's alarm goes off, causing everyone to scramble, but I quickly calm them down by showing them the phone. For a couple minutes, they all clamor to hear the different sounds it makes.

"We have to go," I tell Aamon. "It's almost time."

I say goodbye to Aamon's friends and follow him to the gauntlet.

He grabs my hand, and I squeeze it. "He'll be fine. Madoc's tough."

I don't know whether I'm reassuring him or myself.

Lux grabs my other hand, and I hold on to them both.

CHAPTER THIRTY-ONE

<u>MADOC</u>

Meri strides toward us with Lux and Aamon by her side. She doesn't see the younglings following in the shadows behind her, nor the warriors of the hunt studying her closely. Her ability to adapt and find joy in any environment used to puzzle me, but after visiting a few of her many different homes, I know it's how she coped and found a little beauty in her life.

The relief on Cormal's face is almost comical. "Where the hell have you been?"

"Seeing Aamon's new place and meeting his friends," she replies, deliberately rolling her eyes. "How are you doing?" She scans my face as if she's trying to delve below the surface, but I don't dare show her how much I'm dreading the gauntlet.

"Ready to go home," I growl, needing a reminder of what comes after this. The four of us. Together.

Rivan comes up and joins us.

"We're going to need to find a place," she pertly informs me. "Several places, actually. Cormal needs a sinful city with lots of secrets. Rivan needs to breathe and fly. You need less technology and lots of swords. All those homes need to also have a fantastic rooftop for us to peer at the stars."

"What do you need?" Rivan questions softly.

"I need all of you," she answers before looking at me. "So, go, run the gauntlet. Do not let them take you down. And don't forget to think outside the box. Got it?" Her voice is sharp and full of determination.

"Keep your shield up," I order her. "It's not like I'll be able to come to your aid."

She moves into my arms and presses her lips to mine. "I'm quite obsessed with you, you know."

I press my forehead to hers, then slip on the meanest, surliest look I own.

"It's time," Odin informs me. "Here are the rules. No shields. You cannot use magic to dull the pain. No fighting back. Ten lashes delivered one at a time by weapon, hand, or claw. You must make it past the line at the end. Good luck."

Basically, walk the gauntlet, let them strike me ten times, get to the finish line. Got it. I clasp arms with both Rivan and Cormal. "If something happens…"

"Shut the fuck up," Cormal snarls. "Tell me the rules again." He nods as I repeat the words Odin gave me.

Rivan claps me on the back. "The runes will kick in the second you finish to ease the pain."

Meri sends Lux and Aamon to join the crowd on the sidelines. "Whatever you do, don't interfere." They both promise to stay put.

Not wanting anything to get embedded in the wounds, I remove my shirt and pants. I hear the crowd point and whisper, but unlike most of the Fae, they appreciate the scars on my body. Warrior, I hear them say. I lift my chin and walk to the start line.

The bells strike midnight. When the last one tolls, I step onto the gauntlet. Neither looking right nor left, I stare straight ahead, desperately wanting to brace against the first hit but knowing it will only make it worse. Loosening my muscles, I hear the sound of a heavy chain whooshing through the air.

Wrapping around my arms and torso, barbed spikes embed themselves in my skin. The chain tightens, then loosens, dropping to the ground, leaving sheer agony in its wake. Blood flows like a river to my feet. Breathing through the pain, I swallow several times to give myself something to do besides scream. First hits are always the hardest, right?

Exhaling, I loosen my muscles and step forward again. There is no sound or warning this time. Four sharp points embed themselves in my shoulder and swipe diagonally across my back. Claws. Deep too. The night air slips into the furrows left behind going at least an inch deeper than the skin left intact.

Mother fucker. Son of a bitch. The litany of silent curses continues as I fight to keep my body loose and step forward again.

The gleam of metal flashes in front of me as the scythe slices across my chest, the curved hook doing the most damage as it catches on my side. The wielder grunts and jerks it out, leaving a gaping hole behind. I peer down and see a glint of white mixed in with the blood, tissue, and muscles. Are those my ribs?

Number fucking four.

I take a deep breath and step forward. Bright flames circle around me, then tighten around my calves, burning through the layers of skin and muscle. Gagging, I concentrate on keeping my food down. The wind blows through the gauntlet, and the cool night air brings a new level of excruciating punishment as it sweeps across the charred flesh. My legs weaken, but I lock my knees and thighs to keep myself upright.

Lasso of fire. I know who wields that weapon. Big, bald asshole. I picture myself wrapping it around his neck and tying it to the nearest tall tree. Fury fills me, eclipsing the pain.

Inhaling, I hold my breath, then slowly release it and step forward.

A large swoosh of air and pain explodes in the back of my head. Everything blurs. Stumbling, I fight to not step forward or go down.

Number fucking five was a bitch. My shoulders slump as the thought of five more hits like that one, or worse. Breathing in and out, I think of all I have endured to get to this point. Three thousand years in a pitch black hole tormented by my fellow inmates. Why? Because I was born to be king. *The best rulers always have the hardest paths.* I remind myself. It makes them a better leader. Look at Lucifer. Meri.

Straightening, I breathe in and take the next step. Water pours down on me in a deluge, stripping the air from my lungs, splaying my cuts wide open, running into every wound on my body, and driving nails into the burns with its piercing coldness. I wait for it to stop, but it doesn't.

Breath running out, I step forward... into a shredding machine. Or at least that's what it feels like. Hundreds of small cuts appear across my body. Jaw and fists clenched, I arch my back, trying to get away from the pain, but it's everywhere, and all at once. Blood flows like a river to the ground at my feet.

"I'll take the next hit," Cormal's voice rings out across the gauntlet.

Everything falls silent.

Odin's booming voice rings out. "Madoc must run the gauntlet."

"He is, and he will continue his walk to the end of the line, but nothing in the rules prevents me from taking the next one in his place," Cormal argues.

"Let us confer," Odin says, a note of irritation in his voice.

Voices rise and fall to my left. Swaying back and forth, I wait. At least the knives have stopped cutting.

"This is unprecedented, but you're right, we didn't make a rule against it," Odin concedes gruffly. "Why are you doing this for him?"

"The bastard is family," Cormal drawls. "I sure as hell didn't pick him, but Meri did, so there you go. How is this going to work?"

Odin chuckles. "Meet him on the gauntlet. You step forward first and take the hit. He follows."

Fury rises as he moves to stand next to me. "What the fuck are you doing?"

"Playing by the rules," Cormal retorts. "Kind of surprised me, too. I'm usually looking to break them." He takes a deep breath. "This is going to hurt like hell, isn't it? Got any tips?"

"Why?" I press.

"Because you would do the same for me," he states confidently.

He's right. I would. "Don't brace."

Muscles loosen, and he steps forward.

I watch twin swords pierce each of his sides, skewering him in the middle. Veins pop out of his neck and colorful curses fill the air. He rises on his toes, as if to escape the pain. They retract, and he clamps a hard hand on each side as if he's trying to hold in the pain.

I step to his side. "Brutal. You're right. If I had to watch that six more times, I'd have stepped in too."

Cormal's voice is strained. "Honestly, not as bad as I thought. The scythe and club were much worse."

"Is that what hit my head? Almost took me out," I admit with a pained chuckle.

"I'll take the next hit." Rivan's voice rings out in the night air.

"Mother fucker," Cormal and I say in unison.

Odin curses. "Fuck me! This is the first gauntlet we've had in thousands of years, and you're ruining it. We need to make stricter rules. Somebody write that down. Damn it. Go on."

Rivan steps up beside us. "Can't have you two taking all the glory. Plus, the big fucker taking the next hit appears entirely too happy."

Tempted to look to my right, I turn toward Rivan instead and warn him, "Don't brace."

He flashes a broad smile. "Got it." Taking a step forward, he waits.

Two large hands appear with metal claws attached. They embed themselves at his neck and shred his skin from his shoulders to his feet.

I wait for him to yell or curse or anything, but he's completely silent.

When we step up next to him, there's a painful smile on his face.

"The first time Meri and I met, Nyssa threw one of her tantrums. She hated my runes and the protection they provided against her. In her fury, she shredded my skin," he confides, the darkness of the past straining his voice. "I didn't want to regenerate because it would take me weeks to add them again. Meri understood. She stayed with me for three days until I healed."

He turns his head toward us. "Leandra couldn't have been too happy, but Meri never said anything about it."

Sometimes I wonder if The Below was the better deal. Three thousand years of Nyssa and I would have been completely psychotic.

Odin's voice calls out. "If you move from the line, you'll have to start over. Do you understand?"

Confused, we all three look at each other and it hits us.

Meri's voice carries across the gauntlet. "I..."

We step forward, taking the last hit together. Darts hit our neck. Seconds later, liquid fire courses through our veins, burning everything in its path.

"Step forward," Rivan gasps. "You have to go first."

In a haze, I move, and the second my foot touches the finish line, the pain disappears. The wounds are still there in all their gory glory, but the pain is gone.

Cormal and Rivan step forward and stop the platinum tornado hurtling herself toward us.

"What the hell were you thinking?" I whisper furiously at her. "Never. Do you hear me? I'll never let you stand in and take a hit for me. I would rather die."

Both Rivan and Cormal agree.

Meri laughs. "Never is a long time. Besides, the natives were getting restless." She waves a hand to the ten on the sidelines. Monsters, warriors, and other creatures. "Who knows what they would have come up with next?"

Odin walks over to us. "Congratulations and all that. Unorthodox, but you made it. The power and crown are yours."

He moves to Meri, and I tense. "The younglings enjoyed your visit today. They want you to come back." His face is set as if he expects her to reject his invitation.

Meri's eyes fill with tears, and Odin hurriedly steps backward.

"I would love to," she says with a sniff. "Everybody needs friends, right?"

Odin looks nonplussed, and I laugh. "That's how it starts. You'll never get rid of her."

She glares at me but turns to wave at the stands. "I'll miss you, but I'll return as soon as I can."

Cormal mutters under his breath, cursing me and my unusual lineage.

Rivan steps to the side and regenerates, returning minutes later with smooth skin.

Cormal's sides slowly knit themselves back together.

My skin tightens as the healing process starts, and I can't

help but be thankful for Rivan's runes. If not, this would be near impossible to endure.

Odin steps in front of me, the orb of power in his right hand, and I realize this is the last step of the gauntlet. He slams it into my body. Scar tissue separates, opening a hole for the power. Ancient and dark, it warps and shapes itself, testing the boundaries around it, then settles in, waiting for me to call it forward.

Odin's satisfied nod tells me he's happy. "You're strong like Konnyr. You'll need it. The world is changing, leaving the old ways behind. The Fae need a leader who won't be afraid to forge a new path."

Lux skips over and takes Meri's hand. "Are we ready to go?"

She looks at me, and I wave goodbye to Aamon. "Let's go home."

CHAPTER THIRTY-TWO

<u>MERI</u>

Coronation preparations take a week to pull together. Unlike Denir, Madoc invites all the rulers he favors as a friend or an ally. A show of strength to reassure both the aristocratic dark Fae and the Lesser Fae of his authority to rule and the clout the Dark Fae Kingdom will again enjoy under his reign.

I'm getting ready in the room I claimed because it's big enough for all of us. Huge windows showcase the sweeping vista of the land around us. From the sea on the left to the tiniest glimpse of Winter and its snowcapped mountains on the right, the view is remarkable.

Madoc told me the room hadn't been used in several lifetimes, but when I saw the light from the windows, I was sold. The furnishings and colors, ice-blue and gold, are a bit old-fashioned for my taste. Something I plan to change in the future.

Tonight's theme is starry night, and the dress code is blue. Any shade. Needing to wow, I went to the definitive source of fabulous royal fashion… Solandis. She helped design the dress I'm wearing. Unfortunately, the baby's birth is too close for her to travel, so I'm getting dressed with her over video conference.

I put the dress on and spritz myself with my favorite nighttime perfume, a heady rich mixture of scents like musk, vanilla, bergamot, and orange blossom. Moving close to the camera, I point out the details.

"Stunning. I'm dying. You outdid yourself."

Strapless, the inner dress flows from the tops of my breasts to my toes. The deepest color of night, it has no adornments. Solandis said she designed it that way to give me the illusion of height and the epitome of regalness. From the center column, airy layers attach to the waist. Each one embroidered with a constellation of stars only found in the Dark Fae Kingdom. Under the flickering candlelight chandelier, the diamonds sewn into the dress sparkle on their own, but with a little magic—presto—the stars twinkle with the exact cadence of the actual star in the sky.

She insisted I leave my hair down, and as I pick up the headpiece, I understand why. In the center is a large glowing star.

"That should be centered on your forehead," Solandis advises. She pauses while I slip it on. "That's it. Each strand of diamonds will loop behind your head into a cluster, then cascade down. When you use magic to light the dress, the stars on the headpiece will also light up."

"Amazing," I breathe, staring at the vision in the mirror. "Have you ever thought of doing this for a living? Not that you need the money, but you could make a fortune."

Her twinkling laugh is a melody of amusement. "It's fun. If I made a living, it would be work. Step out farther. I want to see the entire picture."

I move away from the camera and slowly twirl around once with the magic off, then again with it on.

"Absolute perfection," she squeals from the other side of the room. "I believe I outdid myself on this one."

"You certainly did," Madoc interjects in a gruff voice. "Thank you, Solandis. This means a lot to Meri and me."

She sniffs. "Pregnancy hormones. Don't mind me. It's time. Go, darling. Dance and drink champagne for me. Love you."

I blow her a kiss. "Thank you, thank you, thank you. Love you, too. Give Vargas a hug from me and tell him we miss him, too." Ending the video, I close the lid.

Tall, dark, well-built, Madoc is a king in his dark-navy tail-coat jacket with diamonds embroidered down one side, including the adjoining arm. The other half of his jacket, as well as the vest and suit underneath, is the same dark blue color as my inner dress.

"Hmm, guess Solandis felt we should match," I muse, straightening the cravat at his throat. I gather one of the airy panels at my waist. "The constellations of your kingdom."

He stares down at it and clears his throat. "You remembered."

"Of course," I reply with a wink. "I remember everything you do or say. Obsessed, remember?"

Strong hands grab my waist and pull me closer. His mouth descends on mine with passion and need, kissing me until I run out of breath. Releasing me, his eyes dip to my swollen lips. "I want every male in the room to know you are mine. Ready?"

Chuckling, I smooth the dress and flick my hand to turn on the magic. "A little possessive, don't you think?"

"Not in the least," he returns, slipping a finger into his cravat to tug on it. "I really don't want to kill someone tonight. It would ruin my good mood."

"Stop, you can remove it after the ceremony," I order him,

brushing his hand away from his neck. "The man makes the outfit, but the suit emphasizes the king you were born to be. And you're right. You should refrain from killing anyone tonight. Unless they deserve it."

He stops fidgeting as we reach the doors. "Cormal and Rivan are already inside. Once the crown is on my head, you must leave the dais and stand with them."

Surprised to see a glimmer of worry, I lift an eyebrow but agree. "Okay."

The double doors open wide, and we enter the great hall together. Madoc insisted I be on his arm tonight. He refused to listen to any advice on the contrary from his council of advisors. In his words, he wanted everyone to know my importance. When they insisted, he threw them out of the room. Whether he'll let them in again depends on whether they prove themselves to him.

All eyes turn toward us. There are a few sneers from those who aren't happy seeing the former light Fae queen on the arm of their soon-to-be-crowned king. Madoc stops in front of one of the dissenters, tilts his head, and orders him to get out.

The Fae opens his mouth, but I shake my head and whisper to him, "Banishment or death. He's an all-or-nothing kind of Fae."

He swallows hard and walks stiffly out the door.

There's a gleam of approval in Madoc's eye when he looks at me, although his face remains set in its usual harsh lines.

We begin the procession to the throne again. This time, there are no sneers from the crowd. They can try to hide, but I'm sure he's already taken note of them all. Arden and Theron, or rather Lady Arden of Winter and Lord Theron of Winter, dip their heads as we pass by. Her blond locks are coiled in an elegant chignon at the base of her neck, and the teal of her strapless ballgown picks up her green eyes. She's absolutely gorgeous. Theron matches her dress in a suit of the same color. Blond and elegant, both of them.

Fallon stands regally on Arden's other side in a formal navy outfit with a teal cravat. His dark hair and startling green eyes have all the females around him twittering, not that he notices. Beside him, Astor's auburn hair is a great contrast to the outlandish blue ombre suit he wears with a teal flower in its lapel and a devilish smile on his handsome incubus face. Valerian, who usually towers over most of the crowd, actually fits in with the tall Fae. He's striking in his official royal-blue suit that announces his own kingly status to everyone. His only concession is a teal cravat.

On the other side of Valerian is Daire. Almost austere in a deep-navy suit, Daire's blond hair and blue eyes stand out. His teal shirt proclaims him as Arden's companion.

Lucifer is next. Both he and the gorgeous redhead and goddess, Evren, are wearing black, but they've added a small blue star to their outfits to pay homage to Madoc. Lucifer's arm is possessively around her waist as his eyes scan the males nearest to them. She winks when I pass, and I smile in return.

Oryn is every bit as elegant and formal as his brother in a navy suit, which suits his blond hair and brown eyes. Riona, beautiful in a royal-blue dress, holds tightly to his arm, unsure of her place in this gathering. I smile at her, and she flashes a tremulous smile in return.

Torin, Arden's father and King of the Dark Elves, in his official uniform is next. Surprisingly, Odin stands with him, looking extremely uncomfortable in a modern suit, his hands tugging at the shirt around his neck. I glance at Madoc and see the corner of his lips twitch.

Inhaling sharply, I stare at the last two men and lick my lips. Dressed the same as Madoc, there is no doubt we're all together. Both their eyes widen when we get closer. Cormal's appreciative glint is full of wicked intent, and Rivan's amber gold eyes are full of heat.

Moving to the dais, Madoc sits on the throne. Unlike the light Fae ceremony, the crown is simply placed on his head. Once he activates the power inside him, the crown becomes his.

Similar to the throne, the spiky crown is made of black obsidian and shines in the light. There is no other adornment. It's harsh like the land and the king who will bear the crown. I pick it up and place it on his head. Blowing him a kiss, I take Cormal's hand and step off the dais.

Madoc stands and murmurs the incantation to call forth the power. Darkness whirls around him, languidly at first, then with increasing urgency. His body begins to transform, getting larger and larger, until he stands considerably taller than the rest of us. Black hair cascades down his back. Muscles bulge across the length of him. He roars, and a spear appears in his hand. In this form, he's one of The Wild Hunt. Stepping from the dais, he makes his way to Odin and bows.

Odin reaches out his hand and places it on top of his head. "King Madoc of the Dark Fae Kingdom and Magni of The Wild Hunt. Two names. One body. Called to serve both."

Rising, Madoc makes his way back to the throne. His eyes meet mine on the way, and I murmur the word he loves to hear. "Obsessed."

He growls, and my breath catches.

Reversing the magic, his body transforms to his Fae form, scars and all. But instead of returning to the throne, he remains standing in front of the audience.

The entire room begins to bow or curtsy, but he stops them by holding up his hand. "The Dark Fae Kingdom is the only thing that keeps the Fae lands from being overrun with the creatures of the Wilds. We will not fail in our stewardship of this sacred duty to protect them and the people of this land. Nor will we allow our people to force the will of one group over the other. This has been allowed for far too long. The aristocratic lords and ladies have a duty to the entire kingdom, not just the ones they choose to acknowledge. As king, I hereby decree that we are Dark Fae. All of us. No one will be called Lesser. Titles will be held by those willing to find solutions for this kingdom, not given by the right of birth."

He looks at Lucifer and Evren. "Changes are coming. We will learn from the light Fae and The Underworld, building schools for learning and the trades." His eyes find Fallon, who's been building a coalition of trades people in his land. "The days of old are waning. We must be ready to meet the dawn with new ideas and a willingness to serve the entire kingdom. There are plenty of resources and wealth in this land. Enough for everyone to carve a piece for themselves. I plan to create the opportunities, but to succeed, the people must be willing to work and contribute. More to come, but these are the tenants of my promise to the people as their new king."

His words strike a mixed reaction in the crowd, but he knew they would. Nobody likes change. The Fae least of all. But like it or not, they must embrace the needs of the people with a world that better fits with this modern age.

He steps down from the dais and stands at the foot. All three of us walk over, showing solidarity with him. Lucifer walks forward, with Evren on his arm, and reaches out his hand.

"Well done," he assures him. "The Underworld is your ally and will be available if you should need us." It's apparent he thinks war is coming.

Evren reaches out and clasps his hand. "I'm almost done with our university. When you're ready to start planning, give me a call."

Lucifer sighs. "The projects never end, do they?"

She elbows him in the side. "I would drive you crazy without them and you know it." She laughs when he winks and vehemently disagrees with a carefully tossed out "never."

Arden and her men come up, along with Torin, her father.

"I have a feeling we'll be seeing you soon," Torin says with a rueful look. "Even the small rights I've established have caused riots and upheaval, but we don't have an army at our door waiting to wage war."

"If we're going to survive the next millennium and flourish, we have to put a stake in the ground," Madoc states firmly.

Arden and her men offer their congratulations and their support, including the men they lead.

A tall, auburn-haired man comes up with a slender, blond lady on his arm. "This is a disgrace. Denir would have never treated us this way. If he were here…"

Madoc cuts him off. "If he were here, I'd put him in the grave. Never mistake me for my weak cousin. You won't like the consequences, Lord Edsel of the Autumn Court."

Furious, the man stomps off into the crowd.

I lean over and whisper, "You might have to replace him." Then I shrug. "Or send him to war. I doubt he'd survive."

Rivan laughs, but Madoc stares after the Fae with a pensive expression on his face.

At the end of the night, we tally up the wins and losses. It's about fifty-fifty, for and against Madoc. Too bad. He's their king.

Cormal strides into the hall. "The messengers have been sent to every corner of the kingdom heralding King Madoc. Our countdown has begun."

Madoc gives him a solemn nod. "Thanks."

"Did you see Riona? She was beautiful," I tell Cormal. "It must have been hard for her to return. Maybe we can have her over for dinner in The Underworld. She might feel more at home there, like you do."

Cormal runs his hand down the back of my cheek. "Good idea. I'll text Riona in the morning and see how she feels. Oryn's at least got her texting, which is a relief. I like knowing I can get a hold of her."

I gather up my dress and start walking out the door.

"Where are you going?" Cormal asks with a frown.

Deliberately sending the three of them a naughty image of the underwear I had made for this special occasion, I step into the shadows and head toward our room.

CHAPTER THIRTY-THREE

<u>MERI</u>

They arrive seconds after I do. Standing in the middle of the room, wearing a scrap of deep blue silk between my legs and an equally see-through strapless bra, I take a sip of the champagne I left chilling before the ceremony. Bubbles tickle my nose, and I laugh.

"To King Madoc, may your obsessions drive you wild, your tongue lap the sweetest of juices, and your cock last all night long." I giggle, taking another sip. "There's a glass for everyone."

Rivan peels off his clothes in slow motion, and I watch him reveal every inch of his burnished skin. He curls his fingers, and I sashay over to him in my heels and run a finger down his hard chest to his cut abs, then below. I take a drink of the champagne, then tip the glass, spilling a good amount down his body.

Following it with my tongue, I taste and lick every muscle covered in the sweet juice. Then I take him into my mouth and swirl my tongue around him. "You taste better than the champagne."

His hand tunnels into my hair and presses against my head.

Opening wider, he slips in deeper, and I moan around the length of him. My cheeks hollow as I pull back, licking and swirling along the way. He gasps, and I peer up at him as I do it all again, watching the flames rise in the depths of his eyes.

Standing, I push him down to the bed and climb on top of him.

Madoc comes over and pulls my head back, his tongue thrusting into my mouth with a deep kiss, and I moan at the need rising in me.

Shifting, I slide Rivan's cock into my drenched body. Kissing and tasting Madoc as I ride another man is exhilarating. In sync with each other, I'm bombarded with the feel of them both.

Hands wrap around from behind me, covering my breasts as a mouth skims down the side of my neck. The hint of The Underworld drifts to me, and my body quivers with the addition of Cormal.

I remove Madoc's clothes and lick my lips. "I want to taste you, too."

He closes his eyes for a microsecond, then moves forward on the bed. Reaching down, he strokes himself several times. He's longer than either Cormal or Rivan. I open my mouth and take him in one inch at a time, until I hit the base, then I use my tongue, lips, and hand to drive him wild. I hadn't done this to him yet, and it's been a hell of a long time since he's had someone deep throat him.

"You're amazing," Madoc says hoarsely. "With your full lips wrapped around my cock. Sucking and licking. I can't stop watching." He brushes the hair back from my face and holds it in his hand.

Rivan takes over from me, keeping a steady pace that holds

us in a sort of edgy limbo. His hands roam between the two of us, circling where we're joined, then the button near the top. I squeeze him tightly, trying to stave off the desire that's ramping up inside me, but it's like trying to hold off a tsunami.

Cormal pours oil down my back and massages it into my butt. His finger dips into the crack, then down until he rims the hole below. More oil and he presses in up to the knuckle. Working my body, he adds another finger.

"You're so damn tight," he curses. "But fucking gorgeous with your beautiful ass in the air." He slaps my butt cheek, and I squirm as a shaft of desire arrows through me.

Rivan curses. "Hurry the fuck up."

"Bear down," Cormal orders, his voice almost guttural. The beast in him is close to the surface. "Now."

Obeying his command, I bear down, opening for him, and he slips in, but the stretch is tight, making me suck in my breath and hold it. Finally, he sinks all the way in and immediately starts shallow thrusts to get my body used to his. I release my breath in one long moan.

Mouth dripping, I relax my throat and peer up at Madoc. He pumps his hips, taking it slow at first, but after tonguing him for so long, he's straining to stop his release. Thrusting faster and deeper, he fucks my mouth, while Cormal and Rivan fuck the rest of my body.

Goddess, this is better than I dreamed.

My body flies higher and higher, and the smell of the four of us permeates the room with a heady, rich scent that engulfs my senses. Hands everywhere, pressing, thrusting, faster and faster. I tremble, trying to hold onto my control, but the wave crashes over me, and I surrender to the torrent in me.

"Thank fuck," Rivan says with gritted teeth. His body slowing as his own release follows mine.

Madoc jerks my head back to stare into my eyes and comes

deep in my throat. I swallow and his steel-grey eyes flash with satisfaction.

Cormal growls behind me, and with one last thrust, surrenders to the same wave that swept over the rest of us. He bends over and presses sweet kisses on my damp skin, then pulls out.

Hands help me down to the bed.

"Now that was a coronation ceremony. I'm kind of jealous. Mine was spent alone," I lament, rolling over to leisurely scan the three utterly delicious and naked men beside me. "You know, we're just getting started, right? There are a lot of positions I want to try." I point to a book I found in the library earlier this week. "But first, I want an old-fashioned shower. Anyone want to help me wash my back?"

Strolling out of the bedroom, I saunter into the shower I had Cormal create earlier this week. Feet hit the floor behind me, followed by a few thuds and grunts, and I laugh. It's going to be a lovely night.

ALL THREE OF them are dressed and eating breakfast when I wake the next morning. "Where do you find the energy?" I glance in the mirror as I pass and see crazy hair sticking out everywhere. The result of wet hair and lots of sex. Stretching, I push my arms into my robe, and plop down in the nearest chair.

Reaching for the bowl of fruit, I yawn and pop a strawberry into my mouth. Madoc's eyes watch every move, and I smirk, knowing what he's thinking.

"Why so serious?" I ask, grabbing my spoon and dipping it into the yogurt sitting in front of me.

Madoc leans back in his chair. "The Federation for Fae Rights and Independence declared war last night."

I drop the spoon into the bowl. "Who?"

"Basically, the Fire Fae and any additional Fae who've joined their cause," Cormal explains, glancing up from his phone. He leans over and gives me a hard kiss, then hands me a cup of coffee. Black. "You're going to need the energy. We've got a lot to do today."

I raise my two fingers, pinch them together, and thrust forward. When they give me a crazy look, I sigh. "I'm popping my bubble of happiness and post coital euphoria. And here I thought we could try page one hundred and sixteen this morning."

Rivan stares across the table, then jumps up and flips to the page in the book. He groans and brings it over to show the other two.

Madoc scowls. "Fucking hell. I'm going to have a hard-on going to my own damn council meeting."

"Nobody forced you to check it out," I quip in a snarky voice. I can't help it. I'm more than a bit peeved to have my sex fest over this fast. Finishing the coffee, I look at the three of them. "What's first on the agenda?"

"Meeting with the council," Madoc spits out. "As if they will know what to do."

"Red tape. It's why I declared war on the Water Fae," I say with a sympathetic nod. "The council blocks everything. They were a bunch of pansies who didn't know the meaning of fighting for what they want, but they damn sure wanted to dictate my actions."

Cormal darts a glance at Madoc, whose expression lightens.

"Would you mind going to the council meeting in my place? I need to start assessing what's left of the army," Madoc asks, flashing me surly puppy dog eyes.

"I'd love to," I purr. Now where did I put that turquoise low-cut blouse?

Madoc writes something on the pad beside him and tears it off. "You'll need my official approval to be my stand in."

I fold it and slip it into my pocket. "What are you three doing?"

"I'm going to assess the aerial guard," Rivan says with a frown. "If we even have one now."

Madoc shrugs. "I'm going to evaluate the rest of our soldiers. Get a count. See if they're in shape. Nobody has been to war here since…" He stops and winces.

"Since the last Fire Fae Rebellion," Rivan finishes for him. "I've always hated that title. Rebellion. As if we were recalcitrant children throwing a temper tantrum. For two hundred years, we fought. It was war." His hand pushes the red and black strands back from his face.

I lay a hand on top of his. "It was. And there were a lot of lives lost, including your mother's. Maybe we can stop it this time."

Cormal straightens. "We haven't even started thinking in that direction. Our first thought was to prepare for battle, but what if we give them what they want? How many do we think will still want to fight? Especially when they see the size of our army."

Madoc stares at him. "How many did our spies count for their side?"

Cormal shifts around a few papers. "Twenty thousand. Most of it comprised of Fire Fae, but there's a hefty number of other Fae."

Grabbing his pencil, Madoc starts writing out numbers. "Between us, Winter, and Autumn, we should be able to scrounge up… maybe five thousand soldiers. That will give us a start."

"You'll have to remove Autumn's title first," I interject. "He's not a fan."

"He'll either command his soldiers, or I'll bring the army and march across his land," Madoc threatens with a grim expression.

"Go directly to the soldiers and ask," I urge him. "Ultimately, they're yours to command, right? Asking gives them a voice. Something I highly doubt Lord Autumn ever did."

Madoc writes down a note on the pad beside him.

I look at Cormal. "I can't believe you've converted another person to paper. Unreal."

Rivan tilts his head. "Where do you keep notes?"

"In my head or on my phone," I tell him. "Okay, back to the army. Five thousand with Winter and Autumn and, of course, the royal army. Lucifer has how many?"

"At least another five thousand," Cormal states confidently. "Fallon's elite add a few hundred, but honestly, it's like adding another thousand. Ruthless and efficient bastards." His tone is full of admiration.

"A little over half," Madoc calculates. "Valerian has roughly a thousand dragons. Add three thousand for Torin's dark Elves, and we're at fifteen thousand. The creatures of the Wilds, while few, are truly monsters on the battlefield. Giving us the equivalent of fifteen thousand five hundred." He drops his pencil and leans back, cupping his head in his hands. "Technically outnumbered, but only the Fire Fae are likely to be trained, which makes us about even."

Rivan exhales and shakes his head. "At what cost? It took both sides hundreds of years to heal the land. Whole families were decimated. Everything was fractured. And it didn't solve anything. Here we are, three thousand years later, facing the same war." He shoves away from the table. "I'm going for a walk."

I watch him leave, then turn toward Madoc. "War isn't the answer. Fisk knew it. I knew it. Only real solutions, remember. Rights and independence. We need to find a way to offer them what they want and find peace."

I wave a hand until I'm wearing my white suit with the plunging neckline and the turquoise blouse, then grab the note.

Strolling around the table, I bend down and place a kiss on Cormal's lips, then stroll over and do the same to Madoc's. "I'm off to play with your council. Wish me luck."

Madoc looks incredulously at Cormal. "What the hell is she wearing? Is she trying to get someone killed?"

Cormal drawls, "She's fierce, isn't she? I love it."

CHAPTER THIRTY-FOUR

<u>MERI</u>

Déjà vu. Are all council meetings the same? This one kind of makes me sad, though. I miss Solandis sitting regally in the front, silently cheering me on. My heels click on the stone floor as I stride into the chamber and take the black chair at the front that's obviously meant for Madoc.

Conversations cease. I smile.

"Are there protocols here? Roll call?" I ask the lord standing closest to me.

He sputters for a second.

Lord Autumn makes a furious sound and pushes him out of the way. "This is a council meeting."

I hand the prick Madoc's note. "Yes, I know. I'll be sitting in for Madoc today." Several smirk, as if I'm a joke, but I stare them down. "I've done this before, remember? Let's get started."

They turn toward Lord Edsel, whose face is pale. "This is

outlandish. I'm going to find Madoc and remind him we're his council and this is an important meeting."

I take the note from him and pass it along to the serious-looking gentleman in the back. While he reads it, I return to the asshole standing in front of me.

"The meeting is starting. Leave or stay. It's up to you, but today, I hold this seat," I inform him, emphasizing each word so he knows I'm serious. "And Edsel, I suggest you call him King Madoc when you see him. Show him respect and he might kill you quickly."

Sputtering, the Lord of Autumn storms out of the room.

"So, roll call or no?"

The gentleman in the back stands. "I'm Lord Avi of the Woods. The fourteen of us have been on the council for the entire time Denir reigned. There hasn't been a need for formal protocols."

I smile at him. "Thank you, Lord Avi. Let's jump in then. The Federation for Fae Rights and Independence declared war. Thoughts?" I want to hear what they say first.

He shakes his head. "My land borders the Wilds. Letting this kingdom fall would be a catastrophe. I don't like the thought of war, but it might be necessary."

Another brash man stands up. "I fought in the last war. It was brutal, but I refuse to let the Lesser Fae dictate to me."

One by one, they all advocate for war based on one reason or another.

I frown. "What about their rights? Or independence?"

"It depends on what they want," they reply. "If we know specifics, we can determine how to proceed."

"How about the same rights and freedoms you have?" I probe.

Almost all of them shake their heads no. Only Lord Avi is willing to consider it.

I stand. "Okay, I think we're done."

"We haven't talked about the terms we're willing to offer them," one of the council members sputters.

"If you can't offer them the same rights and freedoms you enjoy, then you're willing to accept war. I recommend you go home and kiss your families goodbye," I urge them, walking toward the door.

A bewildered expression crosses their faces. "Why?"

"If you're advocating war, we need every soldier we can get. Being on the council has given you leadership skills that could be useful on the battlefield," I explain with a sweet smile. "I'll let King Madoc know your decision."

They begin shouting as I walk out the door.

Madoc's in the bright sunny courtyard talking to one of his soldiers when I find him. For once, he isn't wearing a scowl.

"Meri, this is General Beld. He leads our army," Madoc says, introducing the fierce-looking barrel of a man standing beside him.

At the word "our", the general straightens and bows. "It's a pleasure to meet you, Lady Meri."

Madoc scowls at the man, and he looks startled.

"We haven't established titles yet," I explain to ease his worry. "I was a little worried about the army, but you seem quite capable."

Madoc gestures to the soldier. "Two thousand highly trained soldiers, according to the general. Thankfully, Denir was quite paranoid. Only the best are selected to serve, and training has remained a top priority." He turns and points behind the palace. "We even have an aerial unit comprised of air elementals, avian Fae, and a few others, though most of the Phoenix and Fire Drakes have left. Rivan's assessing their capabilities."

"That's good news," I state firmly. "I informed the council today that they'll be joining the army. My apologies, General Beld, as I'm sure they won't be up to your usual standards, but

I'm sure you'll be able to find a place for them. I think there are fourteen of them."

Madoc shakes his head. "Thirteen."

I guess Lord Autumn was stupid enough to approach Madoc. "Thirteen. If they don't report for duty, please let us know."

General Beld's stoic face slackens for a second, but he lifts his chin and salutes Madoc, then returns to his men.

Folding his arms across his chest, he peers down at me. "What happened?"

"They all thought war was the only answer and were ready to dictate terms for their surrender or a peace treaty," I tell him. "None of them would consider rights except for Lord Avi. So, I told them every Fae would be needed and they should go home and kiss their families goodbye."

Madoc grunts. "If this war happens, we will need them."

I lean against him. "Is Lord Edsel still alive?"

"Barely, but he's been removed from all duties, and his title stripped from him," he announces in a hard tone. "I need to take a trip to speak to the soldiers under his command and move them here. Will you be all right while I'm gone?"

"Who are you taking with you?" I ask, biting my lip.

"General Beld and a couple of platoons," he states with a wry twist of his mouth. "Does that meet with your approval?"

"Mm, yes, thank you," I reply, lifting my face toward his. "Can I get my goodbye kiss?"

His mouth descends and takes mine in the sweetest of kisses until I'm practically melting into a pile of goo. "Bye. Stay close to Cormal or Rivan. I don't trust anyone else."

"Good. I don't trust anyone here either," I pertly inform him. "Be careful. Keep your shield up." Not once have I forgotten since I got here.

I leave him and cross the courtyard to the rear of the palace to find Rivan. As I turn the corner, I watch him shake hands with a tall female, then walk away.

He meets me halfway. "Is everything okay?"

I give him the highlights of the council meeting and Edsel's fall from grace.

"Why are they so determined to hold on to the old ways? We have talented Fae out there who don't hold titles who could bring so much to this kingdom. The one thing I did like about the light Fae was Meira," he admits. "It gave everyone a glimpse into the future we could have if we got rid of the old prejudices."

"You are Fire Fae. This was your war once," I gently remind him. "Think back to the things you wanted. Two hundred years is a long time to fight. Those things must have been important to you. I'm sure the Fire Fae haven't changed much over the years."

"Madoc knows what they want," he says, his voice full of frustration.

"Knowing and living it are two different things. Madoc was already in The Below when the last war started; he doesn't have the context you have," I state. "Plus, he's the king, and his first priority is protecting his people and the kingdom. If you think there is a better solution than war, you need to find it fast."

CHAPTER THIRTY-FIVE

<u>MERI</u>

Rivan's staring at a map, and I'm texting Cormal when Madoc returns. He strides in with blood on his clothes and the lines of his face set into a fierce scowl.

I jump up. "What happened?"

Madoc takes a deep breath. "Edsel thought he could use his army to hold on to his land. He was mistaken. Lady Dahlia and her children will be relocated to the nearest town. After they bury Edsel."

He pours himself one of Cormal's bourbons and walks over to kiss me hello. My eyes flick to the glass in his hand. The two are becoming more alike each day, and it's quite irritating.

Rivan taps on the map. "What are you going to do with the land?" When Madoc lifts a brow, he clarifies, "There's plenty of available land in this kingdom, but not all of it is hospitable."

"I haven't even thought about it yet," Madoc replies tiredly. "Why?"

"One of things the non-titled Fae want the most is the ability to own land," he informs him.

"Titled Fae, too," I interject, remembering why Lady Estrella fought so hard to keep her land. "I never understood why the titled Fae didn't just claim land for themselves."

Madoc sits up. "Because land lost due to a dispute, an act of treason, or rebellion is returned to the crown. Land lost to the Wilds or a natural disaster or the enemy is never replaced because there is no law to account for those scenarios."

"What if we offered everyone a piece of land? The plots can be reasonably sized, and if they want more, they can purchase more," Rivan suggests. "Autumn probably has enough land for two to three thousand Fae?" He stares down at the map. "If the crown has land originally owned by another, that could also be an option."

He circles a few areas. "Also, what if we tie rights into the land? If you own land, you have voting rights. This gives them a stake in the kingdom and the incentive to vote for additional rights. Those with homes are more likely to commit to improving the kingdom and investing in its future."

Madoc walks over and peers at the map. "I doubt we have enough for twenty thousand." He circles the land the Fire Fae lived on prior to the first war. "One thing I won't do is give them the land that sits between the dark and light Fae kingdoms. It would be like giving my enemy a house in my backyard."

Rivan appears frustrated but nods. "I understand and agree. They're too volatile. Who's to say they won't want more land or better land? Besides the Fire Fae, I think this could work. If we get a thousand Fae to accept the offer, that's a thousand less to fight."

Madoc takes a sip as he thinks through the ramifications. "It also supports the broader vision of equality. I agree. Send out messengers tonight to post the offer in every town. We'll see how many want to own a piece for themselves." He taps the map. "Once we know the number, we can determine the size and location of the parcel."

Rivan takes off, and Madoc comes over and sits next to me on the small settee. He grimaces. "This couch is terrible."

"I plan to change everything once the dust settles," I admit. "Do you think Rivan's plan will work?"

He lifts a shoulder. "I'm not sure if it's too little too late, but we have to try." He cleans his clothes and leans back. "The army fought well. Beld is a strict but formidable commander. His men listen to him, and they didn't hesitate to fight against Autumn's soldiers."

"Where's Cormal?"

I smooth the hair back from his face. "He went to check on his empire." King of a very different kingdom, but a necessary one. If not, the criminals in The Underworld and other places would create chaos. "The bed is probably more comfortable."

Madoc opens an eye. "But you're here."

"That's easy," I tell him, changing into silk pajamas. "I'm exhausted. Worn out from last night." With a wink, I walk over and slide into bed. "Come. Sleep."

He removes his clothes and falls in next to me. Seconds later, he's out.

RIVAN RACES into the room early the next morning. "We have at least a thousand at our door and more on the way."

Madoc opens one eye and glares at him. "The sun hasn't even risen."

"The messengers went out last night with the offer, and it's working," Rivan exclaims. "Fae have come for the land." He walks to the window and points to the ground.

Madoc grunts, then gets up, dresses, and goes to the window. Silent for a moment, he looks at Rivan and grins. Grins. I almost fall out of the damn bed.

He slaps him on the back. "Well, hell. Let's go give away some land." Grabbing the map, the two head out.

Madoc returns a second later, followed by Rivan, to give me a kiss, then leave again. Not wanting the fuss of a shower, I clean and dress the magical way, then head to the library. I remember seeing a record of all land transactions that could come in handy.

A couple of hours later, Rivan comes searching for me. "Thirty-three hundred Fae took the land deal, which is fantastic. The bad news is we have to find those Fae a good parcel of land. It will be tough."

I shove the book and map over to him. "There's roughly seventeen massive areas across the kingdom that are uninhabited and fit your criteria."

His mouth drops open, and he pulls the information closer. "How did you find this?"

"I've spent more time in this library than in any other place," I drawl. "It's my favorite haunt. Nine hundred years gave me plenty of time to snoop into every nook and cranny and find all the best books."

He walks over and pulls me into his arms. "Thank you. This will help tremendously." He bends his head and nibbles on my bottom lip. "Do you think one of those areas is large enough to house the Federation?"

I pull away. "No. If Madoc gives the Federation one of those areas and lets them declare their independence, it will cause a huge amount of resentment with all the other Fae. Plus, we would be sheltering a race who turned their back on both kingdoms. There has to be another solution for them."

Rivan rubs his temples. "Another problem to solve." He drops a kiss on my mouth. "What can I do to repay you?"

"There are so many delightful things, but honestly, I want my rune back," I say wistfully, showing him my blank palm. "Not for the clarity, but because it made me think of you and the day we spent by the waterfall."

He laces his pinky with mine and pulls us out of the library to the room he claimed a couple of weeks ago. Formerly one of the guest bedrooms, it's luxurious with few furnishings but it has a huge balcony. A necessity for Rivan.

He gathers a pile of blankets and pillows and lays them outside. "Is this okay? The lighting in there is terrible, and I haven't been able to go outside today. Phoenix need regular doses of sun and heat."

I narrow my eyes, and he looks sheepish. "Fine. Not all of us need it, but it mentally rejuvenates us." He pats the pillow in front of him. "Sit here."

I plop down. Crossing my legs, I hold out my hand. "That day... I didn't think I'd ever see you again. It nearly broke my heart, but I knew it had to be done. You deserved your freedom and so does the Federation. I know you'll find a solution for them."

He looks sad for a moment. "I hope so, but I doubt there's a realm that will take them. Most of the other lands are trying to find solutions for their own people. Who wants to take in a massive number of Fae who aren't afraid to start a war to get their independence?"

Sad but true. Every kingdom will worry that the Federation won't be satisfied with what they're given and will use the threat of war to gain more.

For the next twenty minutes, I soak up the sun while he works on my rune. It's peaceful here with him. Any place, actually. He has a way of making it feel like it's only the two of us.

"Done," he says, lifting my hand. "What do you think?"

"I love it," I reply with a smile. "Hopefully, I'll be able to keep this one forever. Although, I'll have to remember to stay away from places like Avalon, where the old magic resides."

Rivan's eyes widen, and he jumps up and gives me a kiss. "You're so fucking brilliant. I love you. I've got to find Madoc."

With a sigh, I lean back on the cushions to soak up some more sun.

My phone pings. Cormal has returned and wants to know where I'm at, so I give him directions to Rivan's room.

"On the balcony," I call out when I hear the door shut.

He stops when he sees me lying on a pile of blankets and pillows.

"Join me?"

Seconds later, he throws down more cushions and lies beside me with his face tilted toward the sun. "I've been in the office for two days straight, trying to tie everything up so I can concentrate on the war here. Damn, this feels good." He pulls me in tight. "Mmm, you feel even better."

His hand splays against my back, and he leans in for a long, hard kiss. Breathing heavily, he shifts until his leg is between mine, then continues his assault on my mouth.

"I missed you," he grumbles. "Next time, you're coming with me."

"We should all go," I reply breathlessly. "Rivan and Madoc need to get used to spending time there, too. The Underworld is my home as well."

He tucks my head under his chin and runs his hand down my back. "We could have dinner with my sister and Oryn. Or just my sister."

I tilt my head backward. "Did something happen between them?"

He chuckles. "I think my sister is becoming her independent, feisty self. Oryn will have to figure out if he wants this idea he has of her or the real her."

"She wasn't exactly herself when they met," I drawl.

"Why are you out on Rivan's balcony?" Cormal asks, lifting his head. "And where is he?"

I explain everything that's happened in the last couple of days. "He took off to find Madoc." I shift a pillow under the small of my back. "What's your room like?"

His mouth twists. "Same as this one. Why?"

"When all this is over, I want to redo this entire floor and combine all these separate rooms into one large suite for the four of us. We can spend time together or alone, but we need comfortable furniture and an outdoor space," I tell him ruefully. "The palace hasn't been updated in forever."

Cormal stands and holds his hands out to me. "My bed is much more comfortable than this balcony. Join me?"

I laugh and leap up into his arms, wrapping my legs around him. "If you carry me, I'm yours."

"You're always giving me something to do," he laughingly protests. Then his hands cup my butt, and he presses into me. "Maybe I should carry you all the time."

CHAPTER THIRTY-SIX

<u>RIVAN</u>

Bursting into his study, I stop and stare at Madoc's serious face. An entire battlefield is spread out in front of him. Hundreds of tiny soldiers in the official blue colors of the dark Fae and in the colors of our allies dot the map. My aerial platoon is positioned at the front line to fight against the strongest of the enemy's forces, the Phoenix and Fire Drakes, but our numbers are considerably fewer than our enemy. Hopefully, Valerian's dragons will quickly cut that number down. The Phoenix don't regenerate from a kill by dragon's fire, which means his squadrons will have to be first into battle.

Deep grooves line his face, telling me how weary he is, and the battle hasn't even started. I can't imagine spending all those years in The Below dreaming of crown and kingdom, only to have to fight a war to keep it.

"Are you going to stand at the door forever?" he asks irritably. He rearranges a few of the soldiers from one area to another.

Walking in, I pull a map from the shelf. "I might have a solution for the Federation and their independence. It's risky. They may or may not take it, but I think it makes sense."

Rolling it out on a side table, I wait for him to walk over. "Avalon. The island is awake. There are not enough descendants left to control the wild magic, but if left uncontrolled, it will run rampant and spread across the sea."

Madoc folds his arms. "You think we can give the Federation the island? Won't the magic turn on them?"

"Meri's rune woke the island because it was tattooed by me, a descendant of Avalon, using my mother's magic," I tell him. "Every Avalon citizen wore one. It was a signal to the island of their allegiance. Only two people know how to use that magic— myself and my sister. She wants her independence."

"Yeah, I gathered that during our last encounter," Madoc states dryly. "What makes you think she or the rest of the Federation will go for the deal? Won't they be afraid of the magic? Maybe not your sister, but the rest of them?"

"That's the risky part," I admit with a sigh. "If we make it clear this is the only option on the table, that they will not be given land in either of the Fae kingdoms to claim as their own, they might come to the same conclusion I did. It's either true independence in the unknown or a fierce war that will last who knows how long."

He runs his hand along his chin several times. "Long term, this could backfire on us if the Federation learns to wield the old magic, but I imagine it would take at least a millennium."

I lean in closer. "My mother told me the island stopped sharing its magic with her people because they didn't do enough in return to replenish the resources," I murmur, not wanting to say too much out loud. "I think it will depend on them. Maybe the two will co-exist."

Madoc walks over to the window to view his kingdom. "If we don't offer them the deal, we know blood will run and the Fae will never be the same. Are you willing to be my official emissary and offer them the deal?"

His trust means everything to me, but I have to give him an honest answer. "I'm not sure they'll want to hear it from me. Maybe you should send Cormal or one of your trusted advisors."

He scowls. "You are one of my trusted advisors. But if you think it needs to be someone official, I have an idea for who to send with you."

Tilting my head, I wait for him to tell me.

"Queen Meri," he reveals in a gruff voice. "Do you think she'll accept the crown?"

Thinking of seeing a crown on her forehead, I grimace. "I don't know. Even in her short time as queen, she made an impact."

"Is it Nyssa?" he asks in a soft, understanding voice.

"The memories are always there, under the surface, and sometimes the smallest of things trigger it, like the sight of a crown on Meri's forehead." It's painful for me to admit, but he has a right to know.

He gives a lazy shrug. "Since I'm king and carry my power with me, she doesn't have to wear a crown all the time. Plus, it would be a physical crown, not a magical tattoo across her forehead." He waves a hand toward me, and a more delicate version of his black crown appears in his hand.

"I won't know until I see it on her," I reply.

He motions for me to follow. "No time like the present." Walking out the door, he glances over his shoulder. "Where is she?"

I chuckle. "Last time I saw her was in my room, but she doesn't stay in one place very long." I pull my phone out and send her a text.

"That's the truth," he mutters.

My phone pings a reply. "Cormal's room."

When we get there, they're both eating, and the room is saturated with the smell of sex. I groan. "You could have warned us."

"Why?" she asks with a mischievous expression on her face.

Madoc waves a hand and freshens the air. "Because I would like to ask you an important question."

Meri glances down at her silky attire. "Do I need to get dressed for this discussion?" She takes another look at Madoc's face and immediately gets dressed. "Okay, where are we going? Who are we fighting?"

"You're a damn good queen," Madoc grumbles, and Cormal rolls his eyes. With a sigh, Madoc holds out the crown. "I don't want the general or anyone else to question your place here. This isn't a temporary situation. It's permanent. For as long as I'm king, I want you by my side as my queen. There is no ceremony, just a crown, and a hell of a lot of responsibilities. None of that sounds great, but I know you'll be the best damn queen to our people."

Tears fill Meri's eyes, and she looks at me. "Won't this bother you? And don't lie. You're more important. I know how to get my way without a title or crown."

"Put it on," I reply firmly. When she does, I carefully study her. I hate it, but it's not triggering me. "It's not my favorite look on you, but I can live with it."

She takes it off and hands the crown to Madoc. "I'll accept the title, but not the crown."

When we all stare at her in astonishment, she stares back at us in irritation. "What? I *am* a damn good queen. It surprised me, too. Ever since I gave it up, I've missed it. But Queen of the Light Fae never fit quite right, like a square peg in a round hole. The dark Fae suits me much better. Less protocol, more honest work to be done."

"Is that a yes?" Madoc asks hoarsely.

She laughs and throws herself into his arms. "Yes, my surly king. I'll be your queen." Laying her lips on his, she kisses him deeply until they're both breathing heavily.

"Mmm, we'll have to celebrate later," he huskily informs her. "Rivan has an idea he wants to propose to the Federation, but we'll need our new queen to go with him."

Cormal curses. "Hell no. That's not happening."

Madoc thrusts a hand through his hair. "If the Federation accepts, it will end the war. They won't accept the proposal from Rivan alone. Someone has to go in an official capacity." He shrugs. "I was hoping you would stay here with me and organize the battle, but if you need to go with them, go. I'll get Theron and Fallon to assist or Lucifer."

Torn, Cormal looks at us both.

I'm not oblivious to the leverage we would be handing our enemy if they captured our queen. We need additional back-up. "We'll take Lux and Aamon."

For a second, Cormal opens his mouth, then shrugs. "Sounds good to me. It would serve them right if the little bastard lost his shit on them. Better warn them in advance. Neither he nor Aamon will take kindly to anyone mistreating her."

I smile. "I'll try to remember to tell them."

He runs a hand down his face. "You both better damn well return without a scratch on you."

MY SISTER, along with the council of The Federation for Fae Rights and Independence, accepts our request to present a proposal to them. In the original message, I made sure to include my name so they wouldn't be surprised by my presence, but I deliberately withheld Meri's name and only listed an official advisor, along with two guards.

Standing at the threshold of the Gora Mountain, I watch their sly smiles appear when they see Meri with me, but they quickly disappear when they notice our two rather frightening guards.

The soldier who stood next to my sister at the last meeting steps forward. "Your message said to expect an official advisor." His eyes narrow on me. "Surely, it's not you?"

Asshole. "Sorry, I thought the news would have made it to you by now." Deliberately implying their network has failed them puts them on edge. "Queen Meri and her two guards, Lux and Aamon."

A smug grin appears, and he steps in front of Meri. "Which kingdom are you claiming as queen now?"

She raises her chin and flashes him a warning glare. "I'm not claiming anything." He smirks. "I'm Queen of the Dark Fae Kingdom."

His eyes light up. "Only two guards for such an important person."

"Two is more than enough when they're lethal," Meri cautions him. "Would you like to see a personal demonstration?"

He peers at the two behind her and lifts a shoulder. "If you say so." One of his large hands reaches out toward Meri, but another guard taps him on the shoulder and waves his phone. "The council is asking what is taking so long."

Irritation flashes across his face, but he gestures toward us. "Come. Let's hear this so-called proposal." He pivots on his heel and heads toward the mountain.

Meri eyes him warily then glances at me.

I give her a subtle nod of agreement. He isn't to be trusted.

Thankfully, the walk isn't far. Once we're through the tunnel, the main chamber is right in front of us. With its dirt floor and stone seating, it's pretty primitive, but it will do the trick.

As soon as they see Meri and me, the noise of the crowd gets louder. Some murmuring amongst themselves, while others openly jeer at the two of us.

Directly across from the entrance is a long stone table with twelve individuals sitting at it, scanning us from head to toe. The Federation for Fae Rights and Independence council. Most of the members are Fire Fae, but they've added a few races.

"Queen Meri of the Dark Fae Kingdom," the soldier announces with a sneer. "Rivan. Guards."

Meri smiles at the council. "Thank you for taking the time to hear our proposal. The last war between the Fae and Fire Fae lasted two hundred years. It is our hope this solution will prevent the deaths of thousands of Fae on both sides and give you the freedom to create your own government and laws. Our most trusted advisor, Rivan, will present it."

The entire room goes silent, but I see a triumphant gleam in most of the council's eyes, including Aeris, my sister. Only one refuses to see this as a victory. Lady Brina has joined the Federation in their fight, and they've given her a seat at the table. She must have brought a considerable amount of wealth and influence with her. Her light blue eyes only reflect her hatred of Meri.

"As you may have heard, any of you who wish to stay a part of the Dark Fae Kingdom, under King Madoc and Queen Meri's rule, can come forward and claim a parcel of land for yourself, along with the voting rights it entails. That offer will only remain open until the battle begins," I remind them, hoping some will stay and take advantage of it.

"For those of you who wish to be independent and free of the Dark Fae Kingdom, we offer you one solution. It's an unusual offer, but it gives you complete freedom. It also provides viable land, ripe for agriculture and commerce, and as

Queen Meri mentioned, the right to create your own government and laws." I pause to let the benefits sink in because the next part is going to send them into an uproar.

"We believe Avalon is the answer," I state in a firm voice. "The island is close to both Fae kingdoms, but entirely separate. This solution allows you complete autonomy from any government other than your own."

An older Fire Fae, General Lai, who served under my father, stands. "Avalon will not work. Only descendants are allowed to settle on the island. Surely you jest."

"As you're aware, my father recently held me hostage there," I state in a harsh tone. "Queen Meri came to save me and woke the island up. It welcomed her. She isn't a descendant, but she bears the mark of one."

Meri holds up her hand and turns in a circle for the crowd to see it.

"Both Aeris and I are descendants of Avalon, through our mother's line, and with our blood and magic, we can tattoo each one of you with a mark. The island will accept you," I assure them.

The general glances at Aeris. "Is this true?"

She turns a stunned face toward me. "We're descendants and can use our blood and magic to tattoo runes on everyone, but I don't know the island will accept us."

"I don't expect you to take my word for it. Have Aeris tattoo you with a rune. Travel to the island and test it out for yourselves," I encourage them.

The entire chamber erupts. Jeering and whistling, they present a thumbs down and my heart sinks.

Meri holds up her hand. "Before you decide, you should know we have asked our allies to join this war, and they have agreed. Besides the Dark Fae Kingdom and its soldiers, you will face Lucifer and his Underworld army. Fallon and his elite Elven warriors. King Valerian and his squadrons of dragons.

The Rowan and her coven of witches. King Torin and his dark Elven army. And, of course, the creatures of the Wilds, commanded by King Madoc."

The silence is deafening.

She continues. "Do you realize that without a king on the throne of the Dark Fae Kingdom, the Wilds, including the creatures within it, will be free to escape its boundaries and run amok across the lands, terrorizing and eating anyone and anything in its path?"

Lady Brina stands with a malicious gleam in her eye. "That is a lie. Nothing happened when the Queen of the Light Fae *lost* her crown." Her voice echoes across the chamber.

The muscles in Meri's jaw tighten for a second. "I *sacrificed* my crown for family, and I would do it again and again. But I had that luxury. The light Fae ruler doesn't hold the power of The Wild Hunt inside. The crown doesn't demand allegiance to both the kingdom and Odin. The Dark Fae Kingdom does. Konnyr made a pact long ago, and to void it would be catastrophic, not only to the Fae but the universe."

General Lai motions for Lady Brina to sit, and she glares at him but finds her seat.

He smiles at Meri. "Queen Meri, we are Fae. It is our desire to live with the Fae, not find a new home in Avalon."

She stares at him. "If you wish to reside with the Fae, our other offer is still on the table. Feel free to take it and stay in this land. But if you want your freedom and the right to govern yourself, then you cannot do so here. Do you really think any ruler will allow you to take up residence in their land, enjoy the resources and protection they provide, and remain independent?" She lets the question sit there for a few minutes.

"We could withdraw from the battle and carve out a piece of the Light Fae Kingdom for ourselves," Lady Brina says snidely.

Meri smiles at her in return. "You could try. We promised Hyne and the rest of the Water Fae, our full resources, as well as our allies, if you should decide to take that route. All you'll do is move the battle lines and add more soldiers to our side."

She snarls at Meri but is silenced by the council leader before she can say more.

"Nobody is asking you to give up your heritage," I remind them. "The people of Avalon were still Fae." I nod at Aeris. "This is a way for the Federation to have the freedom and rights you want right now without the astronomical cost of war. Think of how many families were devastated the last time. Mothers, fathers, siblings, and more. All gone."

Aeris jeers at my statement. "Easy for you to say. You weren't there. Instead, you gave up. Accepted the yoke of a queen and now I see nothing has changed."

Meri opens her mouth, but I hold up a hand. "This isn't about me, but if you want to know, as a *free* man, I willingly pledged my allegiance to King Madoc and the Dark Fae Kingdom. I believe in him and the vision he has for the Fae, and I want to be a part of it."

Taking a second to breathe, I get my temper under control. "Last time, you faced two inexperienced rulers who thought like traditional Fae and their equally inexperienced aristocratic Fae soldiers. I should know. I was there. This time, you face a king who will do anything to keep his kingdom intact, including the annihilation of your entire force. Have you trained your soldiers to fight against a lightning-fast vampire or the magical powers of a witch or sorceress? Do they know how to dodge a dragon's fire? Can they stand one on one against Garrett or one of his elite? Or a demon? And this is just the surface. Who knows what lurks within the ranks of Lucifer's soldiers?"

"We don't expect an answer today," I tell them. "You have one week. Go to the island. See for yourself. Give us your answer on the battlefield in one week's time. We'll send you the coordinates."

Meri dips her head in the direction of the council and turns toward me.

Suddenly, the general shouts, and I turn to see a dagger hurtling directly at Meri. Before I can block it, a shadow reaches out and snatches it from the air, then hands it to me. Seconds later, serrated shadows erupt from the ground and brutally shred Lady Brina to pieces in less than a second. She doesn't even have a chance to scream. What follows is scary. Each shadow grabs a remnant and disappears into the dirt, leaving no trace behind. Lux laughs behind me.

The soldier from earlier pulls his sword and rushes toward Meri. Aamon steps in front of her and grabs him around the neck. He lifts him up and snaps off his head with one hand. Shadows slither up from the ground and pull the two parts of his body underground. The crowd waits for the soldier to regenerate, but when he doesn't, they start shouting.

Lux claps his hands in glee. "That was a good one, Aamon. I'll have to try that next time." He scans the chamber as if he's searching for his next victim. "Meri is our friend."

His words silence the entire chamber. Nobody wants his interest falling on them.

I chuckle, and Lai looks at me in astonishment. "There are a lot more like them, and worse, in the Wilds. Trust me. Think about our words. Ask yourself if you're prepared for this war. Avalon is your best offer. I'd take it if I were you."

Handing the dagger to Meri, I watch her run a finger down its blade and whisper, "I've missed you."

"Is that one of the Killian Blades?" I ask, my voice purposely loud.

Based on what Cormal told me, Camon had the blade in his hand when Madoc took his life that fateful day in the court. Brina must have picked it up.

"It is, and it's also my friend, but I'm glad Lux stepped in and took care of Brina," she says confidently, conjuring a sheath for her belt and sliding it inside. "Let's go home."

CHAPTER THIRTY-SEVEN

<u>MADOC</u>

My mind races as I listen to the recap of Rivan and Meri's visit to the Federation to present the proposal. It's a toss-up on whether they'll take the deal, but I like the way the two of them presented it. Not as a plea to avoid war or to sell Avalon as the answer to all the Federation's needs, but as the best offer they will get from us.

"Maybe we can play it up," I start, slowly gathering my thoughts. "We know their spies are watching us. Let's bring in some of the worst. Vampires, monsters, magic wielders, one of the Elven elite, and a demon or two. Get them practicing in the yard. Give them a taste of what they will face in this battle."

Cormal's smile is truly frightening. He's completely enjoying the idea of putting on a show.

"You're in charge," I say, pointing to him. "I'll concentrate on reorganizing our battlefield. Make sure our worst is front and center for the big day."

Cormal rubs his hands together. "I'm going to start with the most terrifying of them all." When I raise an eyebrow, he gives me a droll look. "Lucifer, of course. With a little help from Evren."

I open my mouth to ask why but close it again. Don't get me wrong. Lucifer is truly terrifying up close where you can feel the power he wields and the dynamic force of his fuck you attitude, but at a distance, his appearance resembles an angel. Whatever. This should be interesting.

"Oh, and, Cormal, tell Lux I said thank you. His response was the perfect ending to the proposal," I tell him. "I've already spoken to Aamon."

"I was incredibly impressed with his restraint. Maybe he's finally growing out of his destructive phase," Cormal says with an indulgent smile. "I'm off to find a disguise."

Restraint is always a matter of perspective. I hope he remembers that when he finds a disguise for Lucifer.

"We could hold an aerial exercise with Valerian and myself," Rivan offers. "Most Phoenix are aware of the lethality of a dragon's fire, but they think they'll be able to outfly the large beasts. I want to showcase their speed."

"Perfect. Go for it," I reply. "The Phoenix are one of our most dangerous adversaries in this battle."

His broad grin tells me he's enjoying this, too. Maybe we're the monsters in this story. The three of us find way too much enjoyment in scaring the living hell out of our enemies.

With the two of them gone, I pull Meri closer, careful not to get near the blade at her waist. "Keep that with you at all times. They would have me on my knees if they took you. All of us, really."

She presses her lips to mine. "What can I do to help?"

"How about you work with Arden to set up a show in the courtyard? Remind our foes that the magic witches wield has few boundaries," I murmur against her lips. Pink and plump, they tempt me to abandon everything for a few hours.

"There's never enough time for the fun stuff," she pouts. "By the way, Bianca, one of Arden's coven, is the best portal creator I've ever seen. You know. In case you want to really throw some theatrics into the battlefield and bring the creatures from the Wilds in right before it starts." She pecks me on the lips. "I'm off."

There was definitely a twinkle in her eye when she offered that tidbit. All four of us are pretty warped.

Peering down at the board, I swipe my forearm across it. Their idea to emphasize the differences between the last war and this one was brilliant. We need our force to reflect the worst of our allies. I want complete nightmares to be standing on the frontline, staring at our enemies.

Putting the dark Fae army in the center, I reduce the number of lines, but make them longer. Our entire force is still there, just hidden a bit.

Then I create a large space to the left of my army for Lucifer's bloodthirsty group. Two lines for vampires. Led by Daire, of course, who's well known for his battle prowess. With him front and center, along with some of his ugliest and scariest vampires, that should do the trick. Maybe we can showcase their speed too.

Vargas isn't joining the battle, much to his dismay. Solandis is close to giving birth.

Callyx is taking his place. Equally disturbing, he will lead the demons and shadow wielders. I line them up next. Widening the rows, I make sure there is plenty of room to showcase their beefiest, ugliest, and most brutal-looking demons.

Lucifer is at the front, between the demons and magic wielders. I can't wait to see what Cormal and Evren come up with to showcase the ruthless leader of The Underworld.

To my right, I reserve two lines for Fallon's elite, led by him and that ferocious commander of his, Garrett.

I chuckle. Meri was right. Bringing in the monsters right before the battle will truly set the tone. Waving a hand, I add a portal with a few of their worst at the front and scatter the rest behind them. It's not as if they'll stay in single file once the battle starts, anyway.

Torin's dark Elves are added on the other side of Lucifer.

Last, but not least, Valerian's dragons. I thought to put them in the front to decimate the Phoenix, but if I want to showcase the rest of our gruesome army, I'll have to place them in the rear. Rivan was right. They're fast. As soon as the battle starts, they can fly to the front in record time.

I nod in satisfaction. This is the plan. Rivan was right to warn them. In order to preserve this kingdom, I'll wipe them from the board. I can't afford not to with my allegiance to Odin and the need to keep the Wilds in check.

When I read up on the Fire Fae Rebellion, I realized part of the reason the first war lasted two hundred years was because of all the cease fires to negotiate terms, which would, of course, then fall apart, causing the war to start up again.

I don't intend to offer a ceasefire. Ever. The two offers on the table will end when the battle begins, and no other negotiations will take place. These are all-or-nothing stakes. I will offer no quarter. If they choose battle, it will end with their deaths.

With a heavy sigh, I drop into the chair and stare out the window. It pains me to think of going to war against my own, much less killing them, but they have left me no choice. We can't continue to fight this battle. If they want their freedom, they need to take the offer on the table.

CORMAL'S absent the next day, but I go outside to watch Rivan and Valerian fly maneuvers. Valerian is a beast of a man and the biggest damn dragon I've ever seen. The massive black dragon makes the courtyard of the palace look like someone's yard, dwarfing everything around him. Only the palace itself is bigger. He swivels around and even I swallow at the size of his teeth, and as his golden predatory stare locks on me, I feel the menacing power he wields.

Rivan, in his full Phoenix form, slaps Valerian's tail and takes off laughing. "Catch me if you can, youngling."

I frown, not realizing Rivan was so much older than Valerian, but I guess it's true. The last Fire Fae Rebellion happened prior to Valerian's birth, and Rivan was already almost a thousand years old.

With a huge roar and a gigantic gust of wind, Valerian shoots up into the air lightning fast. I understand why Rivan wanted to showcase this for our spies. Who knew something that large could move at that speed?

The two chase each other through the trees, showing the Phoenix's ability to maneuver barely beats the dragon behind him and only in tight quarters. When they move to the wide open sky, Valerian's ability to use his tail to change course gives him the advantage over a Phoenix.

From a speed perspective, they're pretty evenly matched. Anyone watching on the ground will think they have a shot at defeating Valerian until he wraps the shadows around his opponent and holds him mid-air. Instead of fire, he freezes Rivan to show how easily he could have killed him.

Blowing a warm breath over the Phoenix, he releases the shadows, and the gruesome smile he gives him is absolutely frightening.

The two of them return to the ground, and their human forms, and shake hands. "Brilliant. Thank you, Valerian."

Rivan walks over to me. "That should do it. Even if they know it's staged, it should get our point across."

"Great job," I tell them both, then murmur to Rivan. "Biggest damn dragon I've ever seen. Enough to scare most Fae."

Valerian hears me and roars with laughter. "We have exceptional hearing, too."

Daire strides up next. "Cormal asked us to demonstrate our speed, but I felt we needed to add a little flair to it." He raises his arm, and a hundred straw dummies appear behind him. Turning, he blows a kiss to Arden.

Tossing me a timer, he pulls out his sword and counts down. "Three, two, one." In a blur, he takes the straw heads of all one hundred in eight point three seconds.

Stopping in front of me, he asks for the time. When I tell him, he frowns. "Damn it. I'm getting slower."

Astonished, I scan the field of straw heads littering the ground. "If you say so. Hell of a demonstration. I'm sure a couple of them wet their pants watching it."

He dips his head. "Happy to help. The real show is about to begin."

Arden walks over and pulls her sword. With a flick of her hand, she lights it on fire, then multiplies the one into fifty flaming swords. As her sword engages with the first headless dummy, the other swords follow her command, taking on the enemy. What's most remarkable about this feat is that each sword is moving independently. Thrusting, stabbing, and fighting without a hand on the hilt.

After a few minutes, she changes the swords into one giant lasso of fire and ropes the dummies into a grouping in the middle. The lasso drops to the ground, becoming a ring of fire surrounding the dummies. Lightning strikes them from above. Then, a tornado.

For the finale, she stalks forward, changing instantly from a witch into a dragon, breathing fire. With one exhale, she incinerates the dummies.

Sweat rolls down her temple, but that's the only sign of the tremendous magic she exerted right in front of us. And our enemies' spies.

"Hopefully, that helps," she says, her brow furrowing. "The last thing I know you want to do is fight your own people. Believe me. I understand."

"It does, thank you," I assure her. "And you're right. I hope this works. We've all seen too much death to want this war."

Meri comes up and hugs Arden. "Thank you. One witch of your caliber is worth more than ten coven members. More effective, too. If the power of one can do this, what will ten witches be able to achieve? Even if they know of you, this drives the point home."

A horn heralds at the other end of the courtyard, and we all turn to watch.

Towering over the soldiers around him, the ginormous warrior stalks forward, smoke and shadows swirling around him. His blood-red cloak frames the two thick leather straps crossing his chest, which hold an impressive number of knives and other weapons. He carries a mammoth sword in one hand and a battered gold shield in the other. I narrow my eyes at the words hammered into its surface. "Memento Mori." A Latin phrase to remind his enemies of the inevitability of death. Effective. I'm slightly jealous.

He stops in front of me and tilts his head. Horns rise from his enormous red helmet, and I chuckle.

Meri gasps beside me, and I turn a questioning glance at her, but she shakes her head and mouths "later."

"Lucifer," I greet him. "Truly terrifying." It's so bad. I can't believe he actually wore it. Evren must have used her wiles to get him to agree.

He yanks off the helmet. "It's the helmet, isn't it? I told them it was ridiculous."

Holding up two fingers an inch apart, I nod. "A wee bit."

Evren slides up next to him. "Fine. You're right. The helmet was too much, but it was fun. Admit it. You needed the laugh."

He turns and stares at her incredulously.

Meri leans forward. "What is it with these grumpy men?"

"Who's grumpy?"

Evren nods her head vigorously. "They don't even know." She winks at Lucifer. "Don't worry, the rest of you is fierce."

Cormal appears on my right. "Besides Lucifer, the rest went well. I think that should do it, don't you? And it's only a glimpse. When they stare across the battlefield, they will see what it's like to face death."

The somber words are a reminder of what will come to pass if they force us to fight.

CHAPTER THIRTY-EIGHT

<u>MERI</u>

Lying in Rivan's arms with his hand in my hair, I stare up at the sky above us. "Which one is that?"

Madoc shifts beside me to look where I'm pointing. "Konnyr's sword. See, there's the hilt." He takes my finger and shifts it to the top star. "The cross-guard." He shows me two stars a fair distance below the one, then continues down several stars almost parallel to each other. "The blade."

Rivan listens to him, his hand sifting through the strands. "Once this is over, I'll create something more comfortable up here for us."

Cormal rolls over on the pile of pillows next to us. "This is one thing we don't have in The Underworld. Stars." He taps his watch. "Dawn will be here in less than an hour."

I look at the three of them. Ruthless integrity. Sheer determination. Fierce loyalty. Those are the words that come to mind when I think of them. Love, obsession, mine. Those too. On the eve of battle, I refuse to think of the worst.

"I love you."

They each give me a solemn look and repeat the words with a fierceness that steals my breath.

Not once have they suggested I sit this one out or stay hidden in the palace. I know they've thought about it and even talked amongst themselves. But my place is beside them. No matter what.

Madoc stands and pulls me to him, then reaches out to include Cormal and Rivan. "May the keepers bless us and keep us safe. Thank you for standing with me."

"I pray to the goddess they take our offer," Rivan says fervently. "But if they don't, my wings and sword are yours to command."

Cormal's face settles into an expression of pure determination. "Let's do this." He leans down and gives me a long, hard kiss, then turns me toward Rivan.

Warm and seductive, Rivan's kiss is the sun on my face and love in my heart. He places his hands on my hips and moves me closer to Madoc.

Sweetly powerful, Madoc's kiss reflects the depth of his feelings without uttering a word. "Obsessed," he reminds me.

HERE THE CRISP air from Theron's Winter Court meets the tall, burnished grasses of the Autumn Court. Away from the more populous areas of the kingdom with a completely neutral terrain, this is the place we've chosen to meet our foes.

I stare down the long line of soldiers lined up on our side. Madoc's display of his allies and their strengths is everything he thought it would be. Magic sparks from fingers, beasts and demons shuffle restlessly on their feet, dragons roar from the rear, and swords swing through the air. Warriors, all of them, highly experienced in battle. Our numbers may be fewer, but that only means it will take us longer to defeat them.

Dawn breaks, and the sky lightens. Golden rays streak across the sky, fingers reaching for the farthest point, bringing with it the sight of our enemy. Standing on the other side of the long field are sixteen thousand plus soldiers of the Federation. Fierce, determined faces lined up, ready to fight for their freedom. Above them, the Phoenix and other Fire Fae hold themselves in formation. In the front, members of the council stand, faces stoic, giving us no clues as to their decision. In a moment, Madoc and I will meet General Lai and Aeris in the middle to get their answer.

How many of my friends and family will die today if their answer is war? How many of our faithful soldiers? Callyx winks at me from the front line, but when he turns around to face the enemy, he stares at them with death in those same eyes. How many will we kill?

Madoc raises a finger, and Bianca Perrone, from Arden's coven, and a witch known for her affinity to open portals to anywhere at a moment's notice, throws her arm up high. On her left, a portal opens, spreading wider and taller than any I've ever seen to let in the most terrifying and brutal creatures from the Wilds, including Aamon and Lux. The ground shakes as they stampede to the front of the line, eager to play their part and fight for their king.

Fallon's elite grin at the sight next to them.

Raising his arm, Madoc's magic swirls around him, spreading from the ground to sky, encompassing our entire army until it's hidden from their view. He wants our enemies to glimpse the power he wields over the light. After a minute, he releases the magic so they can see we're still here.

I stride up to Madoc and take his hand. In seconds, we're

stepping from the smallest of shadows into the center of the field. Here, we wait.

The light grows brighter as the dawn streaks across the sky.

Our enemy stands there unmoving. My heart races as we wait. The seconds tick down. Less than thirty left.

Aeris and the general fly toward us at the last possible moment, leaving none to spare.

Madoc quietly exhales at the sight of them.

There's a bitter twist to their mouths that says everything without speaking a word.

Landing, Lai stands stiffly, his face set in stone, and gives us the answer we seek. "We accept the offer of Avalon."

Madoc acknowledges his statement. "It's for the best."

Aeris' tight face smooths after the general's response, making me think she wasn't quite sure what answer he would give us.

"With this many soldiers, it will take us a few weeks to tattoo everyone," Aeris says with a defiant lift of her chin. "We'll need Rivan's help." Not once does her gaze drift in his direction.

"He's already offered to help," I assure her. "In addition, he believes we should offer a reassimilation option if anyone wants to return. We agreed. The land deal can be extended for a year, if you also agree."

General Lai nods, then peers at the army behind us. "We did not make this decision lightly. If we had faced you, this would have been our last battle. Better to be exiled than to see our people dead."

Madoc gives him a hard look. "Start this new path by eliminating the word *exiled*. Freedom will be hard. Governing even more so. In the end, I believe this will benefit all of you. A kingdom of your own is a hard stake in the ground, but it is the definition of true autonomy. Good luck to you all. Who knows, maybe we'll be allies in another thousand years?"

Neither of them says a word in return, but that's to be expected when the pill is bittersweet. They fly back to their army. Portals open across the field, and their army marches into them, disappearing from our sight.

Cheers and roars erupt behind us in a big swell, starting from one end and rolling across to the other. Madoc and I return to our front lines.

He walks over to the creatures from the Wilds and shakes their hands, thanking them for coming to his aid. With a bow, they shuffle into the portal and disappear.

Madoc proceeds to do the same to the leaders of all his allies until all that's left are the dark Fae. A resounding cheer goes up for Madoc, but he stops them.

"There are many ways to defeat your foe. Sometimes we have to sacrifice for the things we want the most. Today, we won the battle, but not the war," Madoc tells them. "Make no mistake, our sacrifice was as great as theirs. Losing fierce warriors and their families is a great loss to our kingdom. One I'll mourn for a long time. I wish them all the best in their new home. And for those who chose to stay and take the land, the past will be the past. We move forward as one. Thank you all for standing with me today."

He holds up a hand. "Oh, and the land deal will also be available to you."

Cheers erupt, and Rivan's eyes widen and he looks over at me with a panicked expression on his face. That's a lot of land for us to find and dispense. I shrug. I'll take a happy problem over a bad one any day.

Callyx suddenly appears beside me. "It's Solandis. She's having the baby."

Madoc, Rivan, and Cormal step forward, but I hold out my hand. "We don't all need to go."

"We're family," Madoc gently reminds me. "Right?"

With tears in my eye, I nod and reach for Madoc's hand. "Family." Sounds good to me. Cormal and Rivan both nod in agreement.

Madoc signals to General Beld to take the army to the palace.

Cormal quickly conjures a portal for us. When we get to The Abbey, we find Arden and her cadre pacing in the hall.

"Any news?" I ask, reaching out to clasp Arden's hand.

She bites her lip. "Not yet. The wait is killing me."

I see the worry in her eyes. And in Callyx's. I'm sure it's in mine, too. Solandis means a lot to all of us. She's the mother some of us never had. An aunt. Friend. Princess. I smile when I hear the word in the same tone she uses.

The door opens, and Vargas sticks his head out. Surprised to see us all, he throws his arms out wide. "It's a boy! Solandis is fantastic. A true warrior. She's in there sitting up, declaring her love for him. Please, welcome our son."

Jumping and crying, we all hug him and each other. Wiping tears from our faces, we clamor to see them both, and Vargas laughs, then pushes the door wide open.

Stepping into the room, we see Solandis smiling serenely at the bundle in her arms. She holds him out to Arden. "Meet the newest member of our family, Asher Kaius."

With tears rolling down her cheeks, she greets the little boy, then passes him to me.

Eyes closed; the pink-cheeked little boy sleeps soundly in my arms. With his blue cap on, it's hard to tell who he resembles, but it doesn't matter. Fisk would be proud to see his lineage continue and get a big kick out of the boy having royal blood, too.

"He's beautiful," I murmur, passing him to Callyx.

Callyx stares in wonder at the tiny baby in his large arms. "He's so small."

Vargas and Solandis glance at each other and laugh. "He'll grow. Give him time."

The baby is passed from one person to another. Each of my men murmur a blessing for the child to carry with him in this world. Today was a good day. One filled with peace, life, and love. A day to cherish and a memory to pull out when times are dark.

CHAPTER THIRTY-NINE

MERI

Sitting across from Ri´, I listen to her tell a story from their childhood when she had to stop Cormal from beating up the kid next door because he had shoved her. Laughingly telling us her other brothers had already hit the poor kid, but Cormal thought he deserved more.

"Cormal has always been a force of nature and the fiercest of protectors," she declares with a smile.

I reach out for his hand as I agree with her. "Absolutely, although I would probably add some additional traits like bossy, always likes to be right, has to plan everything…" The rest of my words are muffled by his hand over my mouth.

She laughs, but there's a hint of envy in her eyes. While Oryn and she have remained friends, the romance didn't survive her transformation from quiet woman to fiery one. I have no doubt that when she's ready, she'll find someone who appreciates her wicked smart brain, boisterous laugh, and fierce nature.

Madoc and Rivan laugh at our antics. We usually try to spend at least a week here every month. The Underworld is my home as well as Cormal's, and we enjoy showing them the wonders of it.

We traded in Cormal's bachelor pad for something larger but retained the modern feel of it. Full of technology, it took Madoc a while to be comfortable here, but Rivan jokingly helped him acclimate. I smile at him. He makes all our lives easier with his easy-going nature and acceptance of almost anything.

It took Rivan and Aeris six weeks to tattoo the soldiers of the Federation. When presented with various runes, they chose the Dagaz rune because it signals change and transformation. The end of one path and the start of a new one. Two triangles interconnected and continuous. It felt like the perfect symbol to represent their new life. That was three months ago. So far, nobody has applied to come back, which, hopefully, means the plan is working.

Rivan's relationship with Aeris never changed. She remained distant the entire time they worked together and didn't even say goodbye when she left for Avalon. Nor did she introduce him to his niece. He's more accepting of her response than I am. If I ever see her again, I'm likely to punch her in the nose. He reminds me she knew nothing of his life with Nyssa, or what he had to endure. She thinks he had it easy. He could have corrected her, but who can say one hardship is harder than another? Who knows what she had to endure with their father? Enough that she felt justified in killing him.

Cormal rubs a thumb across the back of my hand, and I smile at him. We've come a long way in such a short time. The relationship I used to pine for isn't the one we have. Thank the goddess. Instead, it's deeper and stronger than I ever imagined.

"The shop opens early tomorrow," Ri´ says, getting up from

the table. "Next time you're in town, come by and see the new stock. I've got some fabulous things set aside for you."

Her face lights up when she talks about her store. Her obsession with power and magic faded with her capture. She channels all that energy into finding the best clothes for her store. Even Evren shops there.

I stand and give her a tight hug. "Ooh, I can't wait. Thank you."

While Cormal walks her out, I turn and sit in Madoc's lap. "I'm tired. How about you?" It's taken over four months to parcel the land out to those taking the deal, but we're almost done.

He runs a hand up and down my spine. "Exhausted. Are we staying the night here?"

Cormal returns in time to hear Madoc's question. "No, but we're not going straight home. Meri wants to stop and see Asher."

Madoc agrees with a yawn. "We need to go before I fall asleep."

I hop up and tug on his hand. "If we go now, we can be home in an hour."

That's the incentive he needs. Swooping down, he gives me a kiss. "Lead the way."

Solandis and Vargas finally moved out of The Abbey, much to Arden's dismay. She loved having them close to her, dropping by often to spoil her new brother.

Vargas missed The Underworld and, surprisingly, so did Solandis. Their new house is out in the countryside, protected by a magical bubble, of course. The exterior is an aged cream stone found in the quarries nearby, accented with a dark brown roof and door. The interior is massive and full of light. Solandis' effortless style is reflected in the luxurious, but understated, furnishings.

When we get to Solandis and Vargas' new house, she's

getting ready to give Asher a bath. Even though she could clean him with magic, she refuses to do so.

"I made it just in time," I say, blowing air kisses at my favorite boy.

Turquoise eyes bounce with happiness when he sees me. His mouth blows drooly bubbles my way, while his hands happily slap the water around him, soaking everything outside the tub, including Solandis. She laughs, and he squeals.

I bend and give her a kiss. "He definitely loves the water." As I watch, iridescent scales shimmer on his arms, then recede, leaving smooth golden skin in its wake.

"Besides his dark blue hair and the scales, have you seen any other signs of cirein-croin?" If it weren't for those two things, I'd have a hard time believing he had Water Fae in him.

She smiles and shakes her head. "No. With his eyes and skin, he resembles me. I guess only time will tell."

The little boy yawns, and Solandis takes him out of the bath and gets him dressed in the cute octopus pajamas I got for him.

"It's been a long day, hasn't it, my love?" She coos to him the entire way to his bedroom, and his little lids slide shut.

Laying him in his crib, she turns on the sound machine, swearing he needs the ocean waves to help him sleep through the night.

I lean over and place a kiss on his sweet, plump cheek. "Good night, sweet boy."

As Solandis and I start to leave the room, a golden light appears, shining brightly above the bed. Swearing, we rush forward to grab him, but stop when we see what it is. The light Fae crown. Royal blood and cirein-croin. The best of both worlds and the true leader of all the light Fae.

"The crown has chosen the next ruler," I murmur, not wanting anyone to hear us. Her turquoise eyes fill with worry, and I clasp her hands in mine. "We don't have to tell anyone except Vargas. Let him grow up first. Learn all the important stuff. The world can wait."

Solandis gives me a determined look. "You're right. Tomorrow will come soon enough." She walks me out to the living room and kisses my cheek. "Love you."

"Love you," I say with a bright smile as I turn toward the three men waiting for me. "Let's go home. There's a good book I've been reading. But I'm stuck at page one hundred and sixteen."

Cormal's lips curve in a wicked smile as he scoops me up.

THANK YOU!

Thank you for continuing to follow this series! It's hard to believe this is the last book! I've thoroughly enjoyed writing every book in The Killian Blade Series but I'm excited about moving on to new stories! I'd love to hear your thoughts. Whether it's "give me more," or "I want to see a book with…" reviews help me write the next story. Please consider leaving one for this book.

*If you find an error, email me at Stellabrie@stellabrie.com.

*If you see the ebook anywhere besides Amazon KU, please send me an email (see address above) or contact me on social media. Pirating can have severe consequences, preventing authors from creating new stories.

To get a free eBook copy of my first book, My Salvation, just subscribe to my newsletter.

Website: https://www.stellabrie.com/my-salvation

AWESOME PEOPLE

Huge thanks to everyone who make my books possible!

To my readers, friends, and fans! Thanks for all the wonderful words of encouragement, friendship, and love for my books! And for participating in my shenanigans and all the other weird things I post. You guys rock! I couldn't do it without you!!!

My awesome beta readers. They catch so many big and little things, help me with names, show me such amazing friendship, encouragement, and excitement, and they can't even share it with anyone! My books are a thousand times better because of their feedback. Thank you, Nia, Bianca, Iliana, Melissa, Rachel, Sandi, and Debbie for everything!

My ARC team who gives me so much support and enthusiasm even though I drop things on them at the last minute. Ooh, look, cover reveal! Book's launching in a week! Seriously, I appreciate all of you!!

My biggest supporters—my husband and mom. I'm so lucky to have you both! Love you!

And always… a special thanks to all the wonderful authors in the writing community who support each other day in and out. Writing would be a lonely and weird world without you. It would be me and my characters sitting around chatting (drinking) while we plot the next book. Your friendship and support mean a lot to me!

310

ABOUT THE AUTHOR

Stella Brie lives outside of Nashville, TN, with her husband. After mentioning her desire to write a book a million times to her husband, he challenged her to sit down one day and write a paragraph. Instead, she wrote her first book, *My Salvation*.

She traded in her career in digital marketing, working on big brands, for this wildly creative one. Armed with a notebook crammed full of ideas, she's constantly thinking about bold heroines, sexy men, and HEAs. Whether it's a paranormal book full of creatures and magic or a contemporary romance full of heat and drama, she's always thinking about how she can bring her books to life.

Facebook Group: Stella's Stalkers

TikTok: @stellabrie_author

YouTube! Playlists (all books): @authorstellabrie

Instagram: @stellabrie_author

Website: Stellabrie.com - Exclusive sneak peeks, cover reveals, giveaways, and more!

BOOKS BY STELLA BRIE

PARANORMAL WHY CHOOSE

KILLIAN BLADE SERIES

The Rowan (1)

The Rowan's Stone (2)

The Rowan's Destiny (3)

Wicked Savior - Lucifer's story (MF Romance) - Book 3.5

The Light Falls (4) - Meri's story

The Dark Rises (5) - Meri's story

CONTEMPORARY WHY CHOOSE

THE SAVAGES SERIES

Savage Traitor (1)

Savage Ruin (2)

Spin-off:

Lethal Vengeance (Standalone)

My Salvation (Standalone)

To get a free eBook copy of my first book, My Salvation, just subscribe to my newsletter.

Website: https://www.stellabrie.com/my-salvation